SCORE

Also by Kiki Swinson

Playing Dirty
Notorious
Wifey
I'm Still Wifey
Life After Wifey
Still Wifey Material
The Candy Shop
A Sticky Situation
Wife Extraordinaire
Wife Extraordinaire Returns
Cheaper to Keep Her series
Dead on Arrival

The Score series: *The Score* and *The Mark*

Anthologies

Sleeping with the Enemy (with Wahida Clark)
Heist and *Heist 2* (with De'nesha Diamond)
Lifestyles of the Rich and Shameless (with Noire)
A Gangster and a Gentleman (with De'nesha Diamond)
Most Wanted (with Nikki Turner)
Still Candy Shopping (with Amaleka McCall)
Fistful of Benjamins (with De'nesha Diamond)
Schemes and *Dirty Tricks* (with Saundra)
Bad Behavior (with Noire)

Published by Kensington Publishing Corp.

THE
SCORE

Kiki
Swinson

Kensington Publishing Corp.
www.kensingtonbooks.com

DAFINA BOOKS are published by

Kensington Publishing Corp.
119 West 40th St.
New York, NY 10018

All Kensington Titles, Imprints, and Distributed Lines are available at special quantity discounts for bulk purchases for sales promotions, premiums, fund-raising, and educational or institutional use. Special book excerpts or customized printings can also be created to fit specific needs. For details, write or phone the office of the Kensington special sales manager: Kensington Publishing Corp., 119 West 40th Street, New York, NY 10018, attn: Special Sales Department, Phone: 1-800-221-2647.

Dafina and the Dafina logo Reg. U.S. Pat. & TM Off.

ISBN-13: 978-1-4967-1271-4
ISBN-10: 1-4967-1271-4
First Kensington Hardcover Edition: February 2016
First Kensington Trade Edition: September 2016
First Kensington Mass Market Edition: July 2018

eISBN-13: 978-1-61773-967-5
eISBN-10: 1-61773-967-7

10 9 8 7 6 5 4 3 2 1

Printed in the United States of America

LAUREN

Present Day

My feet moved at the speed of lightning. I could feel the wind beating on my skin so hard it made snot wet the inside of my nostrils. My entire body was covered with a thick sheen of sweat and I could feel it burning my armpits. My breath escaped my mouth in jagged, raggedy puffs and my chest burned. My heart felt like it would burst through the front of it. Even feeling as terrible as I did, I would not and could not stop moving.

"Move!"

"Get out of my fucking way!"

"Watch out!"

"Move!"

I screamed command after command at the

nosy-ass people who were staring and gawking and being in my damn way. My legs were moving like those of a swift and agile cheetah as I swerved and swayed through the throngs of people on Virginia Beach Boulevard. I was met by more than one mouthful of gasps and groans and I could faintly see more than one wide-eyed, mouth-agape stare as people gawked at me like I was a crazy woman. I guess I did look crazy running through the high-end shopping area with no shoes on. I had run straight out of my Louboutins, my expensive embellished Balmain skirt was hitched up around my hips, my vixen weave was blowing in the wind, and my Chanel caviar bag was strapped around my arm like a slave chain. I could feel that my makeup was a cakey, smudged mess all over my face and eyes. But I didn't give a damn. I wasn't going to stop running. No matter what. Looking crazy was the least of my worries.

I had run track in high school and it was still paying off now, but clearly I wasn't in the same athletic shape. Still, I wasn't about to go out like this. I wasn't going to get captured on the street and probably murdered for something that wasn't totally my fault. I had been pushed and provoked to do everything that I did. All of the mistakes. All of the grimy shit I had done over the years. All of it was because I was born at a disadvantage from day fucking one.

I didn't want to die. I had always seen myself growing old with a few kids and grandkids surrounding me when I was ready to be settled. I would've given anything to be old and settled at this moment. But, of course, life threw me a curveball.

I could hear the thunderous footfalls of the three men chasing me. If they weren't so damn gorilla big and slower than me they would have caught me by now.

"Hey! Are you okay?" I heard a man on the street yell at me as I flew past him, nearly knocking him over. Why the hell was he asking me such a dumb question when you could clearly see that I was being chased by three hulking goons dressed in all black with their guns probably showing on their waists or maybe even in their hands. Thank goodness I am always so alert or they would've walked right up on me while I unsuspectingly ate my lunch at the posh restaurant and grabbed me. It was the fact that I had only been back in town for a few hours, the disappearance of my lunch companion, and the suspicious looks that had alerted me in the first place. How could I have been so trusting? So naïve and stupid, too.

I could feel the look of terror contorting my face, so I know damn well passersby could see the fear etched on every inch of it.

Finally, I dipped through a side alley and the first door I tried allowed me inside. Thank God! With my chest heaving up and down I rested my back against another cold metal door inside and slid down to the floor. My legs were still trembling and my muscles were on fire in places on my body I didn't even know existed. I tried to slow down my rapid breathing so I could hear whether the men had noticed me dipping into the alley but the more I tried to calm myself the more reality set in about the grave danger I was in. I was probably about to be murdered or worse, tortured and then murdered right in a dank alleyway in the place I thought I would never return to. If I hadn't gotten that call, it would have been years before I crept back here. I thought about Matt and wondered if he was the one who had sent these men after me. But how would he have known I was back? I knew Matt had a lot of selfish ways about him and although shit had gone south with us, I never thought he would try to do something like this to me. I expected that if he wanted to confront me, he would come himself. Even if it was Yancy who had sent the goons, I would think Matt would have tried to spare me.

CLANG!

A loud noise outside interrupted my thoughts and caused me to jump. I clasped both of my hands over my mouth and forced the scream that had crept up my throat back down. Sweat trickled down my face and burned my eyes. My heart jackhammered against my chest bone so hard it actually hurt. My stomach knotted up so tightly the cramps were almost unbearable. I dropped my head. Suddenly I felt like vomiting.

"I don't see her! She's not down here!" I heard one of the goons outside of the door scream to the others. I swallowed hard and started praying under my breath.

Dear God, I am sorry for all of the things I've done. I don't know how things got so far gone. I never meant anything by any of it. I just wanted to live a better life than I had as a child. I guess with the mother You gave me and the hand You dealt me, I should've just handled it. I should've worked harder and not try to take the easy way out all of the time. I knew stealing is wrong. Since the first time I stole a credit card from my foster mother's purse, I'd known it was wrong. But I got addicted to the feeling that I'd gotten over on someone. I felt powerful. I remember the times I'd hear her talking to my foster father about some of the fraud scams she witnessed by working as a bank manager. It was interesting to hear how bank and credit card frauds were being committed on a daily basis. It all seemed too easy, too intoxicating. I had to test the waters. . . .

So here I am today. I'm literally running for my life. Maybe this is Your way of teaching me a lesson. Trust me, I hear You loud and clear. If You let me get out of this, I swear I will change my life. I don't even know how things got this far . . .

MATT

"Ooof," I gagged as another fist slammed into my stomach causing all of the wind in my body to involuntarily escape through my mouth. Acidy vomit leapt up into my throat and spewed out of my mouth right after.

"Hit 'em again!" a deep baritone voice commanded. With that, another sledgehammer-sized fist slammed into my left jaw. I felt the blood and spit shoot from between my lips. The salt from the blood stung the open cuts on my split bottom lip.

"Until he tells me where the fuck every dime of my money is I want his ass to suffer," the deep voice growled. "Break every bone in his body if you have to."

"Agh!" I belted out as a heavy-booted foot crashed down on my ribcage. I think hearing the crack and crunch of my own bones disturbed me more than the excruciating pain I felt.

I coughed and wheezed trying to will my lungs to fill back up with air. Each raggedy breath hurt like hell. I knew then that some of my ribs had been shattered. More fury came right after.

"Ugh!" I coughed as a front kick with a pointed, steel-toe boot slammed into my back. I swore I heard my spine crack. My insides felt like they were being shuffled around by the punches and kicks I'd been subjected to since these dudes had snatched me from my hideout in the thick of the night. I had tried to bounce before they could get me, but I was too slow. Thank God Lauren had up and left or else she would've been there when they broke the door down to get me. Although I wanted to kill her myself right now, I could only pray that she was some-place safe . . . maybe with the police or back on the run. But if these dudes were after me, I would think they would be after her and Yancy as well.

"Where is my fucking money!" the voice boomed again. This time, I forced my battered eyes open and looked at the sharply dressed man that was standing over me. In dim light I couldn't make out his face. But I could see from the flash of his sparkly diamond pinky ring, solid-gold cufflinks, and a clearly expensive tailor-made suit, this dude hadn't even broken a sweat. He obviously took great satisfaction in com-manding his goons to torture me over and over. And like good little soldiers, they did just enough to hurt me, but not kill me.

"I'll ask you one more time, Matthew Connors . . . what the fuck did you and your bitch do with my fucking money?" the boss man growled. His money? Me and my bitch? What the . . . It finally hit me like a hammer to my head. My entire body went cold like my veins had been injected with ice water. The score that was supposed to put me back in the game and set me and my woman up for life had turned into my worst nightmare.

The man who'd been our mark let out a raucous, maniacal laugh. "You petty fuckin' thief," he spat as he moved closer to me. "Stealing instead of going out there and working for your own shit. I can respect a man that hustles for himself, but a man who steals from another hardworking man is a waste of fucking sperm. Your mother should've just swallowed."

The heat of anger that lit up my chest from his words was probably enough to make me kill him with my bare hands. I bucked my body out of anger but that just made shit worse. . . .

LAUREN

Three Months Earlier

"I'll take two of those classics. The red and the royal blue patent leather." I leaned into the counter and pointed at two bags on the shelf behind it. "I think these are the only two I don't have in my collection," I chimed proudly. I could be a snob when I wanted to be. The saleslady's eyes widened at me as she tried to keep a smile on her face. I could tell she was probably secretly judging me. She more than likely instantly thought I couldn't afford these expensive-ass bags. It was amusing to me to watch her struggling to keep it professional because she also knew just as well as I did that my purchase of these two five-thousand-dollar Chanel bags would be a payload of commission for her.

As the snobby saleslady walked away to retrieve my items, I kept shopping with my eyes. Now, I felt like I had a little point to prove. I smirked to myself and for spite I decided to make her piss her pants with jealousy. See, I had worked retail back in my day so I knew that no matter how stuck up these bitch salesladies acted, they were broke as hell and really silently prayed for the commission fairy to bless them. I bet when I walked in she had immediately looked at my race and pegged me as a window shopper and eye hustler. I was about to show this bitch how Lauren Kelly rolled.

"Wow, these are beautiful too. Hmmm, I think I should take every color of these as well," I said, pointing down into the counter at the Chanel cuff bracelets. The saleswoman almost dropped the pocketbooks as she clamored over and grabbed the merchandise I was asking for with the quickness. I could hear the cash register in her head singing *CHING-CHING*. Jewelry sales always brought more commission than things that sold faster like pocketbooks. I chuckled to myself.

"Is that all?" she asked me.

"I think I've done enough damage for one day." I smiled. Then I slapped the newly cloned MasterCard I had down on the counter. The saleslady squinted at my card, picked it up, and looked it over like it was a piece of shit. I could see disappointment in her face that my card wasn't American Express. I quickly began feeling indignant. *How dare this bitch!*

"Do you do that to all customers or just the black ones?" I asked through my teeth.

Her eyes popped wide like I had just dashed a cup of cold water in her face.

"I'm sure if I was a member of any other race you would have picked up my card with a smile and ran to the register. *Now*, do I need to take my business and my commission to another store?" I gritted. It was the worst kind of threat for someone working in sales.

The saleswoman's cheeks flushed deep red and she shifted her weight from one foot to the other. She parted a halfhearted, embarrassed smile and broke eye contact with me.

"No, ma'am, and I apologize if you feel that way," she replied meekly.

"That's what I thought, now ring me up or this store will be all over the eleven o'clock news when I'm done speaking to the media about the blatant discrimination I experienced here," I snapped. She raced to the small suite in the store where they ring purchases over a certain amount. I could tell I had scared the holy shit out of her, which is what I wanted to do. My forcefulness was going to be a great distraction in case anything went wrong with the card. Those credit cards were always hit or miss, although, up to that point (knock on wood) they had always been complete out-of-the-park home runs whenever I used them.

As I stood there waiting for her to return with my nicely bagged and wrapped items my cell phone buzzed inside of my Hermès Birkin bag. I looked at the screen and sucked my teeth. It was my boyfriend, Matt. I wasn't feeling his ass right at that moment and hadn't been for the past few weeks. As far as I was concerned, he was a sneaky, conniving bastard who had it coming to him in the worst way. The only reason I even still fucked with him was because I had a plan that I needed to see come to fruition.

I had just found out that Matt and our other partner in crime, Yancy, had been fucking behind my back. It was a complete blow to my brain and heart because of all of the people in the world, I had trusted Matt. Yancy, not so much. I had basically saved that bitch from a life of stealing and fucking men for money. Both of them seemed to forget that I was the big breadwinner and Matt was living off of me. I gave Yancy a role in what we were doing and brought her around my man. Big fucking mistake. Yes, I knew Yancy was a pretty young girl who knew the art of seduction, but I thought loyalty would be as important to her as it was to me. Unfortunately, I was wrong.

Yancy was one of those video-vixen types who wore a lot of weave, a lot of makeup, and had the fake tits and ass implants. She stood five feet even without heels, had a small waist, wide hips, and a beautiful smooth caramel complexion that I had always yearned for as a kid. I can't say that if I was a man like Matt I would not have been attracted to Yancy too, but I wouldn't be that grimy, either. As long as I live, I will never forget the day I first found out about them. Now, standing right in the Chanel store, I couldn't stop the memory of what happened from crashing in on me. . . .

THE SCORE

July 2013

It was a hot-ass, heat wave–type of July day in the Tidewater area and I was flustered from a day of shopping. Sweat had my hair plastered to my head like I had gelled it down purposely. The twenty bags I was lugging had my body drenched in sweat and pain shot up my arms and down my back with each movement I made.

"Where the fuck is Matt when I need his ass?" I had huffed. I had called him like six times before I pulled into our condo parking garage. You would think that he would answer knowing that I had been out all day getting shit for us to resell in the hood. Sometimes he used our illegal enterprise to buy things to sell on the hot market for some quick and easy cash. It was better than keeping every material thing for our own personal use.

After struggling for ten minutes and fishing around in my oversize Gucci bag for another three minutes, I finally got my key out. I set the bags down at my feet and put the key into the bottom lock of the condo I shared with Matt. At first the door wouldn't open. I crinkled my face in confusion and sucked my teeth. Then I realized why the door wasn't opening.

"Why the fuck did he lock the top lock? He knows we never do that," I grumbled. I pulled the key out of the bottom lock and shuffled through my key ring until I found the top lock key. I got the door open after a few minutes.

"Finally," I breathed out as the cool air from the air conditioner inside hit my face. I stepped inside and dragged my bags in after me. I think it was the music *blasting and the type of music that hit me first. It was the R&B group 112 singing about making love on a waterbed. That was me and Matt's song when we first started dating. It still made me blush hearing it since he and I had made love for the first time with that song on repeat.*

I smirked, immediately thinking that maybe he had planned something sweet like a romantic evening for us since we had been kind of at each other's throats days before.

With a huge, sexy grin on my face, I walked down the long hallway toward our bedroom. I was going to surprise him since I had busted in on him trying to surprise me. I kicked off my Giuseppes and started un-buttoning my blouse. The closer I got to our bedroom door the more the music moved through my soul. I swayed my hips sexily, practicing for the show I was planning to put on for Matt. I started to knock on the door, but I thought it would be sexier to catch Matt in the act of fixing up our room for my romantic surprise. I can't even lie, I was giddy inside for the first time in a long time. Matt hadn't done anything like this in a long time because we had literally been fighting almost every day.

I finally made it down our long hallway and to the bedroom door. I was almost naked, standing there in just my lace La Perla bra and thong. I reached down to turn the doorknob and that's when I heard it. It was like a bomb had exploded in my ears.

"Ewww, Matt. Oh yeah. Right there. Fuck me harder. Harder!" Even with the music blaring I recognized the voice as Yancy's. Then . . .

"Whose pussy is this? Call me daddy! Call me your fuckin' daddy!" I heard Matt growl. Those were words

he had said to me exactly like he was saying them to that bitch. My mind was telling me to bust up in that room and kill the both of them, but for some reason my body was not following directions.

I froze and my feet became rooted to the floor. A tornado of emotions swirled inside of me and I felt unsteady on my feet. Suddenly, I could no longer hear the music blasting and all I could hear was the sound of lovemaking coming from MY bedroom. My heart rate sped up so fast it made my head swirl. I was suddenly unsteady on my feet. My first instinct was to bust in the room and go ballistic on Matt and Yancy's ass. I wanted to fuck her up so badly that no one would recognize her face and cut his dick off so he'd never be able to use it again. My entire body was trembling and then I realized I was standing there half naked still in my underwear like the damn naïve fool that I was. The fucking joke was on me. Here I was thinking my man was surprising me with something sweet. Instead, I surprised myself. Tears involuntarily rolled down my face before what was happening really registered in my brain. I snatched my hand back from the doorknob like it was on fire. Suddenly my body came alive with the heat of shame and embarrassment. You fucking fool! They've been playing you all along! *I silently chastised myself.*

I quickly scooped up my clothes and ran down the hallway to the front of the condo. With my chest heaving up and down and my entire body trembling like a leaf in a wild storm I slipped back into my clothes. Whirling around like a madwoman I located my purse, grabbed it and my cell phone, and rushed back out the front door. I didn't know where I was going but I knew I had to get out of there before I caught a case. Stupid!

Stupid! Stupid! *I chanted in my head. How could I be that stupid not to know that Yancy and Matt had been fucking? No wonder my relationship with him was on the rocks.*

In tears I raced to my car, got in, and just started to drive aimlessly. I couldn't even think straight. At first, I thought about driving to my old neighborhood and buying a dirty gun, going back to the condo, and shooting Yancy and Matt. Then, I thought about calling his probation officer and telling him all that Matt was into so Matt could get violated and sent back to prison. Then, I thought about going to Yancy's little town house and setting that shit on fire. All sorts of things ran through my mind, but finally, after driving around for hours, I came to a resolution that I felt wickedly good about.

"Y'all fucked around on the wrong bitch. I'm not about to be disrespected and played," *I growled out loud as if Matt and Yancy could hear me. At that moment, I had decided that instead of being ratchet and raising hell, I would slowly and methodically plot my revenge. I decided that I would destroy Yancy and Matt slowly and watch their lives crumble to ashes, but not before I got everything I wanted out of the deal at their expense.*

My phone vibrated in my hand again and snapped me back into the moment. I let out a long breath and rolled my eyes.

Yeah. Straight to voice mail, you. Not even ten seconds after I hit the ignore button, Matt was calling again. I furrowed my brows and squinted at the phone. *What has this nigga so hard-pressed?* Still, I hit ignore again. I told myself if he called back a third time it must be important and I would answer it. Well, before the thought could fully leave my mind, Matt was calling again. I sucked in my breath and shook my head.

"Yeah, Matt," I grumbled into the phone.

"Yo, bae, where you at?" Matt questioned, trying to sound all sweet and shit. I rolled my eyes and twisted my lips. He was acting so fucking fake that it sickened me to my stomach.

"I'm at the Chanel store exercising some retail therapy," I said sassily. "But the question is, where you at? I hope you and Yancy are taking care of what you were supposed to do today," I said with a nasty undertone to my words. I wanted Matt to know that I wasn't feeling that bitch. I had sent the two of them on a mission to cash two five-thousand-dollar bogus checks that I had gotten my hands on. Since finding out about Matt and Yancy's little affair, I had been using them for all of the dirty work so I could keep piling and stacking my dough for the big finale I had planned for their trifling, sneaky asses. So far, I was about two hundred thousand shy of the million I needed to make my exit. Matt and Yancy were too fucking dumb and so happy to be together behind my back that they never suspected what I was doing—making them take all the risk and do all of the dirty work. Revenge was a sweet bitch for sure.

"No speaking on this jack. Hit me from your throwaway as soon as you leave the store. What I need to tell you is real important so do it right way," Matt said, sounding like he meant business.

"Yeah, a'ight," I replied. I knew I sounded uninterested.

"No bullshit. This is about the next lick," he said seriously.

In that case, I was all ears. "A'ight, bet," I agreed before hanging up the phone.

My little evil Asian saleslady finally returned with my bags all nicely packed and tied up pretty. Usually shopping made me feel powerful and good about myself, but today I felt indifferent.

"Thank you for your business, Mrs. Hargrove," the saleslady said, calling me by the name on the fake credit card I had given her. "I'm really sorry about earlier. It's just that we've had a string of credit card fraud hits lately and with all of our new training I—" the saleslady started. I raised my hand and halted her words.

"Not every black person lives in poverty, so I hope you learned not to judge a book by its cover," I told her, using the most snobby voice I could muster. I watched her cheeks turn red and she lowered her head in shame. I picked up my bags that contained over fifteen thousand dollars' worth of merchandise, feeling vindicated, and sauntered out of the store with a smile on my face.

When I made it to my car, I threw my bags into the trunk and rushed around to the driver's-side door to jump inside. I popped open my glove box and pulled out one of the TracFones that

Matt, Yancy, and I use to communicate about our little illegal business dealings. I punched in the number to Matt's new throwaway phone and tapped my fingernails on the steering wheel as I waited for him to answer.

"Bae?" Matt answered. I shuddered at the phoniness of him calling me his bae when he knew damn well he was fucking Yancy behind my back.

"Ahem." I cleared my throat and swallowed the hard lump that had formed in the back of it. I took a quick, deep breath so that I wouldn't go crazy on Matt's ass.

"Yeah, Matt, what's up?" I said, closing my eyes to keep my feelings at bay.

"You are not going to believe this shit," Matt said excitedly. I was quiet. Nothing about him excited me anymore. I mean what was he going to tell me? He got off probation or his trifling-ass family had stopped begging for money?

"Believe what?" I asked dryly, rolling my eyes.

"Our girl Yancy Yance came through in a major way today," Matt continued. His voice went up a few notches in pitch when he said that bitch's name. My insides swirled with a quick flash of jealousy and nausea. Hearing Matt refer to Yancy as "our girl" almost literally made me throw up.

"You mean your girl," I said sarcastically. The fucking nerve of him to refer to her as our girl. Matt was really starting to push my buttons. He was so lucky I had an endgame in mind.

"Not only did she cash those stolen checks but while she was in the bank some dude dropped a

Hermès billfold right in front of her," Matt said with pure admiration in his tone. The mere thought of him and her fucking each other behind my back gave me a queasy feeling in my stomach. It seemed like the more he talked about her, the harder it was for me to keep my hatred at bay.

"And?" I said in an annoyed, ready-to-snap tone. It was all I could do to keep myself from going off. Lately, it seemed like Yancy could do no fucking wrong in his eyes.

"*And,* that shit had a stack in it, plus American Express black and plum cards too," Matt said, overjoyed. As bad as I wanted to be mad and jealous that he was giving Yancy props, when I heard what she had found a quick fleeting feeling of excitement filled my chest and my eyebrows went into arches on my face. That excitement quickly faded when I really thought about what he was saying.

"Wait. We don't fuck with American Express cards. American Express monitors their cards like Fort fucking Knox. Anyway, I'm almost sure the owner of the billfold has already reported them lost," I reminded Matt. "So why the fuck would I be excited about that?" I grumbled. I was so blinded by the jealousy of Matt giving Yancy props that I couldn't help but snap on him.

"I know that, Lauren. You ain't let me finish. Damn, so hardheaded," he said in a disgusted voice.

"Then what? I mean, okay, she found a thousand dollars and a Hermès wallet that we can probably sell but we can't use the fucking cards so what is so great about Miss Yancy *Yance,*" I snapped, emphasizing his little nickname for her in a mocking way.

"Yo, you sound mad salty right now, Lauren. I don't know what your fucking problem is," Matt shot back. I had to literally bite the skin on the inside of my cheek to keep from telling him exactly what my problem was.

"No, that's not all she found. She also got dude's bank account information and according to the bank statement he had folded up inside the wallet there is over three million in one of his fucking accounts!" Matt announced proudly. My eyebrows shot into arches on my face. I swallowed hard and suddenly my palms became sweaty. I was hoping I was hearing him correctly. Three million dollars in one account? That was a lot of money. We'd never gotten info on an account that big.

"Oh shit," I gasped. "Are you fucking serious? Wait, are you sure y'all have the account number? Statements don't list the whole account number."

"Yo, for real, Lauren, I'm gonna need you to get on the same page with me because you are not understanding what I'm saying. We're not stupid, we know that. That's what I was trying to tell you—this one does. We have the fucking account number in full! Now all we have to do is get your dude Ryan to do his best hacking and transfer job and our asses will be set for life," Matt preached, elated as hell.

"Stop fucking playing with me," I said. All I

could think about was my endgame. If what Matt was saying was true, stealing three million dollars would be like hitting the fucking lottery. That would put me in the perfect position to snatch the last bit of cash I needed, put the last of my revenge plan into action on Matt and Yancy, and bounce forever without looking back. Leaving shitty-ass Virginia Beach has been my lifelong dream. I wouldn't even go visit my bitch-ass mother in prison to let the bitch know I was leaving. She had left me for dead so many times in my life, I hardly ever thought about her anymore. In fact, I hated her with every fiber of my being.

"I'll be home in fifteen minutes so we can plot this thing out. So I guess you can tell Yancy I said good work," I said to Matt.

"Hurry up. We gon' get this shit poppin' and then we all gon' celebrate," he said cheerfully. I twisted my lips at that. I wasn't celebrating shit with them except my escape and my revenge.

If what Matt said was true about the three million dollars, I was going to make sure Matt and Yancy never saw a dime of that fucking money. I already knew I was smarter than both of them put together. I had proven that shit over and over with all of the checks I had them running around the city cashing and I was collecting most of the money off the top.

I looked up at myself in my rearview mirror and winked at myself. "You got it going on, Lauren. Nobody can't fuck with you," I said out loud, giving myself a little pep talk. As I drove toward home, my mind raced with all sorts of wicked thoughts about how I'd leave those two sneaky traitors behind high, dry, and broke. From day one, I helped that bitch. I helped her escape her pimp, got her somewhere to lay her head, gave her some clothes and food. But what did that get me? A fucking hard way to go and my man's dick inside her every time I turned my back. But it was all good. I'd get my sweet taste of revenge. Yancy would be able to continue fucking Matt and I'd be on my way out of the country with every red cent of the three million dollars. I knew the look on her and Matt's face would be priceless. Too bad I wouldn't be around to see it. It'd be bon voyage, motherfuckas!

MATT

Idisconnected the call with my girl Lauren and I was feeling pretty damn good about the possibilities of getting my hands on some serious cash. I was daydreaming about how I could buy back into the game and about how good it would feel not to have to depend on my girl to come up with ways for us to make money like I did now. The good thoughts and feelings were cut short when I turned around and saw Yancy's face. As soon as I got off the phone with Lauren, Yancy rushed over and got all in my face with her lips poked out and her arms folded across her chest looking evil as hell. I could've just predicted what was coming next as soon as I saw that hater scowl on her face. I let out a long sigh in anticipation of the bullshit. The past few weeks I had noticed that Yancy was finding it harder and harder to hide her jealousy of Lauren. In other words, Yancy was getting that side-chick envy that most niggas dreaded dealing with.

"I just don't understand why you need to tell her everything all of the fucking time." Yancy sounded like the stupid immature young chick that she was. "I'm the one who found the wallet. I'm the one who deserves all of the money. We could've taken that shit and blew town but nooooo you had to tell your precious little Lauren about it so she can get a cut of some shit she didn't work for," Yancy complained.

I shook my head in disgust. She couldn't be serious with what she was saying. Lauren was my main chick and I was going to ride with her to the end.

"C'mon with that bullshit, Yancy. You sound like a little whiny-ass baby right now. You better remember who picked your ass up from the streets." I brushed past her. I wasn't going to say anything else about the subject to her dumb ass. I wanted Yancy to stay in side-chick lane but she was always trying to cross over into the wifey zone. I mean what was the point of having a side chick if she was going to be nagging you like she was your wifey? I'd told Yancy over and over again that I wasn't ready to leave Lauren. Yancy's pussy was tight and good as hell, but I was starting to think that a good nut wasn't worth the headache anymore.

"Don't say it's bullshit, Matt! And don't keep trying to ignore me!" Yancy pressed. "I have a voice and an opinion and I think you should re-spect that!" Yancy screamed and followed me from the living room into my bedroom.

Oh, all of a sudden this dumb bitch wants to have an opinion? It's a little too late in the game for that shit!

At that moment, her squeaky-ass voice sounded like nails on a chalkboard. I felt my fists curling on their own and my jaw was moving from me biting down into it. I could really see myself punching her in the mouth, but then I had to think about how I would explain Yancy's ass being knocked out to Lauren when she got home.

"We could've just gotten the cash and left her ass right here where she belongs. I mean, it's not like you ain't never thought about doing it. You even told me that you were sick of her ass!"

"If you wanna know the truth, I'm sick of your ass, too. Walking around here like your shit don't stink. I know what I said so I don't need you to remind me. Now if I say this is how shit is going to go, then shut the fuck up and accept it. I'm running this show. You hear me?"

"Yeah, I hear you. But you know what? You're worse than her. One minute you acting like I'm all that you need and want, but every now and then, Matt, you act like you truly want to still be with Lauren and the fact that you're still living here with her, playing house with her, sleeping with her every night and giving her more than you give me is *not* all a coincidence," Yancy griped.

I let out a long sigh, shook my head left to

right in disgust, and flopped down on the side of my bed. I picked up my Black & Mild, tore the paper, and started rolling my blunt with some of the best sour weed I had copped in a long time. All I wanted was to smoke in peace and make a plan to get more money. It was that simple, but when you fuck with simple bitches like Yancy, they always make it harder than it really is.

"Matt! I'm fucking talking to you," Yancy raised her voice. But I ignored her. I licked the cigar paper to make sure I had a good seal on my blunt.

"Matt! You better say something I wanna hear because if you don't I swear on everything I love that I will tell Lauren about us as soon as she walks through that fucking door," Yancy hissed with her pointer finger so close to my face it almost touched my nose. Her words hit me like a hammer to the head. I put my blunt down. I glared at Yancy with fire flashing in my eyes.

"Yancy, I wish you would open your mouth. 'Cause if you do, I promise I'm going to beat you to death in here."

"Oh, so now you wanna put your fucking hands on me? You wanna play my pimp now?" Yancy taunted, trying to tower over me.

"Yancy, you better get the fuck away from me right now," I warned her.

"Or what?" she dared me.

"Or I'ma lay your ass out," I told her.

"I wish you would touch me. Because I'm gonna really show the fuck out! As a matter of fact, I'm gonna do you one better. As soon as she walks in here, I'ma tell her everything. And let's see if she'll stick around to collect on that three-million job I brought to the table."

Instead of letting Yancy continue to run her fucking mouth, I rammed into her like a wrecking ball, slamming the palm of my hand dead into Yancy's face. I mushed her so hard she stumbled backward onto her butt. She must have forgotten who she was talking to. I was the same street motherfucka with a different hustle, that's all.

"Don't ever fuckin' threaten me again," I growled, standing over her with my nostrils flaring and my fists curled at my sides. "Bitch, you're gonna shut the fuck up and play along with this shit until we get the money. Now if you keep fucking around you won't get a dime and I'll send your stupid ass back to the track," I snarled cruelly.

"Fuck you, Matt!" she screamed with tears running wildly down her face. "You put your hands on the wrong bitch! You won't get away with this shit!"

"Yeah, yeah, yeah. Get the fuck out of here before I kill you with my bare hands."

"Fuck you, asshole!" she yelled.

She scrambled up off the floor and stormed toward the apartment door. I calmly picked up my blunt and lit the end of it. I needed the shit to calm my nerves before Lauren got home. I didn't have time to be playing with this little dumb-ass chick. What could she really do to me anyway? If she called the cops she would be telling on herself and if she told Lauren anything I would deny that shit until the bitter end. Yancy was harmless. All I had to do was bait her silly ass back in with more promises that I'd eventually leave Lauren for her. In the meantime, I'd keep telling her how sorry I was for putting my hands on her, buy her a few nice, expensive gifts and then I'd give her some of this sweet, hard dick. She'd be back to her normal self in no time. Or so I thought.

LAUREN

The entire ride home from the Chanel store I could not stop thinking about the three million dollars. I figured that if Matt did have the correct bank account number and there was in fact that amount of money in that account then all I needed to do was come up with a way of how I was going to get the entire three million dollars out of that account and away from Matt and Yancy without giving them shit. I had a few ideas in mind, but I knew Matt still had that street mindset so I needed to be real careful. Even though Matt was on parole he still had street connections that ran deep enough to wipe me off the face of the earth if he wanted to, so I would have to tread lightly. His accomplice, Yancy, was just a fucking trick we picked up off the streets so she was harmless. All I had to do to her was call her pimp. I'm sure he'd love to know where she was.

As soon as I put my key in the condo door the door swung open, yanked my hand, and scared the holy shit out of me. I came face-to-face with Yancy.

"Um, Lauren." Yancy gulped like it was a surprise that I was coming into my own place. Her face was scrawled into a disturbed expression that seemed to be a cross between anger and grief. She definitely wasn't too pleased to see me. Too bad though, because this was my fucking house and she was a guest as far as I saw it. And if it were up to me, she'd be gone a long time ago. Lucky for her, Matt kept her onboard for . . . obvious reasons.

"You scared me storming out of the door like that," I huffed. I could immediately see in her face that she was upset. "Where are you going? Don't we have this big score to discuss?"

I wondered if Matt cursed her out and told her to get the fuck out because she looked totally out of it. Her caramel skin was blotchy and red like she'd been crying and her usual perfectly laid makeup was smudged and crazy-looking.

"Ask your man about it because I need some air," Yancy said, sounding like she was using every fiber in her body to hold on to her composure. I had known her long enough to know when she was on the brink.

"Take your time," I replied sarcastically. Truth be told, having her out of my hair was the best thing she could do right now. I've found it very hard to keep up a front in front of her and Matt. To see her anywhere near him made my skin crawl. I loved Matt. So to know that he was dicking Yancy down every time I turned my back felt like a dagger was constantly being thrown at me. So, I hoped she'd find a balcony to jump off while she was out there. Fucking home wrecker!

Once I was inside, Matt came walking down the hallway from the back of our house.

"What's up, bae?" he said, forcing himself to smile. His facial expression was strange-looking. Now that I think about it, it was the same look he wore the very first time I caught him in the act of cheating on me. "You tell me what's up." I cocked my head to the side and answered him. I knew something wasn't right. I knew Matt very well. He was an open book at the time. So whatever went on between him and Yancy before I got here, I wanted to hear about it. But I wanted to hear it come from his mouth. I've learned that when you start guessing shit, you end up putting words in the next person's mouth.

"Why you looking at me like that?" he asked me. I could tell that his mind was racing. He knew I knew something but what it was, he wasn't sure.

"What's wrong with Yancy? What, y'all had a little fight or something?" I asked as casually as I could.

"Nah, she just got an attitude because I told her to keep a tight lid on spending so much money right now."

I knew he was lying. Matt never put a cap on how much money any of us could spend. His deception made my pulse quicken and my insides immediately started boiling. I'd been having this feeling a lot lately. It's so far from the feelings I had around Matt when we first got together. I couldn't help but think back to that fateful day. . . .

May 2005

Matt was the biggest drug dealer in the Virginia Beach area. He was like a king in our neighborhood and everybody knew he had the entire Virginia Beach on lockdown with his premium heroin and the best weed in the South. Matt was that dude who made his reputation off having good product and a no-nonsense attitude. Matt was both the most feared and most admired dude in the entire city. Matt was that dude who drove a different car every week, never wore any of his designer clothes more than once, and lived it up every single night in the clubs and expensive restaurants. I think he was making something like two hundred thousand dollars a week off street sales alone. Matt was the boss and everything about him screamed boss. Matt wasn't the hand-to-hand dude; instead, he employed almost all of the little dope boys in the city. Matt had connections far and wide and even had the police on his payroll. Matt had a criminal enterprise worth millions. His tall, statuesque physique, smooth chocolate skin, perfectly straight white teeth, and the perfect set of waves on his head made every girl in the hood fall at his feet trying to get his attention. Chicks were literally fighting over Matt in the streets, I had witnessed it myself. Mad chicks hated me and wanted to take my position as his girl. Matt had money and *charisma. Not to mention, he had the swag of Jay-Z and Rick Ross put together since his jewelry and watch game was on bling and his clothes were always of the best quality. I don't think I had ever seen him in anything that cost less than a stack each piece.*

Of all the chicks in Virginia Beach, I was the chick who had snagged him and got wifed by him. There were a lot of people in the hood who couldn't understand why he had chosen me. For some reason, Matt had pursued me relentlessly after he first laid eyes on me in the club. I couldn't believe it when Matt was so hard-pressed for my number because I was nowhere near his status. Shit, I was still living in the projects with my crackhead mother and boosting food and clothes just to get by. The one good thing I always did was attend school and get good grades. Later Matt told me that part of the reason he wanted me was because he knew I was one of the few chicks in the hood who went to school every day and he also found it honorable that every other dude around the way hadn't been with me and talked about it. No, I wasn't that type of chick. I was so focused on being the opposite of my drug addict, pussy-selling, trifling-ass mother that I made sure I carried myself totally different. I wanted out of the hood so I figured the only way to do it was to stay in school; who knows maybe I'd go to college and end up with a good job or something.

I mostly stayed to myself, went to school, and never paid the dope boys any mind. Until Matt pushed up. His approach was different, yet I still played hard to get. He had been the perfect gentleman. He was always respectful, sent me flowers, and bought me loads of gifts all before I even agreed to go on the first date with him. Once I did go out with him, I was immediately in love. Matt treated me like a precious diamond and in turn, I was as loyal a woman as they come.

By 2003 and within a year of our first date, Matt had changed my life, but of course, I found out real fast that the good life with Matt came at a high price. I had literally lost my sense of self. I wasn't interested in attending college anymore because Matt had convinced me that we would always have money. I had everything a girl could ask for, except friends and my family. I became the envy of every girl in my neighborhood. I had never really experienced blatant jealousy on that level before. It was a real lonely-ass life. Girls would throw rocks at my windows. Throw shade on my name in the streets. Anything to get Matt for themselves. It was crazy. Matt was busy with his business and slowly but surely he was making less and less time for me. Everybody wanted Matt and in the beginning he made me feel like he didn't want anybody but me. He used to always tell me not to even think about other chicks because I was his number one. He referred to me as the first lady all of the time. During those early months, Matt and I spent lots of time together going out to eat, shopping, fucking, and just being a solid couple. Then it happened, for the first time after we had been together two years, drama and bullshit came into our relationship and it was all because of the hoes.

Another Saturday had come and I was sitting on the edge of the bed watching Matt get his shit together to go out while he was expecting me to stay in the house doing absolutely nothing.

"Why you always get to go to the parties, but you want me to stay home all of a sudden?" I had asked Matt as he got dressed in his finest threads to leave the house. "I mean you used to take me everywhere. Now we hardly do shit together and it's like you want me to stay hidden in the house or something," I griped. "What? You don't like my hair? Did I gain weight? I'm not pretty enough to be out with you no more? What is it, Matt?" I pressed. I could see a look of disgust darken his face.

"Lauren, not this shit again. You already know the deal. The life ain't new to you. So why you actin' brand-new all of a sudden? When you the first lady of a street nigga of my caliber you gotta abide by street rules. I go to these bullshit parties to hustle, to make major deals that will benefit the both of us later, not to be out and about. It ain't about partying, it's about elevating shit for us. I got to keep my endgame in mind. Feel me?" Matt said with a hint of irritation lacing his words. I rolled my eyes and sucked my teeth.

"Yeah right," I huffed. "You can't be conducting business every Friday, Saturday, Sunday, and sometimes during the week, too, Matt. We don't do shit together anymore. And I'm tired of being in this fucking house," I snapped.

"Word to my unborns, Lauren. I can't even believe you trippin' like this right now. You act like I don't try to protect you. This game ain't no place for that pretty-ass face. Sometimes I'm meeting niggas from out of town and I don't know what their real intentions are. A nigga could be setting me up for the downfall and I don't want you in harm's way if that's the case. Niggas who ain't in my circle don't need to know who my girl is. Period. If shit jump off and they can't find me, they gon' come looking for you. I don't need that kind of stress just because you wanted to prove a point about having your ass in the streets. The people who

matter know you my first lady so why you trippin'
about hanging on my arm in a fuckin' hood rat–ass
club? Stop the madness, Lauren. I need you to play
your position and act like a queen. Be easy and life
will always be good for us," Matt preached.

I rolled my eyes and twisted my lips. I wasn't trying
to listen to that fucking sermon he was spewing. I
guess all that talking was supposed to ease the tense
tightening I was feeling in my stomach but it didn't. I
was battling with that gut feeling that women get that
tells them something ain't right with their man. Something was up and I felt it, regardless if he wanted to
admit it or not. I knew what time it was.

Matt walked over and pulled me up from our specially made California King bed. He pulled me into
his chest and the scent of his cologne already had my
pussy thumping. I hated that this nigga made me so
weak in the knees all of the time.

"Just stay home with me," I whined all babylike.

"Stop being like that, Lauren. You know I would
have you with me, but shit is a little sketchy tonight.
I'm meeting a new connect from out of town about
some business and I don't know the nigga from a can
of paint. I need to be on my P's and Q's and if you're
there I will be distracted," Matt said as he softly
stroked my long hair. "I can't have that, baby girl. I really
need this deal to be official with no worrying and no
bullshit." Matt was laying it on thick and I was playing right along too. The whole time I was thinking,
This nigga thinks I'm stupid.

"I hate all of this being alone lately, Matt. Seems
like I'm always in the house. You don't take me shopping now, you just send me with a stack of cash. You
don't take me to dinner, you just send a chef. I mean,

it is not the same anymore. You ain't even giving me the dick like you used to," I whined some more. Matt pulled me away from his chest and looked into my eyes. He started laughing like I had just told the funniest joke. I looked at him and crinkled my face in confusion as to what was so damn funny.

"So that's what this is all about? You want some of this long dick?" he joked. I rolled my eyes, but I couldn't keep the silly smile from forming on my lips. Matt had that good-good. I couldn't stay mad at his ass for nothing once he threw that dick on me. I never turned down a chance to get some.

"Oh, I can give you the dick right now," Matt joked, grabbing a handful of his crotch. I blushed so hard I could feel my cheeks turning red. Matt quickly shrugged out of his jacket and had his pants coming down within seconds.

"No, go to your party. . . ." I started, trying to play hard to get. "I don't even want none if you just gon' dick me down and leave me here."

My words went tumbling back down my throat when Matt roughly put his mouth on top of mine.

"Get off that bullshit and get on this dick," he huffed. I shivered as the heat of his breath sent a ripple of chills down my back. He extended his tongue into my mouth and I accepted by sucking on it gently. Within seconds I was so wet I could feel my own juices soaking the seat of my lace panties.

"Your friends . . ." I whispered. I knew Matt had his crew waiting outside for him.

"Nobody comes before you," Matt huffed. His words made me feel all warm and fuzzy inside. Damn, I loved him so much I could feel it in the deepest part of me.

Matt moved his mouth from mine and trailed his

tongue down my neck. I let out a windstorm of breath and squeezed my eyes shut. I loved when Matt made love to me. Sometimes he liked to rough-fuck me, but that night, he was seemingly taking his time with every inch of me. After a lot of hot and heavy petting, I was ready to feel Matt inside of me.

He pushed me back onto our bed and had me out of my pants in a quick flash. My legs trembled just thinking about Matt's long, thick tool entering my deep, moist center.

"Give it to me, please," I panted.

"You don't ever have to beg for this dick," he whispered as he climbed onto the bed. A single tear drained out of the side of each of my eyes when he said that. I was so in love with Matthew Connors that I truly felt dizzy. I thought he was all that I needed in life, not even food and water could sustain me like being with Matt did at that time.

Matt guided himself into me. "Ohh," I cooed. I arched my back and tilted my pelvis so I could feel all of his thickness fill me up. Matt reared up and slammed into me with the force of a wrecking ball.

"Ahh," I winced. "Yes."

His stroke hurt so good. Matt grinded his hips until his dick was so deep inside of me it felt like we were one.

I tried to match his motion but he was too much for me. I whimpered—a mixture of ecstasy and agony.

"Fuck me," I whispered. "Never stop."

Matt abruptly pulled himself out of me causing my eyes to pop open to find out why. Before I could react or ask, Matt roughly flipped me onto my stomach. I let out a lusty, throaty giggle. It was nervousness that caused it.

"Ahh," I breathed when I felt his tongue against my sizzling-hot skin. Matt was licking from the base of my neck straight down my spine. When he got to my plump, round ass he placed each of his hands on each of his ass cheeks. He gently parted them. The anticipation was killing me. I curled my toes. Then he did it. Matt buried his tongue in the center of my ass crack and began licking like a hungry dog.

"Oh shit!" I gasped. My vaginal walls were pulsing with the first climax. I screamed out Matt's name.

Matt chuckled. "You like that shit, huh?" he whispered. He went back to running his tongue up and down my crack roughly. I clutched the sheets with both hands and let out a series of ohhhs and ahhs. Matt tossed my salad like it was going to be his last meal. My body actually felt like it was floating. Every nerve ending tingled.

"Get up on your knees a little bit," Matt urged.

My legs were trembling so bad I didn't think I could do it.

"I can't. You got me too weak," I huffed. Matt gave me a firm push to help me up onto my knees.

"Owww!" I hollered as Matt slammed his thick dick into my soaking wet center from the back. Instinctively my body inched forward but Matt grabbed me back toward him.

"Don't try to run now. You wanted this dick, now take it," he rasped. He slapped my left ass cheek roughly. I squealed in response and tried to run away from him again.

"Oh God!" I blurted out.

"Nah, you fuckin' playin'. Don't call God now, call out your daddy's name! What's my fuckin' name?" Matt growled.

"Matt," I said, barely audible.

"What? I can't fuckin' hear you!" he barked. He leaned down and while his dick was still buried deep inside of me he lifted me up and fucked me from behind like we were two dogs in heat.

"Uh, ah, uh, Maaattt!" I belted out as I reached the most earth-shattering climax I'd ever had. Within seconds Matt was growling from his climax.

We both collapsed on the bed—me on my back and Matt on his stomach. I rolled onto my side and rubbed his back gently. I was saying a little silent prayer that my pussy would've been enough to keep him in the house with me.

"Just promise me shit is solid with us," I whispered.

"You know I don't make promises, but I will tell you that you my wifey and I love your ass," Matt affirmed. I closed my eyes and smiled. That was what I wanted to hear.

Not even an hour after that beautiful lovemaking session, Matt was in and out of the shower and back into his going-out clothes. My heart was crushed. My prayers had fallen on deaf ears.

I sat on the side of the bed pouting until Matt left. Once he was gone I jumped up and grabbed my cell phone. "Yeah, girl. He's gone. You ready? I can be ready in thirty minutes." I called my girl Daysha and she was at my house in no time to get me.

"Damn, chick, you trying to creep up on Matt or you trying to snag another nigga?" Daysha gushed as she gave me the once-over. "Bitch, you look fucking hot to death in that outfit. I would've thought you was going to New York Fashion Week in all of that haute couture shit you rocking."

Daysha was the one chick from my old neighbor-

*hood who never turned her back on me or threw me
any shade. She and I had been down for years.*

"You like it?" I asked, trying to act all modest like I
didn't know I was the shit in my deep purple form-fitting
Gucci dress and a pair of purple-and-black pointy-toe
python Gucci stilettos. I had pulled my long, dark hair
back into a classy chignon and adorned it with a
beautiful mother-of-pearl Louis Vuitton hair clip.

One thing about me, Lauren Kelly, I was a bad
bitch and I knew it. I was a slim five feet six inches
tall. I had long, slender yet muscular legs, a tight ass
that sat up like a donkey booty, and more than a
handful of perky C-cup titties. My only complaint
about myself was my high yellow complexion. Against
my dark hair sometimes my very fair skin made me
look too light, even ghostly. Growing up, my cousins
always teased me calling me Albino and White Girl so
I developed a complex about my skin color. Rumors
were always circulating in my family that I was a
white trick's baby. I mean you could tell I was a black
girl because of my beautiful mixed features—full lips,
high cheekbones, pointed nose, thick luscious hair,
and round light brown eyes—but if it was just up to
my skin color I could easily pass for white.

"Do I like it? Bitch, I love that Gucci runway dress
and those stilettos are the shit," Daysha carried on excitedly. I laughed. I loved to get compliments. Daysha
was funny as hell too. She didn't look so shabby herself
in a sea-green Donna Karan one-piece flare-leg jump-
suit, a pair of multicolor Brian Atwood sandals, and
her green Chanel mini. Daysha kept a hustle so her
banging outfit didn't surprise me.

"Okay, now when we get in the club I want to hide

out for a little bit before Matt sees me. I just want to see what is going down before I let him know I'm there. Plus, I don't want him to spot me and try to send his people to make my ass leave. You know how possessive and crazy he can be sometimes," I told Daysha. "He is not going to be happy to see me, but oh well. I guess you can just say that I am hard-headed." I laughed. I was playing it off in front of my friend, but that ill feeling in my gut was still lingering. My sixth sense was definitely on high alert that night.

"Bet! I'm with that," Daysha chimed, clapping her hands like she always did to emphasize her points. "Let's go bust up a nigga's party," she cheered.

Daysha and I cracked up as we grabbed our pocket-books and headed for the door.

I had to pay three different corner boys to finally give up the goods about what club Matt and his crew were hanging at for the night. Niggas was being tight-lipped until I pulled out those stacks that I had taken out of Matt's safe. Once we found out, Daysha drove her car over to Club Domino. It was in a seedy part of town but I didn't care. I had a point to prove.

The inside of Club Domino was lit. It was tightly packed with people from all over Virginia Beach and from the sounds of it the DJ was one of the best in the business. The clubs in the worst neighborhoods were always the best ones.

"Damn, everybody and they mama up in here tonight," Daysha screamed over the music. "Shit, I better find a man while I'm up in this piece looking all fine." I laughed at her. Daysha was constantly on the hunt for a man but she was so wild she never kept one for long.

Daysha and I could hardly navigate through the sea of bodies so we held on to each other to make sure we didn't get separated.

"You ain't never gonna find that nigga Matt up in this crowd," Daysha yelled into my ear over the music.

"All we gotta do is find the VIP. You know how he rolls . . . always showing the fuck off. I'm sure he's posted up in the VIP section somewhere with mad niggas and mad expensive bottles. You know, Matt-style," I yelled back into her ear.

"True! True! Well, we have to find out exactly where it's at," she yelled back. "For now, let's head to the bar and see what simple nigga we can get to trick on our drinks," she said. I just laughed. I loved her ass.

Daysha and I headed straight to the bar and ordered our own drinks. I ordered a cosmo and Daysha ordered a Hpnotiq. The simple niggas were swirling around us in no time. It felt real good to be out and it felt even better to know that I could still get attention like that. I didn't realize it until then that I had been cooped up in the house playing wife and living a boring-ass life. Niggas in the club were loving us and of course Daysha was soaking it all up. She had already gotten us another round of drinks for free.

I turned from the bar and looked out into the crowd. Of course I wasn't going to find Matt in that sea of people. But I did peep that there were some real pretty chicks up in the club. Instead of enjoying myself and the attention I was getting, I was preoccupied with taking mental notes on how many of the gorgeous chicks Matt might be attracted to. I immediately started feeling insecure. My gut feeling was back and it was making me feel sick.

"Yo! I just spotted the fucking VIP ropes," Daysha said, excitedly elbowing me in the ribs. She tilted her head and nodded toward the far left of the club. As people swayed to the music and opened up tiny gaps I got a quick glimpse of those famous velvet ropes that everybody knows separates VIPs from the general club-goers.

"C'mon. Let's go bust up that nigga's party," Daysha said, starting to move. I grabbed the back of her jump-suit and pulled her back, almost making her fall flat on her ass.

"Yo! What are you doing? Ain't this what you came here for?" Daysha screamed at me with her face folded into a frown.

"Let's give it a few minutes," I said nervously. "I have to make sure I'm ready for whatever. Matt might act stupid. I have to be prepared."

My nerves were all of a sudden frazzled. I couldn't tell if I really wanted to know what Matt was doing or not. I started second-guessing myself and feeling guilty, like what if Matt was right about keeping me out of harm's way.

"Lauren, I ain't come out here to play stupid games. We came to party and getting in VIP with Matt and them is where I wanna be," Daysha snapped, tapping her foot. I knew that meant it would only be a few more minutes before her ass got real impatient with me and stormed over to the VIP section alone. Daysha was one of those bold chicks who didn't give a fuck.

"Okay. Okay. Let me just get one more drink in my system. I might need my liquid courage," I said.

I downed my drink and ordered one more.

"Oh hell no! What you ordering more drinks for? Are you here to creep on Matt or not? Shit, you acting mad scary," Daysha complained.

"Let me finish this drink and then we will go," I placated.

"Don't be acting scared. This is why this nigga thinks he can keep your ass under lock and key . . . you always acting like you scared to roll up on his ass," Daysha said tauntingly.

"I ain't never scared," I snapped back. I guess her words had put the battery in my back. I slammed the empty glass on the bar, threw three twenty-dollar bills up on the bar, and headed in the direction of the VIP section.

I am not sure why my legs were shaking and my heart thumping, but they were. A cold feeling shot down my spine like something bad was about to happen to me. Even with the dance floor packed with people I felt like I was all alone walking into impending doom.

Daysha got to the velvet ropes first. The thick, purple velvet ropes were all that separated the VIP section from the rest of the club. A thinly veiled material hung at either side of the entrance, too, but those paper-thin sheers did not obscure my vision of all of the people behind them.

There was a tall man dressed in a suit standing guard in front of the VIP entrance and he used his body to block our entrance when Daysha approached.

"Only specially invited guests in this area," the man growled.

"We are specially invited guests. This is Matt's wife," Daysha said sassily, pointing to me like the man should've known that. I was stuck on stupid, unable to even move. I had already peeped what I needed to see. I put my hand against my chest because I felt like I was having a heart attack. My chest literally felt tight like my heart was about to stop.

"What proof does she have?" I heard the man ask Daysha.

Daysha turned toward me. I don't know if she noticed how pale my face had turned or if it mattered to her that my mouth was halfway open in horror.

"Lauren? Tell him you're Matt's wife so he can just let us by," Daysha said to me. Suddenly, my ears began ringing and I could no longer decipher what song the DJ was playing. I blinked a few times and then all of a sudden I felt an unknown force pushing me forward. I swear it was like a demon had jumped into my body and possessed me. I raced around the tall security guard, kicked over the stand that held the velvet ropes, and rushed into the VIP section so fast that even Daysha was shocked. I was pushing and shoving bitches out of my way and I didn't give a damn.

"Oh shit!" I heard some of Matt's dudes say when they noticed me barreling toward Matt like a madwoman.

"Lau . . ." Matt started to say my name but he was forced to swallow it. His eyes flew open as wide as saucers and he didn't even have time to react. Neither did the bitch on his lap. Within seconds I had my hands tangled in her long, wet, and wavy weave.

"Oh nigga this is why you wanted me to stay home!" I barked as I yanked the girl's hair like I was trying to take her head off.

"Ahhh!" she shrieked. It was too late. I had already dragged her off of Matt's lap and onto the floor. I freed one of my hands, curled it into a fist, and slammed it into her face.

"Bitch! You wanna fuck with other people's man!" I growled as I rained punches down on her face.

"Get off me!" the girl screamed. "Get off me!" Her legs were splayed open as she tried to free herself from my grasp. I took the opportunity to drive my pointed toe heel right into her naked pussy. "Argghghghgh!" she squealed gutturally, like a baby pig being slaughtered. I was able to get one more kick in near her ribs before I felt myself being hoisted in the air and pulled off of her.

"Yo, Lauren! You fucking crazy!" Matt screamed at me as the security guard grabbed me up. I kicked my legs and flailed my body wildly. I know I probably looked crazy but that was fine because it was exactly how I felt.

"Fuck you! Fuck you, Matt! I can't believe you did this to me!" I screamed with tears running in streams down my face. "You're a fucking liar! You ain't got no fucking love for me! Liar!" I screeched. As the security guards carried me away I managed to get my left stiletto off. I hurled it in Matt's direction. He jumped back and ducked just before the shoe could hit his ass in the head.

"I fucking hate you! I fucking hate you!" It was a mixture of hurt and devastation that came through in my words. That was just the first of many times I would find Matt cheating and feel so powerless that I would forgive him.

Now, I had to force myself to blink away that crazy memory of the past. "Are you a'ight?"

Matt asked me as his eyes squinted into suspicious dashes.

"Yeah, I'm good. I'm just trying to figure out why Yancy bolted out of here like she did."

"How am I supposed to know? Maybe it's that time of the month," Matt replied nonchalantly, walking over and kissing me on my cheek. It was the exact same shit he'd done all of the other times he was guilty of being unfaithful.

My insides were churning. I wanted to tell him so badly that I knew that once again he was being a fucking dog and cheating on me, although I was the one who had been holding him down after he'd lost everything he used to have.

"Are you ready to plot our next hit?" he continued.

"Sure, why not?" I said as I kicked off my shoes. "But three million dollars in one account sounds a little suspect. But I'm still willing to take a chance and see if we can get it out by wires," I told Matt.

"Think you can call your dude Ryan up north and see if he can crack the account? 'Cause if he can then we can say good-bye to all of this petty fucking stealing and credit card scamming bullshit. And I can finally buy back into the game and get back on my feet. Make money the way I used to do it. Boy it would feel good to be back on my grind. This white-collar shit is a'ight. But it ain't like that street money. That street money comes with power and respect. Not this shit here. Sometimes I feel like a fucking petty-ass thief after we come off with five and ten grand jobs. That ain't no real money to a nigga like me. I need to make the kind of dough I used to make when I was in the streets. I wanna feel like the leader I am," Matt said.

"Oh really?" My nostrils flared and I bit down into my jaw to keep myself from saying what I really wanted to say to him. How fucking dare he talk about buying back into the game and getting back on his feet when I'd been the one holding us down since the drug raid that had ended his street deals. I was also the one who scammed up the money for the defense attorney that kept his ass out of going to prison for life. And because of all the stress I ended up losing a baby I didn't know I was pregnant with until it was too late. I went through the loss of the baby by myself because Matt was locked up behind bars. What's even more fucked up was that I hadn't been able to get pregnant since. The only reason I could think that this was happening was because Matt was too busy shooting sperm up in all the other bitches. Right now, he was definitely treading on thin ice with me.

"Yeah, really. I don't feel like I run this shit. Sometimes it feels like I work for you and that ain't cool. I want my own shit! I wanna rebuild my empire. So as soon as we get this bread, I'm calling my connects and then I'm gonna branch off."

"I see you got everything all planned out. So, I'll call my dude, but you, me, and Yancy are going to have to talk about percentages," I said flatly. "Now I know that she found the wallet but that still doesn't entitle her to the lion's share of the money. It's going to come down to who has the resources to get that money into our hands."

"I figured that you were going to say that," Matt replied. "It's always about who is going to get more and who gets less with you, Lauren. "

"You damn right. I started this whole thing. If it weren't for me, then we wouldn't be living the life we're living. Look at this place. Look at the cars we drive. So, of course, I'm gonna say who gets what," I told him.

"Look at how quickly we forget who took who out of the fucking hood!" Matt snapped. I could tell that he was becoming very irritated with this conversation of ours.

"I haven't forgotten shit. I know what you did for me."

"Are you sure? Because right now, you're acting like you've done everything for me. When in fact, I put you up in a house, paid all the bills, and took care of you."

"Look, Matt, I already said that I remembered what you did for me before you went away and did time. So I'm not trying to go back and forth with you. All I'm saying is that, you can try to get your hands on the money on your own, or you can agree to my terms and we all walk away happy."

"Whatever, Lauren. Just make the phone call and let's make this shit happen," Matt folded.

I smirked and shook my head in the affirmative. "Now that's the spirit," I said sarcastically.

One thing about me, I might have come from the hood but I didn't have a hood mindset at all. I was going to get mine no matter what. Too bad, I was going to see to it that Matt and Yancy didn't get shit.

I left Matt in the room and headed back outside to make the call to my computer geek, Ryan. I needed some privacy so I elected that my car would be the best place for it. As soon as I got into the driver's seat I started dialing his number but before I could press the send button an incoming call came through. I looked down at the caller ID and noticed that it was my homegirl Daysha so I answered it. "What's up, girl?" I said.

"Nothing much. Where you been? I've been trying to get up with you."

"You know me. I don't sit in one place too long," I joked.

"Think you can get me a couple of five-hundred-dollar American Express gift cards? I got this nigga looking for some and he said he's got the money now. So, I'm trying to catch me a lick. I got bills piling up my ass and I need to put some money on my baby daddy's commissary account. Ugh, I just need a break."

She seemed very flustered, but I wasn't feeding into her shit. I've given her plenty of opportunities to get her own cash, but she fucked every last one of them up. Instead of selling the gift cards I had given her, she kept them for herself and lied about them being stolen. Then she almost got caught cashing one of the phony checks at a check-cashing spot. The lady gave Daysha a hard time about the check telling her that she needed another form of ID so instead of Daysha saying that she didn't have it and that she would take her business elsewhere, she starts cursing the lady out and makes a scene. In the end, the lady kept the check and the fake ID and called the cops. Luckily Daysha got out of there before the cops got there, because if she hadn't her silly ass would've gone to jail. And who knows, she probably would've blown my whole operation. From that day, I put her on ice. I never got her to do anything else, even though I knew she needed the money. She was a liability. So, from time to time I'd throw her a few bucks just so she could have a few dollars in her pocket.

"Nah, Daysha, you know I don't do those gift cards anymore. They started becoming a hassle so I just did away with them," I lied. I wasn't dealing with her on that level anymore.

"Well, can you send me on one of those check-cashing jobs? 'Cause I need some money bad."

"Come on, Daysha, why you making me go there with you? You know what happened the last time I sent you on one of those jobs."

"Yeah, but that's been over six months now," she whined.

"It doesn't matter, Daysha. You almost put my business in jeopardy. So I can't trust you handling a job like that anymore."

"Oh so it's like that?!" Daysha said, clearly irritated.

"Yeah, it is. But if you need a few dollars I can come 'round there and give you a couple hundred bucks," I offered. I figured it was better than having nothing.

"What the fuck is two hundred dollars going to do for me? I can't do shit with that, Lauren. I can't even pay my fucking water bill with that."

"It's more than what your baby daddy ever gave you," I hissed. This chick was really starting to get on my nerves. How dare she call me like I fucking owe her something? I didn't tell her to get with that bum she had a baby by. That's her fault she doesn't know how to manage her money. Not mine.

"Yo, Lauren, that was real foul shit to say to your homegirl. You definitely showed me how you truly feel about me."

"Look, Daysha, do you want the money or not?" I asked her. I wasn't about to join her pity party. I had shit to do. I had a phone call to make that was going to bring me a three-million-dollar payout. So, this chump change that Daysha and I were talking about was taking up my time.

"Nah, keep it and give it to somebody else," she said, and then she disconnected our call.

Normally I would call her back when we had our little spats. But this time, I let her go because I had a big fish to catch. And my white boy in Maryland named Ryan was the man to help me do it.

MATT

Lauren had once again worked her magic with her hacker connection. She had somehow managed to get her connect Ryan up in B'more to change all of the account information into the names of Mr. and Mrs. Belton, who would be played by us when we went into the bank. For real, when she first proposed the idea to me, I was looking at her like she was out of her fucking mind. I mean, I thought we were just going to have the money wired to new accounts, but Lauren was talking about us walking into the bank as a rich couple and walking out with a briefcase filled with cash. "I thought shit like that only happened in the movies," I had said to Lauren. She laughed and told me she had everything under control. I guess she did.

All we had to do now was come off as the ritzy Beltons. We'd walk into the bank, meet with the branch manager, and walk out with the cash. At least that was the plan. Sounded easy, but in the theft line of business nothing was ever really that easy. One wrong word, look, or move and you could find yourself trapped in the bank until the cops arrived. I wasn't trying to go back to the joint so Lauren better know what she was doing.

Slinging dope was much easier than making money doing this white-collar shit. At least in the dope game you knew exactly who your enemies were and could try to be ready for a sneak attack. In the scamming business you could've just scored big and never saw that a bank employee or store clerk had hit the button to call the police on you. Who said white-collar crime was safer than street crime?

I flexed my neck and buttoned the top button on my custom-fitted French cuff dress shirt. I stuck my arms out in front of me and admired the shimmery diamond cuff links that were glistening from my wrists. Everything I was wearing felt rich against my skin. A feeling I hadn't experienced in a while. It felt damned good to get dressed up in a custom-tailored Armani suit, brand-new wingtip Ferragamo loafers, and the big H Hermès belt. To seal the deal on my rich look, I slid on the solid gold Presidential Rolex Lauren had gotten me off one of her credit card trips. I took one last look at myself in the mirror behind our bedroom door. It had been mad long since I'd dressed up like this.

"Sharp as shit. Not bad if I do say so myself. Damn, nigga, you still got it. You look good as hell. Like a boss," I complimented myself. I swiped my hand over my freshly lined goatee and made sure the waves on my head were on spin. I was feeling like a boss again. I was ready for whatever. But, to make sure I was definitely ready, I slid my gun onto my belt and pulled my suit jacket over it to guarantee it was concealed. I had already told Lauren if shit went bad at the bank, I was going to shoot our way out. I had made a promise to myself that I would never go back to the joint. I would have rather died.

"Lauren. You almost ready, bae?" I yelled. I was feeling dapper and I knew if I looked this good Lauren was going to be stepping through looking even better. Lauren was beautiful inside and out. I was even more in love with her now than before. She had taken a lot of shit off of me over the years including cheating with other bitches. It wasn't something for her to take personal because I wasn't ever going to feel about the next chick like I felt about Lauren.

Lauren held me down for years. When I got locked up and lost all my shit to the fed seizures, Lauren didn't think twice about coming up with a new plan to get money for both of us. Lauren was one of the smartest chicks I knew. You would've thought she had every college degree there is, but nope, she was just made resourceful and super intelligent.

Lauren was definitely the mastermind behind our illegal credit card and check-kiting operation. When she first introduced me to this shit she never made me feel like I was less of a man . . . until just recently. That's a big reason why I was going back into the drug game. I can't have no chick of mine running shit while I just sit around like I'm her bitch! No way! That ain't how I roll. I was a man of substance. I was a fucking boss! And bosses ran their own show. Aside from all the shit that comes with this white-collar hustle, Lauren was a good girl at heart. She was my ride-or-die chick and she was the realest chick I'd ever had on my team. Lauren was also loyal. Now, we'd had a lot of fights over the years but that came with the territory. I mean, what nigga doesn't go through shit with their chicks? Street niggas didn't do anything the easy way, including loving their chicks. If only Lauren could understand that all that cheating shit was just what I did to make up for my own shortcomings. It didn't mean that I didn't love her because I loved the fuck out of her and my feelings for her weren't going to change.

As I waited for her to come out of our walk-in closet, I sat on the side of our bed with my head in my hands. Things all of a sudden started weighing on me. I was a dog nigga and I knew it. I could probably help it if I wanted but the way I grew up, only weak niggas didn't cheat. As much as I loved Lauren, I had fucked up again. This time it went deep. I was fucking with Yancy behind Lauren's back and now I was feeling like shit about it. It was like I had a sickness. As long as I can remember, pussy has always been thrown at me, so I simply had to take it. Now I'm not making excuses for my behavior, but there was no denying that Yancy was a bad bitch in a totally different way than Lauren. Lauren had that wholesome good girl appeal about her. But, Yancy had that bad-bitch, freak-in-the-sheets, I'll-suck-your-dick-on-camera type of swag about her. It was hard to pass up good pussy when it's always in your face. It was wrong, but I couldn't help it. I knew when Lauren brought Yancy around that Yancy was going to be trouble. I still remember the first day I laid eyes on Yancy. . . .

August 2011

"Help me! Heeelp! Please somebody help me!!"

I heard the screams but I was driving so I didn't see where they were coming from. Lauren had spotted her first as we drove along the street where the Virginia Beach hoes worked the strip.

"Please! Somebody help me! He's trying to kill me!"

I had finally spotted her. She was screaming and running down the street barefoot, flailing her arms over her head trying to get someone to stop for her.

"Oh my God, Matt, that's the girl that always sells me the jewelry," Lauren said to me as we drove toward the highway. "Um . . . her name is Yancy. Yeah, Yancy. Look at how she looks. Somebody must be after her."

"A'ight, so," I said nonchalantly. In my world if a bitch was running down the street either her man or her pimp was chasing her and that wasn't none of my damn business. I was on parole and I wasn't trying to catch no assault case from getting into the next man's business.

"Agh! Help!" We heard more screams as Yancy

caught up to our car sitting at the light. She had a look of terror on her face like an ax murderer was coming after her.

"So you have to stop and help her. See what's wrong at least. It's the middle of the night . . . what if a damn crazy serial killer is chasing her," Lauren said all dramatic-like. I shook my head in disbelief at what my girl was saying. Was she fucking crazy? Were we supposed to just pick up some strange girl off the street?

"Man, listen. You know damn well ain't no serial killer chasing that ho! A pimp, maybe, so that makes it none of my business. Let that chick handle her own shit. She looks like she's got a good lead on 'em anyway. Besides, she probably be robbing tricks. That's how she be getting all those watches and diamond cuff links she be selling," I said dismissively. I wasn't trying to step on the next man's toes if he was trying to handle his business. Bad enough I had lost my entire enterprise based off some jealous nigga shit. I couldn't afford to be in nothing that didn't concern me or Lauren. "If she stole a nigga's shit and he's running her ass down to get his shit back that's on her," I said flatly.

"C'mon, Matt. Please. Stop the car. We can't just leave her out here to get killed," Lauren screamed, whipping her head around frantically.

Yancy was on the side of the street flailing her hands wildly at our car and that's when I could see that her face was all bloody, her shirt was ripped exposing one of her titties, and her hair was tossed atop her head like a wild bird's nest. Somebody had fucked her up pretty damn good.

Lauren kept pressing me to stop for the girl. I

couldn't stand to hear Lauren begging and all upset like that so I finally gave in.

"Gotdamn! You about to get me involved in some shit that might have me catch a fuckin' body out here all for some ho that you don't even know like that," I grumbled. I finally relented, bust a U-turn, and pulled Lauren's whip up to where Yancy was standing. Yancy looked horrible standing there rocking on her legs like she was about to piss on herself. She was bleeding from her nose and mouth pretty bad.

Lauren rolled down her window and without hesitation Lauren yelled to Yancy, "Get in! Get in!"

Yancy frantically opened the door and scrambled into the backseat of the Benz. I could smell the strong scent of blood on her.

"Oh my God! Thank you for stopping. He was trying to kill me! Please don't let him find me!" she cried. She crouched her body down on the floor of the car instead of sitting on the backseat.

"Please don't let him get me! I will do anything to repay you, just don't let that crazy motherfucka kill me," Yancy begged. She was so scared I could hear her teeth chattering.

Just then we all heard the screech of tires behind us. I looked up into the rearview mirror. The headlights of a truck were bearing down on the back of the car like it was about to ram into the back of it.

"That's him! Please drive!" Yancy yelled, kicking her feet and hitting the back of the driver's-side chair. "Don't let him get me!"

"Drive, Matt! Drive!" Lauren screamed too. I floored the gas pedal and looked up into the rearview mirror again. Sure enough, the black Suburban was down on our ass.

"Do you see this bullshit you got us into?" I snarled at Lauren. It was too late for all of that though. We were in it now.

I whipped the Benz into the far left lane of the highway and floored the gas again. I drove right up on the car in front of me and then right before I hit the back of it I swerved in front of the car in the right lane. The car I cut in front of laid on his horn but I didn't care. I was whipping that car like I was a NASCAR driver. I swerved in and out of traffic three more times. The Benz was small enough to fit in the tightest openings between cars. I looked out of my side mirror. I smiled when I saw that the black Suburban was stuck in the left lane behind like three other cars.

"He's coming!" Lauren shouted. She saw the same thing that I saw. The SUV had swerved over in an attempt to get behind us but I was faster.

"Nah, that nigga can't touch me. I'm nice," I said. My adrenaline was pumping now. I threw the Benz into high third gear and laid on the gas. I moved at top speed and slipped into the far right lane. Within a few seconds of missing it I swerved to the right and acted like I was getting off the exit. I waited until the SUV was close and with no warning I quickly maneuvered the Benz over the grass and back onto the highway.

"Nigga thought I was getting off the exit!" I yelled out. I heard horns blaring. It was too late. The Suburban couldn't get out of the exit fast enough. There were too many cars whizzing by for him to jump back on without killing himself. I had stuck his ass in the exit. He had no choice but to get off the exit. By the time he drove around to get back on the highway I was going to be long gone.

"Take that, you dumb-ass motherfucka!" I yelled excitedly. "Wooohooo! Your boy is nice with the wheels! There ain't a nigga alive that can drive better than me," I cheered, slamming my fist on the steering wheel. Lauren's eyes were bugged out and she was holding on to the seat-belt straps for dear life. I started to laugh at her ass because she was the one who'd gotten us into this mess. I can't front; the chase was exhilarating even though I was mad as hell to be involved.

"Oh my God! I can't thank you enough! I can't believe he was going to kill me! Aggggh!" Yancy cried out. "I don't know what would've happened to me! Agggh!" She was screaming and crying like the nigga was still right behind us. She was getting on my nerves with all of that now.

"Yo, chill. You safe now. Just chill. That nigga is lost on the highway somewhere," I told her. I couldn't stand all of that fucking yelling and screaming shit. It was just a crazy situation to be thrown into like that.

I looked at Lauren out of the corner of my eye. She looked over at me and I made a face at her like what the fuck we supposed to do with this chick now? *We didn't know the chick from a can of paint aside from us buying a few hot watches, cuff links, and some nice necklaces from her. That didn't exactly qualify the chick to come chill at our spot with us. I mean if the chick was grimy enough to be stealing jewelry from tricks, what was to stop her from doing some grimy shit to us?*

I was from that street school of thought where we didn't trust nobody, not even a bitch that look like she had just gotten her ass beat. You know how many street niggas I had seen get set up by bitches posing as damsels in distress? Shit, too many to count. That was one of those classic hood setup plots. I didn't trust Yancy from the minute I had laid eyes on her but Lauren was all about it. Lauren was a kindhearted person but I wasn't feeling the whole vibe or motion of helping her.

Lauren turned up the music and leaned over to tell me, "Take her back to the condo. Let me help her get cleaned up and find out where she wants us to take her after that." I look at Lauren like she fell and bumped her fucking head. She had to be smoking some wacky-ass bud if she thought for one minute I was bringing that grimy chick to my crib off the rip.

"Nah, you bugging. You acting like you ain't grow up in the hood. Fuck out of here, Lauren. We not bringing no stranger where we rest at so you better come up with another plan," I said flatly. "I'll grab her a short stay a 'telly if you want. You want to make sure she a'ight once she check in that's up to you. I ain't about to bring no assault victim to my crib 'cause next thing I know she turn crazy talkin' about we did something to her or she have some crazy nigga following her to the crib. Use your brain," I told Lauren point blank. She was really tripping and not thinking straight at that moment. She was acting like this chick was a harmless stray dog or some shit.

"You're right. Take her to a hotel," Lauren changed her mind.

I got Yancy a room at the downtown Residence Inn. I paid it up for two nights just in case she needed an extra day to get herself together. I mean old dude had banged her up pretty badly. I was still curious about how she had gotten away if the dude chasing her was able to inflict that much damage on her. When it came down to it Yancy had two black eyes, two missing teeth, three broken fingers, a fractured rib, and a bunch of scratches and cuts. Yancy was a fighter obviously. I guess that was the first thing that intrigued me about her. She wasn't trying to go to the police or the hospital. She just agreed to stick that shit out like a trouper. Yancy had proven herself as a rider early on.

That night, Lauren went inside with Yancy and took forever to come back out. I called Lauren's cell phone like three times to make sure she was a'ight.

"You know this is some bullshit Mother Teresa shit you on right now, right?" I said to Lauren when she finally returned to the car.

"I don't know, Matt. Something is drawing me to her. Like, I feel like us running into her like this was some kind of fate or somehow meant to be. I just see so much potential in her. The few times I bought stuff from her I just picked up on that hustler spirit in her. I couldn't stand to just drive by and let something happen to her like that. She has a hunger about her that I can fuck with on the real. She really seems like she could be a smart addition to our new shit we starting. It would benefit her and us. Imagine how hungry she would be to do this credit card and check shit so she could get herself off the track," Lauren preached.

I let out a long breath. There was nothing I could say to that. My girl was just kindhearted and equally calculating like that. She wasn't just saving some ho off the side of the road. Lauren was thinking 'bout how she could get Yancy to be indebted to us and use her to our advantage. I liked that. It was her genius brain that I loved so much about Lauren.

"I guess ain't shit I can say to that. You already got stuff all planned out. I respect that though. So that's it? We paid for two nights at a hotel and you think she ain't going back out on the strip?" I asked Lauren. I was a firm believer in that "once a ho, always a ho" saying. Usually chicks like her always find their way back to the streets because that's all they know. It's a waste of time and money to help hoes like her. Those street chicks are addicted to the lifestyle and they find it real hard to give it up . . . even when their lives were on the line. In my mind, it was only a matter of time before she dipped out on Lauren. So I let Mother Teresa have her way for the time being.

"I told her to get some rest and call me tomorrow so we can talk about her getting some money without sucking dick to get it."

"You told her that?" I asked. I knew Lauren was bold with her mouth, but this took the cake.

Lauren chuckled. "No, silly. I told her that if she didn't want to go back to her pimp then she could partner up with us and make some real money. I didn't give her too many details but I told her there was some good money involved if she wanted to get out of the life. Shit, if I can put somebody else on the front lines and make money why not. It's a win-win situation. She gets off the track from selling her ass and risking her life and we get to sit back while she gets a small portion but takes all of the risk . . . why not," Lauren said in a calculating boss-bitch voice. There was nothing I could say to that except that it was a smart-ass business move that even I didn't think of.

The next day, Lauren picked Yancy up from the hotel and we all sat down to discuss our new business. Just like Lauren suspected, Yancy was willing to join our crew and she was willing to take most of the risk and less of the money just so she didn't have to go back *to selling her ass on the streets. The one thing Lauren didn't anticipate was the immediate sexual attraction I had to Yancy and that Yancy had to me. Once Yancy was cleaned up and her bruises were healing, I got to see her real looks. She was fucking beautiful and at some points I couldn't take my eyes off of her. My dick got rock hard just watching her each time I had to be around her. It became harder and harder to deny that Yancy was one sexy-ass bitch. I fought the urge as long as I could out of love for Lauren, but I was a man so that shit didn't last long.*

"What are you thinking about that got you looking so lost?" Lauren asked me, interrupting my daydream about how troublemaking-ass Yancy came into our lives. I blinked a few times to shake off the thoughts.

"You," I lied, giving her a halfhearted smile. Lauren twisted her lips and said, "Yeah, right."

"Damn, you look good," I complimented her. "Real businesslike, but also real sexy. They gon' just hand you all the money in the fucking bank looking like that." I came up from behind her and put my hands on her hips. "You sure you don't want to take off these clothes and let me take care of you before we go?" I asked sexily. Lauren swerved away from me like she didn't want me to touch her. I noticed but I didn't make a big deal out of it.

"You don't think it's too much?" Lauren asked, spinning around like she didn't just throw me the shady swerve. I eyed her up and down. My dick got rock hard too. I had been so busy focusing on Yancy because of the nasty shit she let me do to her, that I had forgotten how gorgeous Lauren really was. She still had it going on too. That flat stomach, those curvy hips, and just enough breasts to satisfy me.

"Dayum!" I huffed as I took an eyeful of Lauren's round ass in the fitted black pencil skirt she was rocking. "Nah, baby, I love that shit," I said, licking my lips lustfully. For real, how could I have forgotten how sexy Lauren really was?

Lauren looked hella classy in a formfitting blazer that hit her at the waist, a white silk blouse with an oversize bow at the neck, and the fitted black pencil skirt that stopped precisely at her knee. Of course, all of her shit was high-end designers. The black Louboutin pointed toe pumps she rocked topped her outfit off. She picked up a black classic Chanel and slung it on her shoulder, looked at her lady oyster perpetual Rolex watch and smiled at me as if to say *it's time.*

Lauren looked like a bag of money as usual and so did I. If I worked in the bank I would think she was a rich lady named Mrs. Belton without even second-guessing it. When Lauren dressed like this it didn't look forced like it did on hood chicks. It looked like she was born with a golden spoon in her mouth and even I was starting to think she was just meant to have it all.

"You look nice too," Lauren complimented me. "I hope this shit goes as smooth as we look," she said. She cracked another halfhearted smile. There was something about how Lauren had been acting lately that was real different. I couldn't put my finger on it but suddenly a feeling came over me that told me I might need to be worried. I couldn't afford another deep betrayal like I had suffered in the past.

"What?" Lauren asked, crinkling her eyebrows in confusion. "Why are you looking at me all strange like that? You want to say something? You nervous?"

"Nah, I'm good," I mumbled. "I'm never scared, baby girl. I'm definitely about this life." I wasn't going to let her know it, but I was beginning to grow real leery about her behavior lately. I had been with Lauren long enough to know that something was eating at her. I couldn't put my finger on it, but I would've bet that it had something to do with Yancy. All I could do was hope that Lauren didn't suspect that I was digging Yancy's back out on a regular. That would be some shit that would take Lauren over the top. Shit, after all I had put Lauren through, if she found out about Yancy she might even kill me.

LAUREN

I was nervous about what Matt and I had to do, but I wasn't going to show it. I had prided myself on trying to be cool under pressure, except of course when I had to fight. When I say I had to be cool I mean for my survival. First, when I was younger and had to steal food from the supermarket just to feed my sister and me, before we were separated by social services and put into two different foster homes after my drug-addicted mother lost custody of us. I'd walk in like a normal little kid and once I had goods stuffed into my pants, I'd walk out just as cool as when I came in. My sister couldn't do it. She was always looking crazy suspicious in the face. Not me, I was all about our survival. Even once we got to foster care, we still had to steal to eat.

Then, as I got older and started boosting clothes and shoes just so I wouldn't get teased in school and in my neighborhood. It was the same for me. Walk in the stores with my rigged bags, get what I wanted, and walk out like I had just purchased everything I had. It was simple.

And, after I was grown, when I started walking into high-end stores with a rack of fake credit cards and calmly buying the most expensive things in the store. I would get into the role of the credit cardholder and everything.

When you have to steal all of your life you quickly learn that showing any sign of emotion could mean the difference between walking away with what you want and being caught red-handed. I was the type who could change faces like a chameleon that changed colors. I guess growing up going from foster homes to group homes and then back to living with a crackhead mother had shaped me in some ways that I wasn't exactly proud of and had turned me into this.

Finally. Matt and I walked into the Regent Bank together hand in hand, smiling like we were the happiest rich couple in the world. It would've been nice for this to be true, but without saying it to each other, Matt and I both knew better. The illusion of a fairy-tale relationship and status in life was all good, but deep down inside, it pained me to admit that this shit was as fake as the identification we held in our possession that said we were Mr. and Mrs. Harold Belton, a wealthy power couple who had money to burn. Matt and I had shared a good laugh calling each other Mr. and Mrs. Belton on our way to the bank. I could tell Yancy was jealous at the mere sight of me but I didn't give a fuck. I figured that whatever thoughts she had about me, she'd better keep them to herself or else.

For a minute it seemed like old times between Matt and me, but it didn't take long for me to remember the time when I walked into our house and heard him fucking Yancy right in our bed. I was literally sick to my stomach. Truly, I still didn't know how I had held it in this long. If it weren't for me having the bigger picture in mind and a revenge plot cooking in my brain, I would've cut Matt's dick off and kicked that bitch Yancy down a flight of steps after I beat her ass like her pimp used to do.

"You ready?" Matt whispered to me as we waited inside the bank. He wrung his hands against each other nervously.

"Born ready," I whispered back. "Now be easy because you look straight nervous," I warned him.

This was one of the biggest jobs we'd taken on in the year and a half since I started our little business. It was also only the second time we pulled a lick together. I usually sent Matt and Yancy to do jobs together. I guess that was my biggest mistake I could've ever made.

But then I figured that it's too late to think about that now. My focus was on being convincing enough to walk out with the cash. Ryan, our computer hacker up in Baltimore, had changed the name on the account of the man who'd lost his wallet. Now the account was in the name of the fake couple Mr. and Mrs. Belton, which was us. In exchange for his brilliant work, Ryan wanted ten percent of the take for his fee, which was three hundred thousand off the top. At first, when I told Yancy and Matt they tried to complain over the fee, but I screamed on them and asked them how else were we supposed to get our hands on the money. After that, neither one of them had shit to say. Now, nothing was stopping Matt and me from walking away clean with a briefcase filled with cash except us. We had to be smooth, cool, and convincing. We couldn't mess this up. One wrong move, body language, or word and the bank personnel could get suspicious and have us like sitting ducks until the police arrived. That wouldn't be a good look at all.

I took a deep breath as I watched a tall, well-dressed white man head in our direction. He looked pleasant enough, but you never could tell with these stuffy suit types. Just like me, they also put on a good poker face right before they set your ass up for the downfall. I was going to be reading him closely.

"Good afternoon, Mr. and Mrs. Belton. I am Adam Schitz, branch manager," the redheaded man introduced himself. He bowed slightly and extended his hand out in front of him. My gut didn't get a bad feeling from him so that was the first good sign.

"The pleasure is all ours," Matt spoke up, and extended his hand to meet his for a handshake.

The bank manager smiled. "Well, I have taken care of your request for the most part. Just a few loose ends to tie up on our end."

"Thank you for seeing us on such short notice. These things come up and you just have to take care of them as quickly as possible."

"Oh, it's my pleasure. Yes, yes. We in the banking industry understand. Our economy is really taking a beating," Mr. Schitz said in a tone that was a little too cheery for me. He turned and extended his hand out in front of him like an usher in a church would do. "Right this way. I have everything set up for you. Like I said, just a few minor things to take care of before we release the funds," he said nicely. *Oh God, a few minor things. That could mean stalling us. That could mean absolutely nothing. Keep cool, Lauren.* My mind raced with all kinds of thoughts as we followed Mr. Schitz down a long hallway to a corridor with what appeared to be executive offices on each side.

Matt just nodded and smiled the entire time. I had already warned Matt's ass to be very quiet and to just nod and smile. Matt was a street dude in every sense of the word so him opening his mouth and speaking his Ebonics would not have been a good look for us. For me, it was easy to switch it up to suit whatever situation I was in. Living with foster parents from all walks of life had taught me that. I was able to turn my broken English on and off, which was also the reason I was able to do so well with the credit card scams in the ritzy stores. I could speak like the most well-educated, high-class snobs in the city. Not Matt and Yancy. Those two were ignorant as hell and most of the time drew a lot of suspicion in stores and banks. Which is why I started just sending them to do transactions that didn't require much talking like kiting the checks at the hood check-cashing spots. And to think Yancy thinks she brings a lot to the table when it comes to getting this money. She'd better sit her ass down before I send her stupid, dick-sucking ass right back to the streets where she belongs.

"Okay. Let's get right down to it," Mr. Schitz said as he closed his office door behind us. He showed us to two nice leather chairs that were situated in front of his desk. Then he briskly walked behind his beautiful mahogany desk. My eyes were immediately drawn to the picture on his desk of his seemingly perfect family—him, his wife, a son, and a daughter. I couldn't help the pang of jealously that flashed in my chest. It immediately made me envy his life, even though I hardly knew him. But the look on his wife's face was one of happiness. She looked like she had the world. And she wasn't even that beautiful. I was prettier than her. I was a damn good woman so why couldn't I have that kind of life? I deserved a husband and kids too. So, where were they? I slowly turned my focus on Matt. All he cared about was getting money in the streets and fucking bitches behind my back, so making me his wife and giving me kids was the last things on his mind, which was why I knew this job had to go off without a hitch. Matt didn't deserve me so I was going to get as far away from him as soon as the money was in my hand. I swear, my life with this nigga was finally over.

"Beautiful office," I interjected after I snapped out of my zone. I cracked a phony smile, but my heart was beating so fast it was making the material of my silk blouse flutter. It was a mixture of nerves and anger together.

Stay focused, Lauren. No personal shit today. Stay focused. I gave myself a quick pep talk. I had to wipe sweat from the side of my head. I shifted in my seat, uncomfortable. Then I looked over at Matt.

Matt was slouched down in one of the chairs like a fucking slob. I cleared my throat and smiled at Mr. Schitz as I furtively kicked Matt's foot to remind him to sit up like a real well-to-do person would. Matt's eyes went wide and he quickly took the signal and sat up straight in the chair.

Can't take this nigga nowhere! I grumbled in my head.

"So this is the release here saying that you want to withdraw a total of three million dollars from your account," Mr. Schitz said, sliding a form toward me. I looked down at the paper and parted a nervous smile. Ryan had really done it. There it was right in front of me in black and white. Sweat beads ran a race down my back and my hands shook slightly. Still, I picked up the black ballpoint pen.

"Great. Everything here looks perfect," I said in the most convincing bourgeoisie tone I could muster up. I scribbled down my alias and slid the paper toward Matt.

"Here you go, Mr. Belton," I said with a chuckle. What I was really doing was reminding Matt's ass of his alias so he didn't mistakenly sign his government name. Matt wasn't the sharpest tack in the box when it came to reading and writing. Matt smirked and scribbled down the signature of his alias, too. We signed about five other forms and then Mr. Schitz smiled smugly and nonchalantly dropped a fucking bomb on us.

"The last thing we need to do is get your thumbprints for our records," he said, still wearing that stupid, phony smile. His words were like small bombs exploding in my ears. I could feel Matt shifting in his seat next to me. I swallowed hard and slowly turned my sight toward Matt. Matt's eyes went wide and his fists curled involuntarily.

"Um . . . okay, sure," I said nervously. "Is this the procedure for all customers?" I asked, my eyebrows dipping on my face. I reached over and gently touched Matt's arm to tell him to calm down and let's just see what was going to happen.

"Oh yes. Whenever a customer wants to withdraw that much money from their accounts and wants cash in hand we have to do this for our records," Mr. Schitz explained. Matt shifted uncomfortably in his chair again. I knew Matt very well and I could tell he was gearing up for the fight-or-flight instinct.

Shit! I cursed to myself.

"Well, great then. I'm glad you have these types of protections," I said, faking like I was perfectly fine with having a thumbprint taken. It was all I could do to keep myself from running straight for the doors.

"Okay then, it'll just be a minute while I set this up," Mr. Schitz said. Matt let out a long windstorm of breath, flexed his neck, and adjusted his tie. I guess I wasn't the only one who was suddenly uncomfortable in my clothes. I hit Matt's foot with the tip of my shoe and gave him the eye. Matt shook his head left to right and swiped his hand over his face. He was showing too much nervousness.

"Okay, ready to go," Mr. Schitz said. He pulled out a fingerprint kit and had both Matt and me press our thumbs into the pad of black ink and transfer it on the documents we signed. We gave the bank manager four prints in total. And as soon as we were done he handed us wet wipes to remove the ink from our fingers. I let out a long sigh. "Well, I guess that's it?" I said, and then I smiled. I was ready to get the fuck out of this damn bank. I felt like a sitting fucking duck. I reached over and squeezed Matt's arm to get him to chime in. "You sound like you're tired, honey," he commented.

"No, I'm just a little famished," I replied. I was giving Mr. Schitz some hints to let him know that I was ready to go once and for all.

"Oh, well, we're done here so I guess you can get you two something to eat," Mr. Schitz said after he closed the fingerprint kit. Then he reached down and used his intercom to call someone to bring us the money.

I balled my toes up in my shoes and I could feel my hands shaking. We were so close. *Please God. Please God. Please God,* I chanted in my head. I could only pray that Yancy's ass was in the bank making sure she didn't see any police cars or any security heading toward the back where we were waiting. All she had was that one job. I had assigned her to be the lookout because I knew that banks sometimes stalled scammers to give the police time to come. I had had a close call once down in South Carolina.

I jumped at the sound of three hard knocks on Mr. Schitz's door. Sounded like a police knock to me. Matt looked at me and I looked at him. I could tell that, just like me, Matt was holding his breath.

Matt furtively pointed to his waist, letting me know that if the bank or the police tried to detain us there we would be shooting our way out of the bank. Matt had already said he wasn't going back to prison, that he would rather die first.

Mr. Schitz jumped up from his desk and rushed to the door. He pulled it open and at first I couldn't see who was standing on the other side of it.

"Thank you, Olga," Mr. Schitz said to the lady at the door as she handed him the two bank satchels with the money inside. There were also two security guards with her. Olga left and both of the security guards stepped into the office. I couldn't even focus. I could no longer see, hear, smell, or feel anything. It was like I was suddenly in another place. All of a sudden the room started to spin and my ears started ringing. My nerves had completely come undone. I could tell Mr. Schitz was talking to me because I saw his paper-thin lips moving but I couldn't hear what he was saying.

"Honey. Honey?" Matt shook my arm. "Are you all right?"

I snapped out of my trance and noticed that the security guards and Mr. Schitz were all watching me with confused expressions on their faces.

"I have both bank satchels. These nice guards are going to walk us to the door," Matt told me. I blinked a few times so that his words settled into my mind.

"We are finished here," Matt said. "We have our cash. We can go now." Matt was speaking like I was a deaf and dumb person who couldn't understand. I let out a long sigh. Finally, everything came together.

"I'm . . . I'm sorry. Just all of a sudden I got the worst headache," I lied, smiling awkwardly at Mr. Schitz and the guards.

"Sorry to hear that," Mr. Schitz said. "Thank you again for your business," he said with finality. Matt stood up and shook Mr. Schitz's hand. Then Matt turned toward me and extended his hand to me in a chivalrous gesture.

I grabbed his hand and let him help me up. I looked into his eyes and suddenly I saw the man that I had fallen in love with all those years ago. Matt held on to my arm and helped me get steady on my feet. I was so nervous and overjoyed at the same time that I could barely walk straight.

When Matt and I exited the bank and the warm Norfolk, Virginia, air finally hit my face tears of joy sprang to my eyes. *I did it! I did it! I did it!* I screamed inside of my head.

"Don't say a fucking word until we are in the car and back in Virginia Beach," Matt mumbled to me as we raced down the sidewalk toward the waiting car. It was the most intelligent thing I had heard him say in years.

Matt opened the door for me and let me into the backseat. Then he slid into the front passenger seat. Yancy turned toward him with greed flashing in her big bug eyes.

"Did y'all get it? Did y'all get all of the money? Is that what's in those two bags?" Yancy fired off questions in rapid succession. She sounded like a money-hungry ho, which is basically what she would always be in my eyes.

"Just drive. Get the fuck from around here and we can speak about it all later," Matt instructed. He didn't dare turn his head to look at her. I watched from the backseat with my insides practically on fire. Yancy snapped her lips shut, stepped on the gas, and headed toward the highway. There was total silence in the car. I was silently going over my plan in my head. This was going to be the sweetest fucking revenge anyone has ever carried out, I was thinking.

I'm sure Matt and Yancy were having some sinister thoughts of their own because, trust me, if there was a way they could get their hands on all of that money without having included me they would have. I was the one with the connection so they had to include me, but that wasn't lost on me.

I wondered if they were both also trying to figure out a way to fuck me out of the cash. It didn't even matter because it would come down to who was smarter in the end. As we got closer to home the reality of the situation finally started sinking in on me. We had just pulled off the biggest bank scam of our lives and we had three million dollars of free and clear cash in our possession! Both bags were heavy as hell but it didn't matter because this was a once-in-a-lifetime type of lick. I had so many plans. I was going to get the next flight out of the country and after I settled down I was going to buy myself a brand-new foreign car, a brand-new condo, and a whole new wardrobe. Who knows, maybe I'd find a new man with more money than I had. What a life that would be. Fuck Matt and Yancy. They could have this godforsaken place. I wanted bigger and better things. A husband and kids and that's exactly what I intended to get.

MATT

I can't front. My stomach was in knots all the way home. I needed a fucking blunt to calm me down. Shit like this just don't happen to regular niggas like me. All kinds of shit was running through my mind like what if we got pulled over and the cops found all this cash or what if someone was watching us and somehow knew we had the loot? When we finally pulled into our building's parking garage a warm feeling of relief came over me. I started thinking . . . *maybe this shit is reality. We got three million fucking dollars in our hands!*

As soon as me, Yancy, and Lauren were all inside of the condo, I clicked on all the locks on the doors and closed all of the shades and blinds. Even though I was home, I still felt a little uneasy. In my mind, I felt like the cops could

run in here at any given moment. This shit was
too good to be true.

I threw both of the satchels with the money in
it on the living-room coffee table, opened that
shit, and stood back for a few minutes so we
could all take it in.

"Gotdamn!" I said, shaking my head in disbelief. "I'm fucked up right now because this shit
just seemed too fucking easy." I didn't have that
kind of fucking luck. It wasn't the amount of
money that had me bugging because I had seen
more money than that when I was on the streets.
It was how easy it was that had me paranoid.

"It wasn't easy at all. This was a lot of work
right here," Lauren corrected me. "It took me a
lot of planning. This kind of lick is much harder
than slinging dope and quick snatch and grabs,"
she continued. I could tell that she was throwing shade at the drug game but I ignored her
ass. Instead of feeding into her bullshit, I stared
down at those neatly laid stacks of cash and I
swear my dick started to get hard. Looking at
that money was probably better than the best
piece of pussy I ever had in my life. I had forgotten how powerful that kind of money could
make you feel. Everybody stared at the money
for a few long moments. They were probably
thinking about how many shoes and Chanel
bags they were going to buy, but I was thinking
about how I was going to take care of my dudes
who were locked up and about how I was going
to buy back into the drug game from behind
the scenes.

Lauren was the first to walk over and pick up

one of the cash stacks. The bills were those crisp, brand-new ones that looked like they had come fresh from the United States Mint.

"This shit right here is pretty as fuck," Lauren gushed. She fanned her fingers through the bills and turned toward me and Yancy. Before Lauren could say another word . . .

"Ahhhhh!" Yancy screamed out in joy. "We are fucking rich! We are fucking rich!" she sang, dancing around the table. I saw when Lauren cut her eye at Yancy. I was thinking, *Oh boy, here comes the bullshit.* Women were so damn catty it made me sick.

Yancy rushed over and picked up another one of the cash stacks and held it up against her nose. She inhaled deeply like she was sniffing a line of the best cocaine. Her eyes rolled up in her head and her lips had a lazy grin on them.

"Ain't nothing like the smell of money to make a bitch high as shit," Yancy said, like she was getting high for real.

"Yeah, and it ain't nothing like the feeling you get when you pull it off with no strings attached. I did it. I fucking pulled it off like a pro," Lauren cheered proudly. Neither one of them was going to let the other have the shine for long. I just shook my head in disgust at both of them.

After that initial shock wore off, I was cool about the money. I didn't scream, dance, or sing about the money. I didn't need to pick up a stack, sniff it, or fan myself with it. Stacks of cash wasn't nothing new to me, but it damn sure felt good to be in that position again. I shook my head and stared at the money, reminiscing on when I had it like that. I hadn't seen that much paper since all my trap houses and my house where I lived had been raided. Back in the days this type of money would've been light work for me. I would have two and three money-counting machines going at the same time in all of my trap houses. I became lost in thought thinking about my manz Ak, Boone, Dread, and Born who were all doing time right now behind a fucking snitch-ass nigga. They had all gotten caught on the bad end of my business and I had skated with almost no time, thanks to Lauren hiring the best defense attorney money could buy at the time. I was going to have to make shit right with my crew. I was a parolee so I couldn't even go see my dudes. I mean, I sent Lauren up there when I could and I kept their commissary accounts on fleek, but that shit ain't the same as knowing your people out in the world were still holding you down. The cash laid out in front of me would be a good place to start. As soon as I got my cut the first thing I was going to do was send Lauren or somebody with a clean record up to the feds to tell my crew that I was about to find the next Johnnie Cochran–ass attorney to work on their appeals. I often dreamt of the day when we would all be a crew again. The street take-over would be real.

"I'm that bitch. That shit was like taking candy from a baby," Lauren bragged, seemingly rubbing it in. If I didn't know any better I would say she was definitely trying to provoke something with Yancy. Lauren had interrupted my thoughts with all the shit she was yapping about. It seemed like she wanted Yancy and me to feel that she was single-handedly responsible for the whole thing.

"We all did it," Yancy snapped back, feeding into Lauren's bullshit. "You ain't do everything by yourself. But that's always you . . . bossy Lauren . . . do-it-all and know-it-all Lauren. Take-all-of-the-fucking-credit-for-everything Lauren. I mean I was the one who was responsible for coming to this lick," Yancy reminded her.

Both Yancy and Lauren exchanged evil glares at each other. Yo, I don't understand why females just couldn't get along. It was so stupid how they acted when it came to dealing with each other. If they only knew how stupid and childish they looked when they took shots at each other.

"We all? I think I was the one who made it happen. You found a wallet . . . so fucking what! A bum in the street could find a wallet and after the bum took the cash out if they were *dumb* what good would the wallet be? That shit would've been useless to you if I didn't have the right connections and the right brains to make a move," Lauren shot back. She moved toward Yancy and I could tell this wasn't going to end well. Lauren had a short temper when she wanted to. I had seen that shit in action many times.

"But your connections would not have mattered if I didn't find the wallet, so what's your point? This bum found a wallet that happened to lead to this lick so you're not the only one responsible. Like I said, we all did it," Yancy went right back at Lauren. She didn't show any signs of backing down. She moved toward Lauren too. The tension between them was palpable.

I eventually stepped between the two of them with each of my arms extended out in both directions. I was literally in the middle. This is how I felt all of the time lately—like the fucking monkey in the middle.

"Yo chill. Both of y'all need to be easy. This shit was a team effort. This is supposed to be a happy time for all of us. We came off lovely. We ain't got no time for pointing fingers and shit. Look what we have in front of us . . . a future. Stop the madness and grow the fuck up," I lectured. I'm sure they could both hear the disgust in my voice.

"People need to stay in their lane," Lauren mumbled. "Bitches think because you're nice to them you like them."

"Oh, I'm in my lane," Yancy shot back. "You just mad because the lane don't belong to you no more." Yancy threw a low blow. I saw the moment when that shit hit Lauren, too.

Lauren moved her head as if Yancy's words had landed like an openhanded slap to her face. Lauren's eyes hooded over with straight malice. Her lips curled into a snarl on her face. Her nostrils flared and her fists curled at her sides. I knew that fucking look. Yancy's words were like the spark that set off the powder keg that had been building. And, BOOM! Before I could say a word the shit exploded. With the quickness Lauren maneuvered around me and grabbed a handful of Yancy's long weave. Lauren yanked Yancy's head like she was trying to disconnect it from Yancy's body. Yancy screamed but she wasn't going down without a fierce fight. She started swinging her arms trying to grab for any piece of Lauren she could grasp.

"Oh that's the problem, bitch, you think I don't know!" Lauren shouted. "You could never take anything that belongs to me, bitch, unless I let you have it!" she hollered.

"Get-the-fuck-off-of-me!" Yancy belted out each word.

"Yeah, bitch, you thought you were so tough," Lauren growled as she walloped Yancy.

"Agh!" Yancy screamed. She swung her arms wildly. I heard a cracking sound when Yancy finally caught Lauren with a two-piece right to the face. Lauren took the blow like a pro boxer and shook it off, but still wouldn't let go of her death grip on Yancy's weave. I saw a trickle of blood coming from Lauren's nose but she was still fighting.

"Bitch! I'm sick of you!" Lauren gritted. "I was the one who was there for you! I took your skank, dirty ass off the street! If it wasn't for me you would be dead somewhere, you ungrateful ho-ass bitch!" Lauren screamed as she pulled Yancy's head down and then lifted her knee until her knee crashed into Yancy's face. Lauren repeatedly kneed Yancy in the face until blood gushed from Yancy's nose. Yancy was still trying to fight but I could tell she was getting weak.

"Enough! Y'all stop that shit! Let go!" I barked

at Lauren. I tried to separate them but to no avail. They were scrapping like two wild dogs fighting over a bone. I took more than one wild slap, punch, and kick in the midst of me trying to break up their fight.

"Get off me!" Yancy screeched. Lauren wasn't letting go though. Yancy got a few hits in but she was clearly taking a dusting from my girl. Yancy tried to bite Lauren but she wasn't able to get a good grasp. She did manage to inflict a long scratch across Lauren's left cheek. I had seen enough. This time when I rushed in I took a fist to the face from Yancy but I wasn't going to let them keep fighting.

Finally I was able to grab Lauren around her waist and hoist her up. She was literally going crazy. I almost dropped her a couple of times because she was thrashing so wildly.

"Enough! Let go, ma. Let go of her hair. C'mon with this bullshit. We are supposed to be a team. Let go. You won. You always win. Let go," I urged. I was saying anything to get Lauren to give up. I knew if I didn't separate them they would fight to the death.

"C'mon, Lauren, you won," I said again.

Finally, Lauren released her grasp and Yancy crumpled to the floor in a bloody heap.

"I'll kill that ungrateful bitch! I took that bitch off the street . . . out of the gutter! Everything she got is because of me!" Lauren screamed, flailing and kicking her arms and legs trying to get back to Yancy. I wouldn't let go of her though.

"Shhh. C'mon, ma, you better than this. You

got way more going for yourself. C'mon," I placated as I carried Lauren out of the living room and into our bedroom. Once inside I dumped her on our bed. She was still going crazy. She was snorting and breathing like a bull ready to charge. Her face was red and blotchy, she had scratches on her face and neck. Her hair was a bushy mess on her head. Lauren literally looked like an escapee from a mental institution. She was acting like one too.

"Calm down, bae. It's not that serious," I told her. Lauren glared at me with her chest heaving up and down.

"You would say that," she huffed. "You would take up for a bitch like her."

I don't even know what Lauren meant by that but right then I needed to secure the money. Fuck all the dumb catfighting.

"Let me go get the money and take care of her and then we will take care of everything together," I said in a comforting tone. Lauren squinted her eyes into dashes and pursed her lips. At that moment, Lauren looked at me with the most evil, vengeful glare. That look scared the shit out of me and sent a cold chill through my body until I shivered a little bit. I hadn't seen that type of hatred and malice in a person's eyes since the day one of my workers had looked at me like that. He had shot me that exact look just weeks before he ruined me. Out of nowhere and out of my control, the day someone I had once trusted promised vengeance with his eyes started to replay in my mind. . . .

June 2010

"C'mon, Big Matt, I swear on everything I love I didn't short you. I wouldn't steal from you. I'm telling you I got robbed," Young Dane pleaded. He would say anything now that my crew surrounded him with guns pointing in his face.

"Nah, nigga. Robbed once maybe, but two and three times . . . nah," I snarled. I could tell the little nigga was lying. He was trying to insult my intelligence, which wasn't a good look. I was a good read of people like that, plus, mad dudes in the street reported back that this nigga Young Dane was flapping his gums about being on the come up. I had heard that Dane told more than one person he was stashing so he could branch out on his own. The one thing I didn't tolerate was shorting my paper.

"Listen, nigga, I was born at night not last night, feel me?" I growled. I nodded at Ak and Boone, my two right-hand men, to do their thing. They had been my enforcers for years.

"Where is the stash at?" Boone snarled in Young Dane's face. "Last time we asking."

"I'm telling you—" Young Dane started like he was trying to be tough. WHAM! Boone brought his gun down on the bridge of Dane's nose before he could even finish his sentence. I heard the cracking sound before Dane screamed out in pain like a little bitch.

"Agh! I swear! I swear, Big Matt," he cried, holding his face and trying to stop the blood from gushing from his nose.

"Don't swear, nigga. I ain't tryna get hit by lightning fucking with your lying ass," I laughed sarcastically.

"*Now, I'ma ask you one more time. Where is the money you stole? 'Cause we know you stole it, mother-fucka,*" *Boone gritted.*

"*Let me get at him. I ain't catch a body in a minute,*" *Ak said as he walked over and put the barrel of his Glock to Dane's temple. Young Dane's bladder involuntarily emptied and piss soaked his pants. We all started laughing.*

"*Oh, now you wanna be scared and pissing on yourself? Nah, you wasn't scared when you decided you was gon' violate that man right there,*" *Ak growled, pointing to me.*

"*I . . . I . . . didn't,*" *Young Dane stammered. Boone rushed over and drove his fist right into Dane's stomach. Dane's frail, skinny body doubled over at the waist and he coughed and gagged.*

"*Stand up like a man, nigga. Matter of fact, you ain't no fucking man, so I take that shit back. You a pussy and I'ma show you how pussies get dealt with 'round this fuckin' hood. Take off your shit, nigga!*" *Ak barked using his gun to hit Dane's chest for emphasis. "I want you to strip down 'til you ain't got on nothing but your fucking boxer shorts. As a matter of fact, take them shits off too. I want you to look like you did the day your sorry ass was born.*"

Dane was shaking but he knew the drill. He wasn't no stranger to me and my crew. He had been around us when we had made examples out of other lame-ass niggas before. So, this beatdown wasn't nothing new to him. When we stripped a dude and sent him on the street it was our way of telling other crews and stickup niggas that the dude was open for the taking. Trust that the street vultures would be waiting to make an example out of a nigga like Dane.

"Pl . . . Please . . . I ain't do nothing," Dane pleaded. His eyes were starting to swell shut from his broken nose. His mouth was filled with blood too.

"Nigga if you don't . . ." Ak began. He didn't even need to finish his sentence. Dane began to comply because he knew what was up. I was laughing the whole time watching this show.

First Dane removed his long, iced-out Jesus piece and chain. Boone snatched it from his hand. "Oh, a nigga went to see Mr. Ice the jeweler, I see. Don't this look like a Mr. Ice piece?" Boone said, swinging the chain so me and Ak could take a good look at it.

"For real. I thought only bosses get to go see Mr. Ice. How you affording that blood?" I said to Dane. "Shit that make you say hmmmm."

"Take off everything!" Ak ordered. Next, Dane slowly removed his Maison Martin Margiela jacket. I could tell by looking at it that it cost at least a grip and better. This nigga was really out shopping with money he had stolen from me. I just shook my head in disgust.

"This shit look like my little brother size," Boone said cruelly as he grabbed the expensive jacket and examined it closely. "Looks like this little nigga been living better than all of us. Take off that fucking Gucci T-shirt too, nigga. You like to be runway shopping I see."

I was taking delight in watching Dane get what was coming to him. My hand definitely didn't call for Dane, of all people, to be stealing from me. I had literally taken his little dirty ass off the street. He was like twelve years old when I saw him outside of the takeout begging for change to get two chicken wings. I could see the hunger in his eyes. I handed him twenty dollars *and told him to come see me the next day. He was there before I even arrived at my trap. I gave him a job as a biker runner so that he could just feed himself. I was paying Dane more than any of the other little dirty boys I had on my payroll. It was out of respect for his lineage. See, Dane's pops was doing life but before he got knocked he was one of the most revered niggas in the game. Dane's mother was another story. Back in the day when she was with his pops she was the bitch everybody wanted, but as soon as all the glitter and gold was gone, she realized she had no skills, no money, and no man. She quickly became the neighborhood ho and niggas started running up in her guts just to throw shade on her man who they knew would never see the light of day. By now, she not only had Dane; she had mad kids and didn't give a fuck about none of them. It was a sad situation to say the least, but it was the hand the nigga was dealt. I understood that shit better than anybody so I gave the nigga a job and let him move up to holding his own package.*

"A'ight, nigga, run them Jordans too," Ak demanded, pointing his gun at Dane's feet menacingly. Dane took off his sneakers. Before long, he was standing in front of all of us butt-ass naked, balls out and shivering.

"Now, nigga, you see how you standing here naked as the day you were born?" Boone asked. "Well this is how you gon' be for the rest of your life. You can't work in this town. You can't eat in this town and you can't buy shit in this town until you bring the boss every dime you stole with interest," Boone said with feeling.

Dane had his hand covering his dick and balls with tears running down his face. "This ain't right, Big Matt. I ain't even do nothing," Dane cried.

CRACK! Ak slammed his gun into the side of Dane's head. The skin split like dropped watermelon exposing the white meat. Even I winced seeing that shit.

"Ahh!" Dane crumpled to the floor. Boone used his size thirteen Timberland boot to stomp on Dane's ribs.

"Aghghgh!" Dane gurgled, then started coughing and wheezing from the force of the kick. He rolled onto his side and rocked back and forth pitifully.

"Don't address the boss unless you get permission!" Boone barked, kicking him again, this time in his spine.

Ak and Boone hoisted Dane up from the floor. They dragged him over until he was eye level with me.

"I guess the next time you decide to bite the hand that feeds you your ass will think twice. I suggest you get the fuck from around here and never come back. The only reason I ain't spill your brains is because I got respect for ya pops," I said to Dane.

He lifted his bloodied, downturned head so he could meet me eye to eye. I was kind of taken aback that the little nigga wasn't scared to force eye contact with me. The look in Dane's eyes was one I had never seen before. There was not one ounce of sorrow or remorse in that kid's eyes; instead, the piercing glare he locked in on me with was filled with so much hatred, jealousy, and vengeance it literally gave me the chills. I couldn't let my crew know that the young kid had actually scared the shit out of me.

"Toss his sorry ass in the street just like that . . . butt-ass naked. Let's see how far that nigga gets before the desperate stickup kids grab his ass and fuck him up," I commanded, breaking eye contact with Dane.

Dane didn't cry out. He didn't beg for mercy anymore. He didn't show any emotion as Ak and Boone dragged him to the door. I had to admire the nigga's bravado, though. As I turned away from watching them toss the kid onto the street I felt real uneasy. I had a feeling deep in my gut that it wouldn't be the last time I seen or heard from Dane. I was right.

Not even two weeks after Dane's beatdown, Lauren and I were asleep in my mini mansion on the outskirts of the city. We were both stark naked after a night of hot and heavy fucking. Life was still good back then.

BOOM! BOOM! BOOM! It sounded like the house was being bulldozed.

The thunderous noises had yanked me out of a deep, alcohol-induced sleep.

"Oh shit! What the fuck?!" I huffed and immediately grabbed for the gun I kept at the side of my bed. The first thing that came to my mind was a stickup kid robbery. That's how hood niggas rolled—middle of the night so they could catch a nigga sleeping. This was the best way to catch a nigga off guard. And if you're lucky, you'd probably walk away with a big payday. Dope, money, and drugs.

"Oh my God, Matt! What was that?!" Lauren screamed, her eyes round and wide. We were both dazed and confused by the loud crashing sounds coming from downstairs but I wasn't trying to let shit happen to her.

"Yo! Go out on the terrace and climb down," I whispered. "You need to get out of here."

"I don't want to leave you," Lauren cried.

"Get up and fucking go!" I whispered harshly. I gripped my gun, but I still needed to put some clothes on. I could hear the footsteps getting closer and closer with each second that passed. With one hand I kept my gun trained on the door. With the other hand I reached down for my clothes that were scattered on the floor. The whole time I was thinking, I can't let niggas take me out with my dick hanging.

Before I could fully get into my boxers I heard the words that all hustlers and street niggas dread all their lives.

"Police! Search warrant! Don't fucking move! Let me see your fucking hands!"

I gasped in a lungful of air and never let it back out. My world came crashing down around me minutes after those words sunk into my mind. The footsteps and the crashing noises never stopped after that.

Police officers and federal agents in raid gear swarmed our bedroom and our entire house within seconds. They were smashing my expensive Italian furniture with sledgehammers. They were drilling holes through the walls. Throwing our clothes and shoes out of the closets. It was massive chaos and all I could do was stand there with my mouth hanging open and my insides burning.

"Matthew Connors, we have a warrant for your arrest and a search and seizure warrant for the property," a burly, white DEA agent said to me, just before he threw me down on my stomach, dropped a knee into my back, and handcuffed me like an animal. I don't think I had ever seen that many law enforcement motherfuckas in my entire life. You would've thought they had come to pick up a serial killer or some terrorist.

I could hear Lauren crying and saying something but I knew she wasn't snitching or telling those pigs anything. Lauren knew the drill. We had been over this shit many times. I had always coached her on the what-ifs of my business. Police raids was a big one.

My mind raced with all sorts of thoughts but I was confident that Lauren would get off. She wouldn't say anything about my business. She didn't really know that much anyway. I was sure there was nothing in the house for them to find because it was a new crib and I never shit where I ate. I was too smart for these fucking pigs. I was going down, though. Just them having enough PC (probable cause) to be up in my crib was already a parole violation for me. Lauren was going to get off though. Those bastards wouldn't have shit to hold her for. Far as they knew, she was an innocent girlfriend with no ties to the criminal activities of her man. It was a role I was confident she would master.

"With friends like the ones you have who needs enemies, huh, Connors," a tall, white fed I recognized as Agent Stiffly said to me in a sarcastic and demeaning tone. I just closed my fucking eyes. I knew then that somebody close to me had snitched and cooperated with the feds and the cops. There was no other way for the cops and the feds to know about my new house.

"Maybe you should've stayed focused on keeping everyone happy rather than humiliating them and acting like a king," Stiffly taunted with a wink. He was trying to let me know that he had an insider working with him. I immediately thought back on who I had dealt with lately. Who did I have to straighten out?

"Dane," I whispered under my breath as I was dragged up off the floor and led down the winding staircase in my house. I was thrown into the back of *a police vehicle and before it pulled out I got one last look at Lauren. She was shaking and her face was red from crying. It broke my heart to see her like that.*

"You fucked up, Dane," I mumbled to myself. "You really fucked up." That little nigga had blown the whistle on my entire operation. Jealousy was a motherfucka but so was revenge.

I left Lauren in our bedroom brooding like a crazy person. She was something else once that temper flared up. I returned to the living room to deal with my other problem. Yancy was holding a rag to her face and pacing the floor when I walked in.

"I want my money now!" she barked at me.

"Yo, you just have no chill button, right?" I gritted at her. "I told you to be easy, but you just can't do it. I told you shit was going to work out but you couldn't just hold that tongue and let it ride."

"That bitch attacked me. I'm so sick of how she's been acting lately. I'm telling you she knows. But, I don't give a damn; she fucked with the wrong one," Yancy spat.

"We have to settle out the fees for the hacker and then split up the money, Yancy. Nobody is going to cheat you out of shit. Give me twenty-four hours and I will hit you off. Just go home and relax until shit settles down. Just do that for me. Please," I said, trying to keep my voice in a comforting tone. I realized if I didn't change my tone this bitch would never go away. She was

playing hardball all of a sudden and it was starting to wear on my nerves.

"Matt, I swear you got twenty-four hours to
make shit right. I want my third of the money *before* the hacker fee. Fuck that, I found the wallet.
You and Lauren pay him out of your take," Yancy
said flatly. She was truly bugging. Yancy was letting her feelings over being the side chick cloud
her good judgment once again. I was regretting
that I ever fucked with her like that.

I squinted my eyes into dashes and my nostrils flared. Now she was rubbing me the wrong
way. I didn't like to be threatened. This was the
second time Yancy had hurled threats at me and
at Lauren.

"A'ight, your time is up. Go the fuck home.
I'll see you in twenty-four hours," I said through
my teeth. Then I ushered that bitch to the door.
Before she left she turned to me with fire flashing in her eyes.

"Don't fuck with me, Matt. I'm not who you
think I am. You have no idea what I am capable
of. I'm not that little prissy bitch you got back
there," Yancy said with a lot of feeling. She had
this crazy strange look on her face.

"Yo, get the fuck out of here, man. I said I
would contact you tomorrow. But if you keep
threatening me you won't hear from my ass at
all," I spat. I slammed the door right in her face.
I should've known right then and there that I
had gotten in bed with the fucking devil. Her
pussy was good as fuck. But she was fucked up in
the head. As much as she thought that I wouldn't

seriously hurt her, she was wrong. My alliance was with Lauren. Yancy needed to understand that, but I knew it was a long shot. This situation might finally get me to change my ways. I was starting to think I'd never fuck with another dingy-ass chick again behind Lauren's back. I was now seeing that it wasn't worth it.

LAUREN

Matt tried all night to be up my ass and make everything all good. He was all "baby" this and "baby" that. "You a'ight, baby. You need anything, baby?" Matt was being the perfect gentleman all of a sudden. I probably could've gotten him to eat my shit if I'd ask him. But I was tired of being phony with him too.

I could tell by how guilty he was acting that he thought I might know something about his little affair with Yancy. I kept my mouth shut, though. I couldn't let him screw up my plans. I was so very close to executing it flawlessly. All I needed at that point was a few more hours. I would be a rich woman. Just thinking about having that much money had lightened my mood. Being around Matt suddenly became bearable. I guess that's the light-at-the-end-of-the-tunnel thing people always referred to that allowed them to get through tough situations.

Matt and I had fun together counting the cash without that bitch Yancy. "We should lay it all out on the bed and fuck on top of it," Matt had joked. I can't front, I thought about doing that ghetto shit too.

"Nah. Let's lock it up and get some rest," I had told him instead. Matt took the cash and locked it in the built-in wall safe he had installed last year. It was one of those times when he thought he was "getting back into the game" so he needed a safe to secure the money he hadn't made yet. As usual that shit never panned out. I was happy now that we had the safe, though.

Matt and I had both agreed that we'd get together in the morning, count out everyone's share, and take things from there.

"Yo, life is going to be fuckin' great for us from now on. We won't ever have to use another bootleg credit card or scam another bogus check again," Matt said to me. I had just smiled at him with a phony loving face and nodded my agreement. Matt seemed to trust that we were on the same page, which is exactly what I needed him to do. It gave me great satisfaction that Matt thought I was the one in the dark about his affair, when in fact, he was really the one in the dark. When he found out what I had planned for him he was going to see just how dark shit could really get.

"To us and the fact that we constantly land on our feet when it comes to these come-ups," I made a toast, handing Matt a special glass of co-

conut Cîroc and pineapple juice—the ghetto champagne. He was amused. He took his glass and held it up.

"Word. To having the smartest chick in the game and the most loyal chick in the game. To the good life to come and to watching a nigga get back on his feet," Matt professed, raising his glass and clinking it against mine. We smiled at each other. I guess you could say we were smiling for different reasons. Matt, because he thought shit was perfect and me, because I knew my plan was perfect. So far, things had played out just like I thought they would.

I took a little sip of my drink but Matt downed his with one gulp. I gladly poured him about three more and watched him take all of them to the head. A woman who didn't know their man's favorite drink was useless.

"C'mere, girl. I fucking missed you. We been so focused on making money I ain't been giving you this good ol' dick," Matt slurred, grabbing me and pulling me into him. At first I felt funny letting him, but I had to remember to put my actress hat on. *This is all for the bigger picture, Lauren. In a few hours none of this shit won't even matter when you're counting that paper,* I told myself. I guess that was how prostitutes got through the agony of fucking tricks.

Matt couldn't keep his hands off of me. That's how it used to be for us back in the days. Matt and I would spend three and four days straight in the house just fucking, sleeping, eating, and fucking some more.

"Damn. Where you been, girl?" Matt whispered into the skin of my neck. "You been hiding this pussy from Daddy, huh? Where you been hiding this pussy at?" Matt garbled his words.

A cold feeling shot down my spine. *No, nigga, where you been? Up in Yancy's pussy, that's where!* I screamed in my head. I let out a phony giggle to keep from saying what I was thinking. The thoughts were keeping me from getting into the act of having sex with him. But, just like that, the scent of Matt's cologne, the heat of his breath on my neck, and the yearning in between my legs helped me decide that since I knew this was the last piece of dick I might get for a while I was going to enjoy it. Besides, I still felt like Matt's dick belonged to me.

"You ready for this shit," Matt panted as he pulled the crotch of my panties to the side. His touch was like electricity against my skin.

"Mmm. Hmmm," I moaned as Matt's fingers began exploring the soft folds of my pussy. I shifted my waist until I felt his fingers dip inside of me. He finger-fucked me until I was begging him for more. Matt moved lower and lower. I was ready for the real deal.

"Give it to me," I panted gruffly.

"You sure," Matt whispered. He moved his hot breath over my mound, which sent a shockwave of sparks down my spine.

I placed one of my hands on each side of his head and guided his face. Matt took the hint and buried his face between my legs. I moved my ass to the very edge of our bed until it was almost suspended in the air. I wanted to make sure nothing came between my pussy and Matt's mouth.

"Yeah, that's what I'm talking about. Feed it to me," Matt wheezed as I gyrated my hips slightly. I had my legs bent but was standing on my tiptoes so the muscles in my calves were burning but I would not let him stop. Matt took great care slowly and gently parting my labia with his hands first, then with his warm, wet, lizard-long tongue.

"Sllll. Yes. Oh yes. Lick it. Right there," I hissed, throwing my head back and closing my eyes. My head was spinning with all sorts of thoughts. Maybe I didn't want to leave Matt after all. Maybe I could forgive him again for the one hundredth time. Maybe he did love me. Maybe it was only one time with Yancy. Good loving could make a woman forget a lot of shit. I had forgotten how well Matt ate pussy. I could barely keep my composure, it felt so good.

Matt blew on my wet clit, then flicked his tongue over it roughly, then blew on it again. "Oh God!" I huffed, grabbing on to his ears. I was moving my pussy over his face and the pressure on my clit was driving me wild.

Matt began flicking his tongue and using it to put pressure on my love button. Short bursts of electricity traveled from my clit to my ass. I knew what that meant.

"Oh shit!" I screamed out. I was on the brink. That shit drove me wild and made me thrust my pelvis forward toward Matt's mouth even harder and faster. When I did that Matt took that as his signal that I wanted to be tongue-fucked. He extended that God-given thick, long tongue and darted it in and out of my dripping wet hole. My legs trembled so fiercely it rocked my entire body.

"Oh Matt. Don't stop. Please, I need it. Don't stop," I pleaded. I knew I was about to bust all over Matt's face and in his mouth.

"I'm about to . . ." I started but suddenly I lost my words.

"What?" Matt mumbled as he ate me out like I was his last meal.

"I . . . I . . . I'm . . ." I stuttered, unable to get the sentence out.

"Mmmm. Mmmmm." My moans and groans seemed to make Matt more and more excited by the minute. He was going crazy now. He licked and sucked my pussy with the expertise of a porn star. I could feel the climax welling up in my loins. This was going to be one of the biggest cums I had ever experienced with Matt. It was a mixed bag of emotions for me. I let go of Matt's ears and clutched two fistfuls of the bedsheets.

"Here it comes!" I yelled out. "Here it comes!"

"Ahhhhhh. Ahhhhhh," I screamed as I busted my nut. I could feel my juices escaping my body onto Matt's lips and chin. His face was soaking wet. I opened my eyes so I could look at him. He smiled at me and then licked all of my love juice off of his lips.

"Yeah, that's what I'm talkin' about. I love it when you cum right in my mouth," he whispered. Then he put his fingers in his mouth and licked my juices off of them, too. That shit drove me wild. For a minute it was like old times between us. That seemingly symbiotic connection, the fidelity, the friendship, and just pure love that we used to share seemed to come back for one fleeting moment. I felt like I was in love with Matt all over again. I felt like I had never found out that he'd hurt me in the worst way. Suddenly, I was that little, naïve girl who had fallen for the bad-boy hustler all over again. Tears welled up in my eyes because although I was lost in ecstasy, reality was right at the corner of my mind telling me shit wasn't ever going to be like it was back then.

"Now, let me get mine," Matt said sweetly. He stood up in front of me and pulled out his thick, long, chocolate love tool. *Damn!* I cheered in my head. That thing was still as beautiful as ever. I licked my lips just looking at it. Then, like a jolt of lightning something hit me. Just that fast Yancy came into my mind. Yancy had enjoyed that fine specimen of a penis. It was supposed to be mine! Suddenly I grew angry. I turned my face to the side so Matt couldn't see the tears draining from my eyes. I didn't stop him, though.

Matt was oblivious as he climbed on top of me. I couldn't connect with him anymore after my mind started playing tricks on me. I made noises but clearly I wasn't into it. I just lay there stiff as a board and let him get his rocks off because I knew it wouldn't be long before it was all finally over. Matt never noticed that I wasn't into the sex or into him, for that matter. Like always, he was clueless to my feelings. Matt rolled off of me and flopped onto the bed on his back. He was mumbling something to me one minute, the next minute there was silence. The mixture of a good nut and the liquor he had consumed had Matt knocked out in no time. I lay there for a few minutes until I couldn't fight my sleep any longer.

A few hours later, I shifted in our bed and moved my body away from Matt's. I opened my eyes in the dark and squinted to see the cable box across the room. The bright red numbers read 3:30 AM. My head felt a little wavy from the drinks I'd had earlier. Plus, I was exhausted from everything that had happened.

I closed my eyes back for a few seconds trying to stave off the slight throbbing at my temples. *Damn!* I cursed to myself, opening my eyes again. I had to get up now or else. I was slipping. I had definitely overslept. The music was still playing lightly in the background. The burnt smell of the faded candles Matt and I had lit during our lovemaking still lingered in the air. I told myself it was time. I knew it was now or never. There was no getting weak this time. I had to stay on track with my plan or else I'd never get another opportunity like this one.

I slowly slid up onto my elbow and peeked over at Matt again. That nigga wasn't just asleep, he was in a dead sleep. I watched him for a few seconds to make one hundred percent sure.

I took a deep breath, swallowed hard, and

said a quick silent prayer. I knew that I was taking a chance. I reached over and shook Matt gently at first. I told myself that the worst that could happen was he'd wake up and I'd lie and say I was waking him up for some more dick. He didn't budge from the first shake. I shook him a second time, this time a little more vigorously. Matt didn't move at all. I was confident then that he was truly out cold. Since the police raid Matt hadn't really been a solid sleeper so any little thing would wake him up. He often awoke during the night to make sure the house was quiet and safe. Any little noise in the night would also wake him up and have him reaching for his gun. I would have to be careful now.

"Matt," I whispered his name softly, and shook him again for the last time. "You awake, baby?" Not a budge.

He was still but for his chest rising and falling. A wave of excitement mixed with the craziest dose of fear I'd ever felt came over me until I was shaking a little bit.

Yes! It fucking worked! I screamed in my head. I loved when a well-laid plan worked out for the good. I bit down into my bottom lip nervously and eased myself out of the bed. Now it was time for me to move swiftly and thoroughly. I didn't trust a soul so I still couldn't be sure whether or not Matt was playing like he was knocked out or if my cocktail of crushed Ambien and Cîroc had really worked like a charm. It seemed to be the latter because Matt was sprawled out on our bed, limp dick lying on his thigh, mouth hanging open, snoring like a bear. He looked so vulnerable at that moment. If I was a real vengeful bitch I could've caused him some bodily harm like slicing little cuts into his dick since he liked to share that shit with bitches all of the time. Or, I could've tied him to the bed so that when he woke up he'd be stuck there for days or even months before anyone could find him. It would take Yancy busting down the door like a superhero to save him. I mean that would be the only way someone would find him since we didn't usually have visitors at our house and not too many people knew where we lived since Matt was paranoid about people knowing.

I had a million wicked thoughts going through my head, but I decided not to carry them out. What I was about to do was enough of a "fuck you" to send the message.

I crept over to my treadmill where I had laid my stuff out from the night before without Matt even noticing. That's how stupid he was because if the tables were turned I would've noticed if he had an outfit perfectly laid out like he was planning on going somewhere. Not Matt, he was just so sure that the little dumb Lauren Kelly he had met back in the days would just always be here taking his bullshit.

I took one last look at him to make sure he was still knocked out. I shook my head in disgust. *What a waste of a man. I thought you would always take care of me. You made so many promises that you couldn't keep that I stopped counting. I hope you know that none of this is my fault; this is all your fault. Karma is a bitch,* I said in my head as I shook it from side to side.

Matt had really turned into one big disappointment since he'd lost everything. I mean I had put up with a lot of shit from him when he had money, but I guess that came with the territory of having every material thing I could dream of including trips to several exotic places that I would have never been able to travel to on my own.

I guess I thought once I started being the fucking breadwinner this nigga Matt would have just chilled and been good to me. Nah, he was still the same ol' ho-ass Matt Connors, minus the bankroll, cars, clothes, and expensive trips. I just couldn't live with a nigga being broke and being a nasty cheater sharing his dick with the world. I deserved a better life and trust me I was about to buy a brand-new life.

I slid into my clothes as quietly as possible. Then, I tiptoed into our closet and opened the safe. I quickly stuffed all of the cash into a duffel bag that I had stashed on top of the safe earlier that night. Another thing that Matt hadn't noticed. I think an empty duffel bag on top of a safe would be a red flag. But, once again, Matt had slept on me.

I raced over to the far corner of the closet and dug out the suitcase I had hiding behind some of my long coats. I'd packed the suitcase months ago right after finding out about Matt and Yancy. At first, I had packed it to leave right away but the more I thought about it, the more I began thinking with my head instead of my broken heart. I wanted to really exact revenge on the two of them. I just had no idea it was going to be with two point seven million dollars free and clear in my possession. That's right. I was taking all of the money. I could've left Matt and Yancy a couple of hundred or even a couple of thousand dollars but I didn't. Fuck them!

After I took out what I was to pay Ryan, which was three hundred thousand dollars for his work, I'd be left with the rest. The entire take was all mine. I wasn't leaving Matt and Yancy a dime and they would never hear from me again.

My heart skipped several beats just thinking about that shit. Sweat was running a race down the sides of my face and my back. My legs shook with each step and my stomach was in knots. I took several deep breaths trying to keep it together but it was really hard to fathom. This was real. This was really happening. I was leaving Matt forever. I was never looking back. I had been with Matt since I was a teenager and now at thirty years old, I was finally breaking free. It was bittersweet to say the least. I had been through so much at his hands. Like a wimp, tears sprang to my eyes. I couldn't believe it was coming down on me this hard.

I could feel my heart breaking as I hoisted my suitcase up and started walking out of our bedroom door for what I knew would be the last time. In the doorway I turned around and took one last look at Matt as he lay there helpless and in his most innocent state. I wished he was really all that innocent. *Stay focused, Lauren. He is the same nigga. No matter how much you give of yourself, he will still be out there fucking other chicks. He will still be that same shiftless-ass nigga that won't respect you. This is for the best,* I said to myself in a stern pep talk.

It wasn't that hard to remind myself that Matt was a disgusting, ungrateful, lying-ass cheater. I was fighting tears of anger, joy, hurt, and relief all in one. This wasn't the first time I'd attempted to leave Matt but it was going to be the last time. Standing there I started thinking back to the first time. . . .

November 2005

I had paced the floor of our apartment until the bottom of my feet ached. My fingers were raw, bloody, and sore. My eyes were red-rimmed and swollen. My voice was hoarse. My head pounded from a massive self-induced headache. I had no one else to blame but myself. I had trusted, believed, and loved Matt even when I knew he was a lying-ass bastard. But this latest thing was just too much. I looked down at the pictures that I had sprawled out on the floor in front of me. I bent over at my waist and dry-heaved. That's how disgusted I was by what I was seeing. I stood up, closed my eyes for a few seconds, and began pacing again.

"Motherfucka. Wait until you get here," I puffed. "You gon' do this to me again? Not even six whole months later? Oh no. This is it, Matt! I am not a fucking doormat. You have fucked Lauren Kelly over for the last fucking time, you piece of shit," I screamed out loud as if Matt was right in front of me and could hear me. I walked to the corner of our living room and wrapped my fingers around the handle of an autographed Louisville slugger Matt had gotten from a sports mem-

orabilia auction. I gripped the baseball bat in my hand like I was about to hit a home run.

"Argh!" I shrieked as I hoisted the bat in the air and swung it with all of my might into the center of the fifty-five-inch plasma TV that was hanging on the living room wall. "Argh!" I growled, hitting it again. Finally the screen shattered and glass rained down around my feet. I could feel several shards pierce the skin on the top of my left foot. I was probably bleeding but I didn't care.

With my chest heaving up and down, I sniffled back the snot threatening to escape my nostrils.

"Stupid! You stupid for forgiving this nigga the first time," I chastised myself cruelly. I threw the bat down and began sobbing harder. Just like earlier, each time I destroyed something an overwhelming feeling of guilt would seemingly choke me until I could barely breathe.

I stopped moving for a second and tried my best to take a deep breath. I raised my hands to either side of my head and tugged on my hair until it hurt my scalp.

"Why? Why, Matt? I'm not good enough?" I sobbed. "I have done everything to show you that I'm with you one hundred percent! Why?!" I screamed through wracking sobs. "You ain't no better than my fucking grimy-ass mother! You never loved me just like she never loved me! Always picking people over me. She picked all her men and her fucking drugs over me. You picked bitches over me!" I cried out.

Through teary eyes, I looked around at the rest of the mess I had made just thirty minutes before. Suddenly I felt a mixture of fear and shame at what I had done. I cupped my hand over my mouth as I looked around. Matt was going to kill me when he found out.

"What did I do?" I said, whirling around to take in the mess.

A pile of Matt's most expensive clothes were heaped in the middle of the floor. I coughed as I stepped closer to the at least two hundred thousand dollars' worth of items that were now covered in every cleaning product I could find in the house—Clorox, 409, Pine Sol, Dawn, Soft Scrub—you name it, I had dumped it on Matt's most treasured clothing items including a vintage Pelle Pelle jacket that had belonged to his uncle who'd been murdered. The mixture of all the chemicals had smoke rising from the clothes like they were about to make a bomb and explode. I could also see that most of the clothes had begun changing colors or the material had begun eroding into shreds right before my eyes. I made a ninety-degree turn and my eyes went wide. "Lauren," I gasped. "What did you do?"

I had completely lost it. All of the beautiful glass and crystal accessories that usually adorned the tables and shelves in our living room lay in shards throughout the room. I had either thrown the glass and crystal against the walls or against the hardwood floors in one of the many fits of rage I'd experienced that night. All of Matt's jewelry was in a bag that I had packed by the door along with every stitch of clothes that I owned. Matt's prized sneaker collection, including at least twenty-five pairs of Air Jordans, were ruined from me either cutting them with scissors, slicing them with a box cutter, or pouring bleach on them.

"Oh my God, Lauren," I gasped as I took in more and more of the damage I had caused. I had started thinking about what Matt was going to do to me when he found out. Especially when he found out about his uncle's jacket.

I walked over and bent down next to what had been a large canvas portrait Matt had paid a local artist to paint of him. It was now sliced down the middle, across the side, and from corner to corner until barely any canvas remained attached to the wooden frame. I swore if Matt was in front of me his face might've looked the same as that damn picture.

I slid down to the floor and buried my face in my hands. I was exhausted. Finding out about yet another chick Matt was sleeping with had made me emotionally and physically spent but finding out that he was having a baby with someone else had literally broken my heart into a million little pieces. It hadn't been that long ago that I had miscarried our first child. I felt so betrayed. At the moment, I felt confident that as soon as Matt walked in the door I would slap the shit out of him, spit on him, then grab my bags and leave.

"This is the last straw, Lauren. You have to leave him or this nigga will never stop," I told myself. I don't know why I sat there waiting to confront Matt instead of just leaving. Each hour that passed that Matt didn't come home my confidence dwindled and dwindled.

When Matt finally arrived, I was sprawled out on our leather couch that now had stuffing spilling from it like a gutted pig from me slicing it with my box cutter. I had the pictures laid out around me. I was staring straight at the door when Matt turned his key and walked through it. He was speaking to someone on his cell phone and had the nerve to be laughing. That didn't last long. I don't know if it was the pure evil showing on my face or the damage that Matt saw first.

"What the fuck?" Matt clucked, his face immediately folding into a confused frown. "Yo, son, let me

hit you back," Matt said, and disconnected his call. I swallowed the hard lump that had formed at the back of my throat. My mind was telling me to get up and attack Matt but my body wouldn't cooperate. The tears immediately began rolling down my face again. Seeing Matt's face, smelling his cologne, and just thinking of being without him was too much to take. My insides ignited with a mixture of fear, anger, hurt, shame, and just total devastation.

"Yo, Lauren! What the fuck did you do? You fucking bugging?!" Matt boomed as he whirled around and around taking in the destruction. I swear it was like someone had pulled a red veil over my eyes and shocked me with a jolt of electricity. I jumped to my feet and charged into Matt like a Spanish bull.

"I hate you! I hate you! I can't believe you did this to me again!" I screeched until the back of my throat itched. I hurled wild punches and slaps at Matt's face, neck, and head. I swiped my fingernails across his left cheek and caught nails full of skin.

"Ah! Get the fuck off me!" Matt barked, clutching onto my wrists. He squeezed them so hard I thought he'd break the bones inside. Although I felt the pain in my wrists it was nothing compared to the pain I was feeling in my heart.

"You got her pregnant! I hate you!" I screamed. Matt used his strength to push me backward until I landed on my back on the couch. He was too strong for me but I wasn't going to give up the fight.

"Get off of me! I'm leaving you! I hate you!" I screamed and cried at the same time. I knew my face was red because I could feel the blood filling up under the skin of my cheeks. The hot tears ran down my face like a newly opened faucet. Since Matt was holding *my wrists I began kicking my legs. I really wanted to inflict the worst kind of pain on his ass.*

"Yo, chill. Fuckin' chill," Matt growled. He pinned his body on top of mine so I couldn't kick him anymore. I didn't give up though. I wriggled, flailed, and bucked against Matt.

"What the fuck are you talking about, Lauren?" he grunted. It was taking all of his strength and effort to hold me down because I was going wild bucking my body, spitting, crying, and cursing.

"She came here, Matt. I saw her belly. I have all of the pictures of y'all together. I have the fuckin' sonogram pictures," I wailed.

"I saw the sonogram pictures of your first child," I whimpered weakly. Just saying those words had defeated me. Suddenly my body went still and I closed my eyes. The only sound filling my ears was my own rapid breathing. At that moment I really wanted to die. I would have rather given up my own life than to think of Matt bringing a life into the world without it being with me.

"Why? Why did God punish me and take my baby but let you have one with her?" I croaked pitifully.

"Lauren, baby, stop. I swear, I don't know what you're talking about," Matt said calmly. I felt my insides going soft. "You are the only one I'm with. Somebody is lying. These haters want to break us up. None of that shit is true. I ain't got no baby on the fucking way," he said softly. I remained silent. "Do you hear me?" Matt asked. I stayed quiet and still.

Finally he loosened his grip on my wrists and got up off of me. I lay there a few minutes completely still.

"Lauren?" Matt said my name. "Did you hear what I said?"

Like a demon possessed I sprang to my feet before Matt could really react. I turned toward him and with all of the force in my body I slammed my fist right into his mouth. Caught off guard, Matt slumped over and fell off the edge of the couch.

"You're a fucking liar! I'm leaving!" I screamed, hurling more punches and kicks at him. Then I ran straight for the door. I wasn't fast enough. Matt had gathered himself and gotten to his feet. He tackled me from behind, turned me toward him, pushed me up against the door, and crushed his bloodied mouth on top of mine.

"Mmmm," I moaned, trying to fight him. Matt had my arms pinned up on either side of my head.

"Stop. Stop. I'm not letting you go nowhere. I love you and only you," Matt whispered as he tried to force his mouth over mine again. I was trying to fight him, but he had overpowered me again. Then he began undressing me. With tears running down my face like a waterfall I let my body melt against his and let him take my clothes off.

"I only love you. Nobody else means shit to me," Matt said. I cried and cried but I stayed. I had tried my best to leave but I just didn't have the strength to leave him.

I snapped out of my thoughts of the past. As I finally crossed the doorsill of our bedroom with my suitcase and the money from our scam in tow, I held back tears. I didn't know if they were tears from thinking about the hurts of the past or tears of joy about what was coming for my future, but I was crying like I was at someone's funeral.

It wasn't easy leaving Matt even now but I was ready to show him that I was strong enough to break free of his bullshit after all of these years. I think I held my breath until I finally made it out of our condo, out of the building, and safely to my car. I let out a long windstorm of breath as I climbed into the driver's seat and locked all of the doors. I looked up into my rearview mirror to make sure I had really gotten away without Matt knowing a thing. There was not a soul in that parking lot at that time of morning but me. That's when it finally sank it. I had done it! I was the last one standing!

"Owww!" I howled and slammed my fists against my steering wheel. "You fucking did it, Lauren! You fucking got your revenge and all of the fucking money, too! Fuck 'em. They can't touch you! You are that bitch! Owww! Catch me if you can, Matthew, and tell your new bitch Yancy Yance to eat shit and die!" I was talking shit like Matt could somehow telepathically hear me.

I let out a raucous, maniacal laugh and let a wide toothy grin spread across my mouth. I turned on some music and I swerved my Benz out of the building's parking garage. I swiped my key card one last time and then tossed that shit out of the window.

"Won't be needing you ever again," I said as I heard the key card hit the ground.

Once I was out on the street, I mashed my foot on the gas pedal and let my car zoom through the streets. I can't even explain the sense of freedom I felt as I got farther and farther away from home. I was on my way. I only had one stop to make before I put the rest of my plan into motion.

I was making the first part of my getaway by car. Flying would have been faster, but there were two drawbacks. It's easy to track someone's air travel and I knew I couldn't carry that much cash to an airport because the limit you could travel with was ten thousand dollars. Those TSA fuckers had dogs that could sniff out if you had more. I couldn't put the money in the bank because of course it wasn't mine. I was going to have to be smart about stashing this much cash. I was getting as far away from this hellhole as possible.

"Oh, I won't be needing you anymore either. I know you can be tracked with that Find My iPhone bullshit. Not fucking with you, iPhone," I said to my phone, and then I tossed that shit out of the window too. It shattered into several pieces as it hit the street. Each time I threw away an essential piece of my life it was like shedding dead weight and felt oh so good. Whatever contacts I had in the phone were all considered a part of my past now. I would get in touch with my sister once I got settled. She and I hadn't been in contact for years, but I still needed to be able to touch bases with her from time to time. Just like that phone, I was leaving all the broken pieces of my past life behind. At least that was my plan. I never anticipated that stealing that money wasn't going to be the best thing that had ever happened to me like I thought. I could've never guessed that while I drove off into what I thought would be a new and improved life, I would actually be putting my life in serious danger. After all, Yancy had said she'd found that Hermès wallet and swore that no one could ever trace it back to her, Matt, or me. I guess just like with everything else, Yancy had fucking lied.

YANCY

Fuck, yeah, I'd lied. Got no damn reason to tell Lauren the truth. Her snobby ass needed to be taught a lesson and I was just the bitch to do the teaching.

Lauren thinks she saved my ass, but I was used to the ass kicking my pimp handed down weekly. This was just the first time she'd seen the aftermath, and yeah, I'd put on a good show of being a damsel in distress. Yeah, that shit wasn't as real as she thought it was. I was just angling to get all up in her business. See, I'd dealt with Lauren a couple of times, peeped her lifestyle, and decided to give it a try. She was living easy and sometimes a bitch just wanted to trade spots for a minute. I wanted a taste of her man. Simple as that. I didn't expect to start crushing on him, but now that he's stomped on my heart, fuck 'em!

Everybody knew Matt. He'd been the man in the streets before one of his soldiers turned on him and got him locked up. He'd been free for a minute, and everybody could see he wasn't feelin' playing wifey to Lauren, driving her around in her car and having her bring in all the cash. Shit, he wasn't no chauffeur and everybody knew he was itching for a return. Like a phoenix or some shit. But he was tainted . . . and busted! I don't know where his mind was, but I can tell you what word on the street was. Matt had lost his edge and was pussy-whipped by Lauren's high yellow ass. Wasn't no way the niggas in our hood were gonna follow behind that shit. So he was locked out of the game and if it weren't for Lauren he'd probably be living with his mama. Oops, my bad. His mama's dead. Anyway, Lauren turned her man into a bitch, but he was still hot and I didn't see nothing wrong with giving him a ride and helping him spend Lauren's money. That's what hoes do!

So yeah, I let Lauren save me. Funny thing is, for a pushy bitch she sure is soft when it comes to dealing with bitches. Might be because of her little sister, but that's her problem, not mine. Sure, she gives me some friction 'cause I come off as a dumb ho and we both know I'm screwing her man. But any other chick woulda split my head open over the shit I was doing to Lauren. I'm practically living in her condo and giving her man the best brain he's ever had. I keep thinking about the night Lauren and Matt scooped me up off the block and wiped the snot from my nose . . . shit, it was all I could do not to laugh in their faces. They have no idea what I'm about.

"Agh, help!" Humph! I'd screamed that word so many times it was my motto. "Help, help!" I sang again, like I was busting a nut, leaning back in the driver's seat of my red Mustang convertible. I was headed to see my man one last time before the shit hit the fan. That's right. I wasn't just fucking Matt. You can't count on one man for ya come-up.

I pulled up in front of Nik's ultramodern glass mansion and revved my engine a couple of times before jumping out. I loved that car. It was just one of many gifts I'd earned since hooking up with one of Virginia Beach's most successful businessmen. Rolling in dough. Dripping in gold. That kind of shit. He might be claiming Virginia Beach right now, but he was not from around here. And any fool could see that the money he rocked did not come from the businesses he claimed. Didn't add up. But that was okay by me. I wasn't his accountant or the fucking IRS, so I didn't need to track his dough. It was my job to spend it.

Which brings me to today's final visit.

Dude decided he was gonna cut me off. Kick me to the curb. End the affair. Whatever you wanna call it. I didn't expect our arrangement to last forever, but what happened to my parting gift? Consolation prize. Something! I mean, we'd been fucking for almost a year, and he didn't even want to get me a house. Stingy motherfucka!

I wasn't 'bout to hang around when my time was up. I was done livin' like that.

But I got something for that ass. Last week I ran through his office and picked up just enough info to lighten his wallet by three million dollars. I didn't have the connects to get that money out of his account and into my hands, but Lauren sure did. I just needed a little cover story on how I got the goods, 'cause I sure didn't want her in my business and that bitch always got a lot of questions.

As I walked through the door one last time, I said under my breath, "That's what he gets for letting a ho in his house. He shoulda just got me my own place."

MATT

I was dreaming that a huge boulder was rolling behind me when a sound like thunder caused me to stumble and fall. But the boulder didn't catch up to crush me. Instead, I jerked out of my sleep and heard the thunderous sound again.

BOOM! BOOM! BOOM! That's when I realized I was no longer dreaming.

My heart was racing while my brain struggled to connect the sound with its source. Scared as hell, I forced my eyes open to the constant loud noise coming from somewhere in the condo. I tried to lift my head, but could barely move. The pain that shot through my skull from just opening my eyes was unbearable. It felt like somebody was standing over me hitting me on the top of my head with the pointy part of a hammer. The noise came again. After being fully awake for a few minutes, I realized it was coming from the front door. I reached into my nightstand drawer for my gun.

"Oh shit," I croaked, barely able to move my dry, cracked lips. My mouth was so parched it felt like I had swished a cupful of sand around and tried to swallow it. I was experiencing a cross between a bad hangover, the day-after effects of an ass whooping, and a bad case of the flu.

BOOM! BOOM! BOOM!

Damn. Whoever it was, they weren't going away or giving up. I cocked my gun. Then I heard the familiar, high pitch of Yancy's voice. My shoulders slumped and I put the gun down on the nightstand.

"Matt! Lauren! I know y'all fucking in there!" If Yancy's screaming sounded that loud to me and I was in the back of my condo, I could only imagine how it sounded to our neighbors. This bitch was really wearing out the little bit of patience I had for her.

I tried to gather up enough strength to stand up from the side of the bed, but it wasn't easy. "Awww fuck," I groaned. Not only was my head throbbing with pain, but I felt completely off. The room was on tilt. This was crazy because I hadn't had a hangover in years. And from Cîroc? Nah, I wouldn't feel this fucked up from that mild-ass drink.

"Lauren?" I mumbled. "You here?" I struggled to move my pounding head so that I could look around the room. "Bae?" I called out to her. No answer.

"Maybe she ran out for a minute," I said under

my breath. But why wouldn't she have woken me up? It suddenly dawned on me that we had business to take care of, hence the reason Yancy was pounding on the door like a madwoman. Speaking of which . . .

BOOM! BOOM! BOOM!

"Matt! Lauren! I'm not fucking playing! Open up this door!" Yancy. Again.

"Fuck!" I huffed.

I squinted at the cable box and it read 4:55 PM. I swiped my hand over my face and shook my head. I couldn't have possibly slept all fucking day.

"This bitch," I rasped. I gripped the side of the bed for support and slowly got to my feet. I almost fell backward. That is how bad my equilibrium was off. I felt like somebody slipped me a fucking roofie. I ain't never feel like this from no damn Cîroc.

I lumbered down the hallway to the condo door, barely able to lift my feet. I yanked opened the door to find crazy girl Yancy looking like a maniac on the other side. Her eyes were bugged out and had dark rings under them like she hadn't slept in days. Her hair was wild on her head. She had the illest look on her face too. Scary as hell.

"Why the fuck are y'all playing games with me?" Yancy barked as she bulldozed her way inside. Shit, she slammed into me so hard I almost fell flat on my ass.

"What are you talking about, man? I was sleeping. Lauren must've gone to run some errands," I growled. "Fuck is you out here banging like the gotdamn police? You making it real hard to have a chill button around your ass."

"Run some errands? You let her leave? You can't be that stupid, Matt," Yancy spat. "Why would you let her leave without you? You really think she just went to run some fucking errands? I've been coming here since early this morning, banging on the door. I have been sitting outside and I haven't seen her come or go," Yancy screamed at me. At first her words didn't quite sink in.

"Wait. What?" I asked. I felt dazed.

"You heard me. I've been here since like ten this morning. Banging. Sitting outside. I left and came back. Started banging again. You just now hearing me? There's no way Lauren was here this morning and left."

I moved my head left to right, trying to shake off the fog that seemed to be looming over me. I looked around the living room and nothing seemed out of place. Then I checked the key hook and noticed that Lauren's car keys were gone.

"Let me call her," I grumbled. "Because you bugging right now. You mad paranoid and shit. I told you she probably ran out for a reason. Damn."

I slowly walked back to my bedroom to get my cell phone. Of course, stress box– ass Yancy was hot on my heels like she was going to miss something. She was mumbling and grumbling, but I wasn't trying to hear her.

I picked up my cell phone from the night-stand on my side of the bed. As I dialed Lauren's number, I watched Yancy peek into our master bathroom, walk over to Lauren's vanity, snoop on her nightstand, and finally walk over to our closet. She was like the fucking feds on a search warrant, I swear.

"It's going straight to voice mail. Maybe her battery died. I'm sure she will be back in a few," I told Yancy. Even though I was trying to act like I believed that Lauren's battery had died, something in the pit of my stomach was telling me I might need to be worried. Lauren carried her phone around like she needed it to live, so she never let that shit go dead. I was still playing it cool in front of Yancy, though.

Yancy squinted at me, folded her arms across her chest, and tapped her left foot impatiently. "Matt, she's gone. I bet you she took the fucking money and left," Yancy said calmly, taking a break from her panicky octaves.

"Nah, she wouldn't do that. And where she gon' go? I'm all that she knows. Lauren ain't got the heart to leave me. You ain't gon' understand what I have with her, but I know she can't stand to be without me," I said confidently. But as the words left my mouth, I didn't know if I even believed that myself.

"You were all that she knew before we fucking stole three million dollars! But I bet you that bitch is gone and I bet you even more that she has the fucking money, too!" Yancy yelled, her face turning all sorts of shades of red. She started fidgeting her legs like she had to take a piss. "Matt, where did you put the money?" Yancy asked with panic lacing her words. "I want to see the fucking money. I want to see that shit right now, Matt. Where is it?!" she pressed me.

"It's in my fucking safe, Yancy," I retorted. I walked over to my closet and stepped inside. My entire body was cold. My head was pounding. I wasn't up for this bullshit.

"It's probably gone," Yancy taunted from behind me. "Every fucking dime is probably long gone. That bitch got us. I'm telling you she took it."

I don't know if she was trying to convince me that it was gone or convince herself that it wasn't. My jaw rocked and I bit down on the skin inside my cheek. It was all I could do to keep myself from turning around and knocking Yancy's ass out. She wouldn't shut the fuck up and that shit was getting on my nerves.

I pushed my shoebox collection out of the way and moved the clothes I had blocking the wall safe. Nothing looked out of place to me. I punched in the combination code and listened for the beep. When the safe beeped and the lock clicked, I pulled back the small, heavy metal door. Yancy was still yapping from behind me, but all of a sudden I couldn't hear her. My ears were ringing. My heart pounded. I rubbed my eyes to make sure they weren't deceiving me. Heat rose from my feet and climbed up my body until it exploded out of the top of my head.

"Fuck!!!" I hollered. "Fucking bitch!!"

The safe was empty but for a lone piece of paper. I reached inside with a shaky hand and grabbed the paper. It was a note from Lauren. I held it between my fingers, but I couldn't even bring myself to read it.

"See! I told you she fucking took it! I fucking knew it!" Yancy cried out. She snatched the paper from my hand and began reading it out loud.

Matt,

I guess by now you've figured out that I'm gone and that I've taken the money too. You had this coming to you. I think right now you feel the same way I felt when I found out about you fucking Yancy. Yes, that's right. I knew all along. I've been wanting to get back at you, and stiffing you for three million dollars is the ultimate fuck-you.

I hope you realize that you lost a good one. I hope you can put that whore Yancy back out on the track to make you some money. You'll never find another one like me, boo.

Sending a big FUCK YOU to you and her.

Lauren

P.S. Life with these millions is going to be the shit! I hope you enjoy fucking that broke bitch for the rest of your life.

After she finished reading the letter, Yancy stood stock still for a few seconds. Then, as if someone had kicked her in the backs of her knees, she collapsed onto the closet floor.

"No, no, no!" Yancy shrieked over and over. She started kicking and screaming like that possessed bitch from the exorcist movie. I couldn't even understand what she was saying, nor did I care.

"I'm going to kill that bitch!! I will find her and I will fucking kill her!" I screamed. I began going crazy, swiping clothes onto the floor, kicking over shoe boxes, and finally sending both of my fists through the long mirror on the back of the door. I was so angry the pain from the glass cutting up my knuckles didn't even register. I punched the glass over and over until there was nearly no skin left on my knuckles.

"Lauren Kelly, you better hope I never find you. You fucked with the wrong man, you fucked with the wrong man," I said over and over. I didn't care if I died trying, I was going to find Lauren and blow her brains out.

"You let this happen!" Yancy screamed at me. "You promised me that you would take care of it. You're so fucking stupid!"

Her words exploded in my ears like someone had detonated bombs in them. I grabbed a fistful of Yancy's weave and pulled her up from the floor.

"Get the fuck out!" I roared, dragging her toward the door. My hangover symptoms were long gone. I no longer had the pain in my head or the weak feeling in my body. I was feeling like the Incredible Hulk. My adrenaline was high and I felt like I could snap someone in half with my bare hands.

"Get off of me! I'm not leaving until I get my money!" Yancy cried out. She swung her arms wildly, trying to break free. She twisted around, trying to bite, kick, and punch me.

"You better stop and just get the fuck out!" I roared. With the anger I was feeling, I knew that if I really hit her, the blow would be fatal. Once we reached the front door, I opened it and tossed her out by her hair. She fell forward onto her hands and knees.

"Matthew!! You will see me again! This is not over!" Yancy cried. "This is not over! You motherfucka! It's not over!"

I wasn't trying to hear none of that bullshit she was spewing. I had too much shit on my mind to even care what Yancy was yapping about. I slammed the door in her face. Once I was inside of my condo alone, I put my back against the door and slid down to the floor. I felt like a bitch sitting there with my knees pulled up into my chest, rocking back and forth. For the first time since my moms had been murdered, I cried. I had not felt this kind of pain, grief, anger, and betrayal since that day, but now all of those emotions were back. I was crushed. Lauren had really fucking hurt me. I wasn't the type that could take this kind of hurt and just bounce back like shit ain't happen. Nah, I still had pride. I still had an ego, too.

"This ain't over. Somebody gotta die. Either you or me," I said through clenched teeth, speaking to Lauren like she could actually hear me. "Somebody gotta die." Little did I know those words would become a very true prophecy.

LAUREN

"*G*et up, bitch! Get the fuck up right now!" Matt barked, pulling me up off the bed by my hair.

"Agh! Please!" I pleaded. Stabbing pains shot through my scalp causing tears to leak from the sides of my eyes. I couldn't believe Matt had found me. But how? I had covered all of my tracks. There was no way for him to hunt me down through the cell phone. I had left the state.

"So you thought you could just take all of the money and get away with it? Huh? You really thought a street nigga like me would let you get away with crossing me like that?" Matt snarled with his gun pointed at my right eye. He tightened his grip on my hair. I put my hands on top of his to try to ease some of the pressure pulsating through my scalp and head.

"Just blow that bitch's brains out. Fuck all of this talking." Yancy stood behind Matt talking shit. She *would've loved nothing more than to see Matt finally choose her over me.*

"Where's the fucking money, Lauren?" Matt asked, tightening his grip on my hair even more.

"Ahh. I . . . I . . . I don't have the money," I said, wincing. "It's gone. All gone. I had to get rid of it," I lied. I would never give up where I had stashed the money.

"Gone? Gone where?" Matt asked, pressing the cold steel of his gun harder into the skin of my forehead. My bottom lip trembled and my heart thumped wildly. I knew even if I told Matt and Yancy where the money was they'd still kill me just to get me back for leaving them behind. If I was going to die anyway, why give them the satisfaction of having the money after I was dead. If I couldn't have it, nobody could have it.

"I put it all away. I can't touch it and neither can either of you. If I can't have it, y'all can't either," I replied, blurting out what I had been thinking.

"What, bitch?" Yancy spat. "Kill her fucking ass, Matt! Kill her I said!"

"Stop fucking playing and tell me where the money is," Matt gritted. I watched him move his finger into the trigger guard on the gun. I could see in his face it was paining him to hurt me. Even though I had done some grimy shit to him, I could tell Matt was struggling against the little devil and the little angel on his shoulders. I closed my eyes. I didn't want to die. Not like this. Not at the hands of the man I once loved.

"Please, Matt, don't do this. Everything I did you deserved. You did so many things to me over the years. I was just trying to give you a taste of your own medi-

cine," I pleaded. "I really don't have the money. It's all gone."

"Fuck that! Shoot that bitch!" Yancy screamed at Matt over his shoulder. "She conned us out of all of the money. She don't deserve to live," Yancy pressed.

"Matt, please. I always loved you," I begged some more.

"Tell me where the money is or die," Matt said heartlessly. I could see little flickers of our old love in his eyes.

"I can't do that. It's gone . . ." I started to say.

BOOM! BOOM!

"Noooooooooo." I bolted upright in the bed gasping for breath. My chest heaved up and down fiercely. I clutched my chest and felt that it was soaking wet. Fear gripped me in a suffocating hold around my throat. I was scared to look down at the hand that I had placed on my chest. Slowly I raised my trembling hand in front of my face and widened my eyes.

"Ahhh," I let out a long exasperated breath. It was only sweat on my hand and not blood like I had dreamt. I looked down at my nightgown and there were no bullet holes in it. Another sigh of relief escaped my mouth. I whipped my head around and realized I was still in my hotel room alone. The same recurring nightmares of Matt and Yancy catching up to me had been paralyzing me for the two weeks since I'd left them high and dry with not even a dime of the money we had stolen.

"Damn, Lauren, you have to get it together.

You can't keep running off of one hour of sleep every night. You have the entire city to explore," I mumbled to myself.

I tossed the duvet aside and climbed out of the bed. I raced to the safe in the hotel closet and punched in the code I had made up. The safe clicked open. I peeked inside. I pulled out the stacks of money that I had there and held them up against my chest.

"No one can take you away from me," I spoke to the money. "You're all I need in this life." I laughed to myself at the fact that I was actually talking to the money like it was a person. It was something I had seen Matt do back in the day when he had it like that. Back then I thought it was the craziest shit I had ever witnessed. I couldn't help but think about one of those times now. . . .

January 2006

The sound of the five money counters flipping through stacks of bills had given me chills. Not in a bad way, but in an inexplicably good way. I felt like I was in some fairy-tale dream being around that much money. Yeah, I knew every single bill was dirty money but just being around it gave off such a powerful feeling. I had been with Matt a lot of years and never realized shit was this serious. It was an eye-opening experience to say the least.

Matt was trying to rebuild my trust at the time after being caught cheating again only two months before. Things he never allowed me to do with him were no longer off limits. I was with him everywhere he

*went so that he could prove to me that he was being
faithful.*

*It was the first time Matt had allowed me to stay
while his crew counted their daily take-in. They had
been dumping bags and bags of money on three long
tables. Coming out of the bags some of the money was
in rubber bands, some was loose, and some was folded
into bundles. The sound and the smell of the money
had actually made the hairs on my neck stand up.
Matt smiled at me when he noticed the look on my
face.*

*"Why you looking so amazed, baby girl? You ain't
know how your man was getting it out here in these
streets?" Matt asked me as he walked around like a
proud peacock. I shook my head, but my eyes stayed
stretched wide. I must've looked like a kid in a candy
store with excitement shining in my eyes. Only a damn
deaf, blind mute wouldn't have been in awe of all of
that money. There was another table right in front of
me where the already sorted money was placed. It had
piles and piles of cash on it. Crumpled bills, crisp
clean new bills, big bills, and small bills were all piled
in stacks that were the same height. I didn't know how
they got all of the stacks to look so perfect. Everything
was moving like a well-organized business when it
came down to counting the money. No one else in the
room, aside from me, seemed fazed by the amounts or
the process. They all had a job to do.*

*Matt's crew members Ak, Boone, and Dread were
all walking over, picking up large stacks of the cash
and putting the stacks in the money counters. They'd
listen to the money being flicked and counted by the
machine, then they'd pick it up, slide a rubber band*

around it, and call off the digital number on the counter. There was a female sitting on the side of the table taking down the numbers each time a stack came out of one of the counters. She would then yell it back out loud for confirmation. I had to give it to them, they were moving like real professionals. It looked like what I would picture a bank doing at the end of the night before they put all of the money into the vaults.

"Fifty thousand," was the last number the girl had called out. My eyebrows went into arches on my face. One stack had equaled fifty thousand and there were plenty more to be counted up. Up until then, I had never been in the presence of that much cash in my life. I had been with Matt for years, but he had always meted out money to me in increments that satisfied him.

I watched Matt walk over to where Ak stood placing the already rubber-banded stacks into several large black duffel bags. Matt dug into one of the bags and picked up a couple of the stacks. He held them up to his nose and inhaled deeply.

"Ahhh. The best fucking scent in the world," Matt said. Then he held the stacks up to his face and came eye level with them.

"They say y'all are the root of all evil but for me y'all are my savior. I'm always going to worship you. I'm always going to be good to you. You keep being good to me and I'll keep putting you first. Nobody can't take you away from me unless I let them. You're all I need in this life of sin, fuck everything else," Matt spoke to the money. I squinted my eyes and watched him. He was seriously speaking to the money like it was an actual person or like it was an actual

higher power like God. I thought it was crazy then, but I slowly but surely began to understand. When you're a slave to money nothing else really matters.

"You look crazy talking to that money," I had said to Matt. He had a serious look on his face when he walked over to where I stood.

"It may look crazy but it's reality, baby girl. Everybody in this world worships money. We can say whatever we wanted to say with our mouths but in our hearts and with our spirits we worship this motherfucka money more than any God, Allah, Yahweh, or Buddha. I'm just real enough to show it. Trust me, when you make enough or get your hands on enough of this shit you'll become a believer. A motherfucka who says he wouldn't kill his own mother for money is a lying-ass bastard, baby girl," Matt preached to me with feeling.

I should've believed every word he said that day because over the years I would find out that it was true. Money ran the world . . . at least the one I lived in.

I rushed around the hotel room and quickly got dressed. I needed to get out and stop giving in to that lingering fear about Matt and Yancy finding me. I'd planned to leave the country via New York so that I could do some shopping before catching an international flight. Plus, New York was a huge city. What were the chances that Matt and Yancy would even think to come look for me here?

"Can't stay cooped up in this room any longer. Maybe a little retail therapy will help me get rid of these jitters," I said to myself aloud as I slipped my feet into a pair of pumps.

I finally stepped out of the Millennium Hotel in New York's Times Square and inhaled a lung-ful of the smoggy city air. I had my ivory and black Chanel CC monogram scarf tied around my head and my eyes were covered in a pair of black oystershell, oversize, round sunglasses—all Jackie O. style. I had an off-white cap jacket thrown over my shoulders to dress up the dark blue fitted skinny jeans and pointed toe pumps I was wearing. It was a classic, high fashion, but still a not too dressy look. Perfect for New York City, the fashion mecca of the world.

I had always dreamed of moving to New York City when I was a little girl. For some reason as a kid I thought that the streets of New York were paved with gold and everyone who lived here was rich and famous. I used to watch shows that were based in New York and dream of one day standing on the streets of Manhattan and looking up at the crazy tall skyscrapers. Now, I couldn't help but look up at all of the tall buildings just like a little kid would.

Even when I got older and after I got with Matt, he and I would come to New York to shop for all of the newest clothes and shoes, since it took forever for new styles to get to Virginia Beach. I remember those trips would leave me feeling full of life, but I still didn't feel like I had gotten the full effect of being from the city. It was always a quick run up and back down south.

Not now. This time I was here on my own

terms. I might even be here to stay. I jumped from a loud car horn blaring in front of me. I had to smile at that. In Virginia no one ever blew their horns unless it was to warn someone that they were about to be run over.

This little old country girl was big city living right now. The blaring of car horns, the brightly lit up billboards, the throngs of traffic and all of the people crowding and rushing up and down the sidewalks, all gave me life. The city that never sleeps was very fitting for me since I hadn't gotten a lot of sleep since arriving in New York. I inhaled one more time. It was off to be a New Yorker for the day for me. First things first, I had to get around.

"Taxi!" I yelled, and waved at one of those famous New York yellow cabs. The car pulled to a screech at the curb. I hopped into the back, smiling like I had just gotten on a roller coaster at an amusement park.

"Where to, lady?" the driver said rudely. All I could do was keep smiling. Even the rudeness of the native New Yorkers was fascinating to me.

"Fifth Avenue . . . where all of the high-end stores are located," I instructed. The taxi rushed out into the traffic and of course a bunch of other cars and taxis blew their horns at him. I just shook my head.

I watched the cityscape whiz by out of the window. I was in amazement. There were thousands of people on the streets and everyone looked like they had a purpose. Everyone looked like they had money in New York City too. I was down with that. I was trying to fit in too.

I touched my pocketbook where I had three stacks of cash, just waiting to blow it all. I know that was probably the ghetto thing to do since I was kind of on the run, but I had decided that before I settled down someplace for good, I was going to enjoy myself. I had given a lot of time to being Matt's girl and it was my time to focus on myself.

I wanted to see and feel exactly how the other half lived and this time I was going to do it with my own money, not with Matt's drug money or with fake credit cards. Today, I was paying cash for everything that I wanted.

The taxi dropped me off in the heart of Fifth Avenue. Every single high-end store you could name was there. The first store I went into was the Saks Fifth Avenue flagship store. I walked in and my eyes grew wide. I couldn't believe I was standing in the very first Saks Fifth Avenue store ever to be created. I don't know why Matt and I had never come to Saks in New York. It was something to see, too. I whirled around on the balls of my feet in amazement. The store still had its old vintage feel. The ceilings were grand with intricate swirly designs and the most beautiful crystal chandeliers hanging from them. They were still the old, wooden ones with the large steps. There were a few modern touches to the store, but for the most part the store had kept all of its original woodwork and style. It was nothing like all of the smaller, newer, not-so-grand Saks stores everywhere else. As soon as I walked in three women dressed up in black pencil skirts, white blouses, and black blazers rushed over to me. They looked like triplets, which I found amusing.

"Good afternoon, ma'am. Thank you for coming to Saks Fifth Avenue today. We are in-store personal shoppers. If we can be of assistance today please let us know. We are happy to help you with whatever your needs are during your shopping experience," the tallest of the three women spoke up. The other two nodded and smiled brightly. It must've been the oversize new season Chanel bag I had slung on my shoulder. Or maybe it was the Rolex gleaming from my wrist. Maybe I just looked like I had money. There had to be a reason these women rushed up to me all willing to wait on me. I'm sure they didn't do it to every customer that walked in. Whatever the reason it had made me feel great. I hadn't had the personal shopping experience since Matt had lost everything.

"Oh thank you," I said, smiling back at the three women. "I think I will use the service," I told them proudly. One of the women who had introduced herself as Rosy ushered me to a sitting area that was past the jewelry, perfume, and makeup counters. Damn I felt special as all of the different saleswomen smiled and nodded at me. I'm sure they were hoping I made a purchase from their department so they could get their commissions.

"You can sit here and we will bring you our catalogs. As you find items that you're interested in you can request them and we will bring them here to you for fittings and try-ons. You are not obligated to buy anything," Rosy said cheerfully with that same warm and inviting smile she had greeted me with. Then she introduced the other two women as Deana and Chris. They were also smiling brightly. It was an amazing feeling having these three white women wait on me hand and foot.

Chris handed me a silver tray filled with small French pastries and chocolate-covered strawberries. Then she asked if I wanted champagne, water, or any other beverage. Of course, I went for the champagne. This might've been a once-in-a-lifetime thing. I was going to take everything they were offering. I had so much fun trying on clothes and shoes. The ladies helped me put together more than one beautiful expensive designer ensemble that was complete with matching shoes and handbags. Within an hour I had tried on about six different Diane von Furstenberg dresses, two Nicole Miller pantsuits, a few Topshop sporty tops, and at least ten different styles and cuts of all of the newest designer jeans. I was in shoe heaven, too. Rosy, Deana, and Chris were laughing, saying they would have to live vicariously through me as they brought out every designer shoe you could think of—Valentino, Christian Louboutin, Altuzarra, Brian Atwood, Charlotte Olympia, and Jimmy Choo—to name a few. I wanted to buy every pair I tried on. When I was finished shopping, I finally plopped down on one of the comfortable recliners in the personal shopping suite and I looked around.

"I did some real damage in here today, huh?" I said to Rosy. There were about forty shoe boxes scattered around the floor, at least ten pairs of jeans that all cost over three hundred dollars folded for purchase, and more than one mink vest laid out on the chaise longue for me to pick from. Forget about the handbags. All of the newest premier designer bags were neatly placed atop a glass countertop so that I could choose which ones I wanted to buy and which ones I wanted to leave.

"I just cannot leave this Christian Louboutin and Louis Vuitton collaboration bag here. I have to have it," I said to Deana.

"Oh yes. There are only two hundred being made worldwide. It's an exclusive, that is why I chose it for you. I can tell you must love bags," she replied. The scene was probably every woman's dream. I felt like a real rich person. This is how they got to live every single day. It was a thought that made me mad because I did have to beg, borrow, and steal just to be on their level.

I made all of Rosy, Deana, and Chris's efforts worth their while. I purchased over sixty thousand dollars' worth of shoes, clothes, handbags, and perfumes. I also gave each of them a two hundred dollar tip. By the time I was ready to leave Saks the three of them were clamoring to get me anything I wanted. I didn't even have to carry my items back to my hotel myself. Rosy used the Saks-to-home service and told me my items would be delivered to my hotel room that evening. I think if those chicks could've carried me back to my hotel they would have, that is how much they appreciated my business.

I left Saks feeling like I was sitting on top of the world. I was a little tipsy from downing all of the champagne in the personal shopping suite too. I stopped in a few more high-end Fifth Avenue stores and purchased a couple of little things but nothing compared to the damage I had done in Saks. I was still feeling nicely buzzed but I was also hungry. I decided to stop at a swanky little restaurant and bar down on Sixth Avenue to grab something to eat and maybe a few more drinks. I figured the more tipsy I got the better chances of me getting some sleep later that night. Shopping and drinking, a combination that was sure to be an exhausting sleeping potion. I hoped.

When I exited my cab I noticed that another cab had pulled right up behind me. Out of my peripheral vision I could see a man racing to get in front of me. I paused for a minute and my heart rate sped up. I mean, New York was still considered a dangerous place too.

I paused for a few seconds and noticed that the guy was going to the same place as me. He smiled at me and as I approached the door, he pulled it open and allowed me to step inside first.

"You didn't have to do all that," I said to him, finally taking a good look at him. He was a tall, handsome, cinnamon-colored hunk. He was dressed neatly in a collared shirt open at the neck, a sleek, neat-fitting blazer, and a pair of jeans that looked like they were custom-made for him.

"Beautiful ladies shouldn't open their own doors," he said with the sexiest deep baritone.

"Why thank you," I said, flashing my gleaming white smile at him. The sound of his voice got me feeling good and flirtatious at the same time. It had been a long time since I'd had those feelings.

"No thanks needed," the sexy stranger said. His smile was perfect and so was the one dimple in his right cheek.

As hot as he was, I wasn't interested in starting something in New York. I was just passing through, so I put him from my mind and I walked over to the bar. As I sat down, I could see that the place wasn't crowded, but it wasn't completely empty, either. There were quite a few people there for it to be so early in the day. This was why I loved the feel of New York. There was just a different type of pulse to the city. I looked around thinking if I were still back in Virginia Beach this place probably wouldn't have a soul inside. Those guys down there were so into chain restaurants and bars that a place like this wouldn't have done well at all.

"Let me have a cosmo, please," I said to the female bartender. She smiled at me.

"Getting your *Sex and the City* on?" she joked, nodding at the bags I had on the stool next to me.

"I'm trying," I replied, returning the smile.

"Where are you from?" she asked. I crumpled my face a little. I thought it was a little forward and nosy of her to be asking me a question like that.

"I'm asking because I can hear your accent. It's definitely not from up north," she clarified.

"Damn, is it that obvious? I'm trying to fit in 'round here," I said with a little nervous laugh. I didn't want it to be that easy for people to call me out.

"Yeah. Definitely a Southern accent. If you're trying to pass yourself off as a New Yorker you better go take some lessons because I knew right away you were an out-of-towner. I'm sure everyone you've spoken to can tell you're not from here," the bartender said. It was something I had never thought of. As I started my new life, did I really want people to peg me as a Southerner? She was right, I needed to work on my accent.

"Trust me, I'm not trying to pass myself off as a New Yorker, I'm just not eager for everybody to know I'm an out-of-towner," I told her. We both laughed.

"I'm Delilah. Born and raised in Brooklyn," the bartender said.

"Laur . . . um . . . Lauriel," I said, stumbling. I had almost slipped up and told her my real name. Shit, I'd have to be quicker and smoother with my responses. After spending two weeks on the low in the hotel room, I hadn't had a chance to try out the new persona I'd created for my new life outside of Virginia Beach—my fake background, new accent, etc. I needed to be really focused about my new persona. I didn't want to fuck up and drop info that would lead Matt to me. Since I might not ever see this bartender again, it was good practice for me to get used to using the alias that Ryan had put on the fake identification I had purchased from him.

I chopped it up with the bartender about good places to go out and things to see in New York. It wasn't until I felt someone lightly brush me as they moved in to sit next to me at the bar that I realized the stranger from the door had decided to act on our attraction. I had caught him staring at me a few times since we'd been there but I had acted like I didn't see him. Honestly, I couldn't help but see his fine ass. He was definitely a gorgeous man. All of the women in the bar were ogling him too.

"Can I buy you that next drink?" he asked me. I felt my cheeks flush red. I had been out of the dating scene for so long I was blushing as soon as he opened his mouth to speak to me. I had to play it off.

"How about we do this the reverse way and let me buy you a drink?" I replied smoothly. His eyebrows shot up on his face.

"A lady who likes to take the lead. I like that. I knew there was something about you that I liked from the time I saw you get out of your taxi," he said.

"He will have a Hennessy sidecar," I told Delilah. The gorgeous stranger started laughing.

"Damn and you just order what you want me to drink, too," he chuckled.

"Well, I'm paying so I'm saying," I joked. "Plus, you look like a Hennessy type of dude."

"I hear that," he said. "I'll take that."

"By the way, I'm Drake," he said, extending his hand.

"Lauriel," I said without any hesitation this time.

"Lauriel . . . hmmm . . . nice name. Sounds like a fake one though," Drake said, followed by a little awkward chuckle. A quick flash of nerves flitted through my chest but I played it cool.

"I could say the same about the name Drake," I told him. "Sounds real fake."

We both laughed. I spent hours laughing and talking with my new friend Drake. I had no idea that there was no such thing as real chance meetings like this one, but I would soon find out.

YANCY

Oh shit!
I. Did. Not. See. That. Coming.

I slid down in the seat of my Mustang. I was across the street from Lauren and Matt's condo, waiting to see if that bitch changed her mind and came home. With my money. I still couldn't believe she'd got the jump on me. I knew I shouldn't have left without my cut.

I'd been there a couple of hours, even ordered food delivered to my car. I never imagined I'd witness this crazy shit.

Lauren and Matt's condo was on a pretty nice block and you usually didn't see people hanging out. Most folks got where they're headed by car, so that's why I noticed two black ops–looking motherfuckas when they jumped out of a van. If I hadda blinked, I woulda missed them enter the condo. Real quick and stealthy. That shit didn't look good.

About two minutes later, I saw the lights go on in the place and shadows dancing in the window. But they weren't doing no fuckin' waltz. That shit looked crazy. I saw Matt's shadow tossed across the room, then held up by the collar. Looked like they were asking questions and not getting the answers they wanted. The whole thing looked like the bloodiest fight since Mayweather . . . no Tyson . . . no it was more like *Kill Bill* shit, 'cept Matt could hardly get a lick in. I think I heard Matt scream like a bitch but I couldn't be too sure.

Then there was the smoke. Yep, they torched the place. Probably to cover up Matt's body, 'cause they sure did a number on him. As the black plumes snaked out the windows, I saw the van pull up again. The goons popped out of the condo, jumped in, and sped off. If I'd taken a break to piss, I woulda missed the whole thing.

When I heard the sirens in the distance, I decided it was time for me to leave the scene too. I put my Mustang in gear, hit the gas . . . and hit the brakes when I saw Matt in my rearview window, crawling along the sidewalk outside the condo. How that nigga got out so quickly was anyone's guess. But I laughed like the Joker at his broke-down ass. Madness! I'd have to come back later and get Matt's story, but right now, I needed to bust the hell up outta here!

LAUREN

I hadn't planned to be in New York this long, but after meeting Drake, I was in no hurry to leave.

Our drinks at the bar turned to dinner and before I knew it, we were strolling along the Brooklyn Promenade on the most romantic date I'd ever had. Actually, my first day with Drake was more romantic than any date I'd ever been on. Made me feel as if what I had with Matt was nothing but knocking boots.

I spent every day after that with Drake. And little by little, my plans began to change. I didn't let Drake know that I was living in a hotel. Instead, I told him I was between places and asked his help in looking for a neighborhood. The search for my new crib led us all over the city. I was surprised at how hard it was to find a place in a nice neighborhood. New York was a world-class city that everyone wanted to visit, but even in a "good" area, you might have to step over a bum and trash on the curb. And the apartments were mad small.

Drake laughed at me. "Sweetie, people don't come to New York for the apartments. They're here to follow their dreams."

"Yeah," I said. "But how can they sleep at night living above a bar and with the subway beneath their window?" We were walking along Avenue of the Americas in the Village, where stars like Hugh Jackman and Sarah Jessica Parker live.

Drake paused in the middle of the sidewalk and pulled me into his arms. "Lovely lady, don't you know New York is the city that never sleeps? Besides, I'll show you such a good time you'll never want to sleep."

I smiled and leaned in for a kiss. "I look forward to many sleepless nights."

MATT

I took a long pull on the fat blunt filled with purple haze that my man Buddha had just passed to me. I inhaled the sweet bud into my lungs and held it in for a few minutes. I could feel the effect right away. When I blew the smoke out of my mouth, I passed the blunt back to Buddha. He did the same thing. It was a little like old times. I had come to see him because he was the only dude left on the streets that I could trust to help me get what I needed to find Lauren. He was also the only nigga that might be able to front me some funds so that I could try to get out there and find Lauren's grimy ass.

Buddha was one of those behind-the-scenes dudes that made a lot of money, but wasn't flashy so he always rode under the radar of the feds and the local police. He was almost five hundred pounds and could barely walk so that might have something to do with why he was so unsuspecting. Don't sleep though. Buddha had turned into a deadly cat over the years. He ran his business from his couch but the gang of loyal dudes he had working the streets for him were bangers in every sense of the word. I was there asking for a nigga to throw me a bone . . . for old times' sake.

He didn't believe me when I told him what Lauren did to me. He laughed because he thought I was pulling his fucking leg.

"Wait. Hold up, nigga. I don't think I'm hearing you right. Maybe it's this bomb-ass Kush talking, nigga," Buddha said in disbelief. I shook my head left to right.

"Nah, nigga, you heard me right," I affirmed. My eyes low from the weed.

"So you tryna tell me that your girl, who you took out the hood way back when, stiffed you for like a million dollars? She just got up in the middle of the night, cleaned out the safe, and bounced and a nigga just slept right through that shit?" Buddha reiterated what I had told him as he let out a mouthful of gray smoke. He made it sound like I was just making up some fantasy. I looked at Buddha's obese body and his triple chins through squinted eyes. That shit sounded much worse when it was repeated back to me. Still not worse than it felt to experience though.

"Nigga, I ain't tryna tell you shit. I'm telling you this is fact, nigga. She fucking drugged me so I would be knocked out. Then she up and left with all of the paper after I put in work helping her get the funds. I mean she was kind of the mastermind behind the lick because she had a computer hacker from B-more that was able to get us to the money, but I had to take a risk to get that shit too," I replied. "Truth be told, I never thought Lauren would do no shit like this to me," I said, lowering my head in shame.

Buddha shook his head left to right, his fat cheeks jiggling like a bowl of Jell-O. He let out a snorting grunt that I guess was supposed to be a laugh.

"It ain't that hard to believe, nigga, trust me. When money is involved a bitch would cut all their own mother's organs out. You know I was always a nigga that got to the paper, but I loved the bitch so I got caught slipping this time. I mean after years of putting in work and showing her how to live, I didn't think she would turn on me like this," I said. I took another toke off the blunt. The weed was starting to help me finally feel relaxed after two long weeks of straight bugging. Having this conversation was already threatening to blow my fucking high real quick.

"A'ight, so what you need me to do, nigga? I mean, I ain't no private detective or nothing. If you don't know where to look for her ass, I damn sure don't know," Buddha asked and told me all in one breath. "But if you find the bitch I got some niggas that will body her just off GP."

"Nah, I'm not asking you to find her. This one I gotta take care of myself. I need to look that bitch in the eyes before I give her ass wings," I said.

"A'ight, then what?" Buddha asked again. I

felt sweat on my forehead. I hated asking niggas for anything.

"I need you to front me some ends so I can go find her. I mean there are a few places I got in mind to look but a nigga is left with nothing right now. She took my jewelry so I don't even have shit to pawn. My condo burned to the ground for no fucking reason I can figure out and I ain't got no car because after all my shit was seized Lauren got a car and I just drove it . . . she left with that shit, too. Man, a nigga's dick is in the dust right now," I said, being as honest as I could. My situation sounded bad enough without giving Buddha all the details about the beating I got before my shit burned down. I hadn't been in the street game since my release, so I had no idea who would want to fuck with me like this. But I was going to get to the bottom of it and dole out my own ass kicking once I lined my pockets with a loan from Buddha and got my hands on a piece.

Buddha let out a long grunt followed by a long sigh. He rubbed the turkey wattle that doubled as his chin. I could see the shade of doubt darkening his eyes. Before he even thought about telling me no I needed to remind this nigga of what I had done for him.

"C'mon, son. I know you not gon' act like a nigga didn't save your life back in the day," I said. "I ain't never ask you for no favors in return for that. But, I'm sure you remember that if it wasn't for me your ass wouldn't be sitting here right now."

Buddha looked over at me and we locked

eyes. Both of us seemed to be drawn back to that day. . . .

July 2008

Laughter resounded loudly in the night air. It was always nothing but laughs when I was with my dudes. We ain't have no worries in the world.

"Damn, Ak, you dissed that bitch hard. She was trying to be your baby mother, nigga, you ain't have to do her like that," I joked as me, Ak, Boone, and Dread all came out of the hole-in-the-wall strip joint called Benny's in Norfolk. We all busted out laughing again.

"Nah, nigga, I ain't making no bullet-hole-having ho wifey," Ak joked back. "When that bitch got up from the lap dance I swear I saw six bullet holes in her ass." Everybody laughed again.

"Nigga, there wasn't no pretty chicks in that spot. This the hood hole for real," Boone declared. "My dick shrunk and went into hiding up in that motherfucka, son."

I was laughing so hard I almost pissed on myself. Those niggas was funny as hell.

"Damn, hold up. I gotta take a piss and I can't make it home," I told them. "I'll be right back."

I walked around to the dark alley at the back of the club. Just as I went to pull my dick out I heard voices. I lifted my head and listened as the piss drained from my tool.

"Run that shit, nigga! Run all that shit!" I heard the muffled voice bark. "You don't run that shit your brains gon' be on the ground."

"C'mon, man. I ain't got nothing," I heard another voice plead. "I don't walk around with shit on me."

I stuffed my dick back in my pants and I immediately put my hand on my burner. I peeked around the side of the building and that's when I saw two stickup kids holding guns on Buddha. His eyes were wide and glistened with fear. He had his hands up in defense. I could tell from a distance that nigga Buddha was trembling.

I remembered Buddha from going to high school with him. He was always that fat nigga that everybody teased, but I always remembered that he kept his clothes fresh and always had about a grip in his pocket even back then. I was always cool with him. I fucked with his little weed hustle in high school. He had the best bud in the city.

"Run it, motherfucka, or get ya fat-ass head blown off," one of the stickup kids said. Then . . . CRACK! He hit Buddha in the head with the butt of his gun.

"Ahh!" Buddha hollered. I saw the skin split open and blood dripped down his face.

These motherfuckas ain't tough, I said to myself.

I crept around the side of the building with my gun out. There was no hesitation in my response either.

BAM! BAM! I busted two shots into one of the stickup kid's legs. He had never seen me coming. He folded to the ground like a deflated balloon.

"Agh! Oh shit!" he screamed, writhing around on the ground. The other kid tried to turn his gun toward me, but my dudes were right there with theirs drawn first. We were real like that. Always had each other's backs.

"*Drop that shit, bitch,*" *Ak snarled at the other stickup kid with the gun wavering out in front of him. I could feel the fear coming off of him like stink off shit. He dropped his gun.*

"*Please. We . . . we . . . wasn't,*" *the stickup kid started. WHAM! Ak hit his ass.*

"*Shut the fuck up, little bitch-ass nigga,*" *Ak growled.*

"*Yo, you a'ight?*" *I asked Buddha. He looked pale as hell like he was about to faint.*

"*I . . . I . . . I'm good now,*" *he stammered with his lips trembling.*

"*You know these two was about to put your ass on ice tonight, right?*" *I asked.*

Boone walked over and told Buddha, "*Yeah, you was about to be ghost. These little niggas ain't got nothing to lose or to live for.*" *Ak and Dread started kicking and punching the two stickup kids. They went through the kids' pockets and took all of the money they had stolen from other people that night. They took their guns and their jewelry, too.*

"*Now get the fuck from 'round here before I put more bullets in y'all asses, this time in the dome,*" *Dread told them. The kid I shot couldn't walk so his friend had to drag him.*

"*Th . . . th . . . thank you,*" *Buddha huffed. "That . . . that shit was crazy. I usually have my gun but you know how it is in the club, they ain't tryna let you in with no burner,*" *Buddha explained. I could tell he was still shaken up. The club rules about guns didn't apply to me and my crew.*

"*I hate bitch-ass stickup kids. Think nothing of it. Just make sure if I ever need you out here in these*

streets you got me. Oh and make sure I get that good
weed hookup next time I see you too, nigga. I remem-
ber that you be getting that straight from the bud, hy-
droponic shit," I told Buddha. Me, Ak, Boone, and
Dread walked Buddha to his ride and watched him
pull out.

"That nigga was made shook. Fat as his ass is he
could sit on them two skinny little niggas," Ak joked.
We all started laughing again.

"A'ight you got that one. How much you
need?" Buddha relented after thinking back for a
few minutes. I knew that memory would get his
ass back on track.

"I'm thinking ten stacks should take me over
for a minute. Or at least until I can get my
hands on a few dollars more," I said.

"Gotdamn, nigga! You thinking a lot!" Buddha belted out. I had also forgotten this nigga
was mad cheap.

"I told your ass I'ma have to travel. You know
the bitch didn't stay local. She ain't that fuckin'
stupid. In fact, she's real smart. I'm telling you,
once I find her, I will be able to pay you back.
This ain't a couple stacks she got on her. This is
millions that she owes me, nigga," I said.

I could see Buddha contemplating and calculating what I was saying at the same time. With
hood niggas you always had to show a benefit to
them before they would help you.

"Damn," Buddha gave in. He pulled his fat-
ass body up from the couch, which looked like it

was painful. He was breathing all hard like to even walk was hard work for him. He could barely lift his feet.

This nigga need to lose weight before he drop dead. Damn, I thought as I watched Buddha struggle to walk to the back of his apartment.

"I got eight stacks and that's all I have in the house," Buddha lied when he returned. My eyes hooded over, but I thought better of arguing with him. I wasn't going to split hairs with the cheap nigga over two stacks but I was going to remember this shit. I snatched the money from Buddha's hands.

"Thanks." I paused for a moment before throwing in my last request real casual. "I'm also gonna need a place to crash until I leave town. How about that condo you got downtown?" Buddha gave me the side eye, probably wondering if he'd regret helping me out. But I pressed on, 'cause I wasn't about to take no for an answer and I was serious about getting Lauren and setting things right. "I'll let you know when I find her . . . because I will fucking find her," I said.

I stuffed the eight thousand dollars in my jacket and left Buddha's apartment. I wasn't expecting to have anybody watching me or following me. I guess a nigga should've kept his guard up a little better than that.

LAUREN

"Here are your keys and your lease, Ms. Kelton," the nice Realtor said as he handed me the things I needed to take possession of the new Brooklyn apartment I had just rented. I'd been able to get around the usual credit check and income verification by paying for the year's rent upfront. At thirty years old, I finally had my own place. And it felt good.

"Thank you so much," I beamed, practically snatching the keys from the Realtor's hands. I whirled around one more time and took in an eyeful of my new place. It was absolutely the perfect place for me. The beautifully restored crown moldings and shiny refaced hardwood floors made it feel so rich inside. I could already picture what type of furnishings and décor items I wanted.

Drake had recommended the rental, which

was the entire first floor of a brownstone in the swanky DUMBO area of Brooklyn. Drake and I had been almost inseparable since the night I met him at the bar. I had learned so much about New York City from him and he had been showing me around the city. Drake was a welcome distraction from thinking about my problems. He had been showing me a good time and I let him. He had worked wonders at taking my mind off of Matt and Yancy and my past.

"Didn't I tell you that you would love it," Drake said into my ear, coming up from behind me and placing his hands around my waist as we both looked out of one of the three floor-to-ceiling windows in the apartment. I closed my eyes for a few seconds and smiled. I inhaled the scent of his cologne. It was Issey Miyake, my favorite scent for men. I turned to face Drake.

"You sure did," I giggled. "And everything you've told me so far has been right on point," I said. He gently put his mouth over mine and I slipped my tongue between his lips. We kissed passionately for a few minutes, our tongues doing a sensual dance with each other. Then he moved his mouth from mine. I opened my eyes to see why he had stopped. I was already flushed with heat. I could also feel the moisture building up between my legs. Drake was looking deep into my eyes, which melted my insides and made me feel tingly all over. I hadn't had that tingly feeling from a man in years. I had lost that with Matt.

"You ready to christen this place?" Drake asked me with that sexy gaze in his sleepy eyes. I smiled at him coquettishly. Drake took that as a yes. He put each of his hands on my cheeks and pulled my face closer to his. He kissed me again. After a few minutes, he slowly pulled his mouth away from mine. Still holding my face in his hands, Drake kissed my chin, then my neck, then moved to my chest. Before long, Drake's hands and his tongue were exploring my body without one bit of protest from me. It may have been too soon, but I couldn't resist his sex appeal. I was longing for a man's touch. I was also desperate to feel safe, protected, and loved again.

"Christen? Is that what you call it when you let a sexy-ass stranger take your clothes off in your new home?" I whispered to Drake.

"No. It's what you call it when you let a man who is feeling you treat you like a woman should be treated," he replied in that smooth sexy-ass voice of his. He slowly unzipped my BCBG dress and used his mouth to slide each sleeve off of my shoulders. He was so fucking sexy!

"Ohh," I gasped as I felt his tongue trail over my sizzling-hot skin. I threw my head back and closed my eyes. I was breathing hard. Just then Drake took in a mouthful of my right nipple. I had no choice but to bend to his will now. He had me right where he wanted me. I didn't even realize that I was gyrating my hips, too. My breasts were my weak spot and Drake had found it. He moved from the right nipple to the left. I let out a long hissing sigh.

"I want to feel you," I panted. Drake ignored me and continued to lick every inch of my body. When he trailed his tongue from my chest straight down the middle of my stomach to my belly button I almost lost my mind. I arched my pelvis to let him know I was ready for him.

"Not yet," he whispered. "Let me take my time with you. You deserve every minute of my time."

I truly felt like crying. This man just seemed to drop out of the sky and was so perfect. I hadn't found one thing about Drake that I didn't like.

Drake finally made it below my belly button. He kissed the inside of each one of my thighs. My legs were trembling. No man had ever gone down on me besides Matt. I started to feel nervous and uncomfortable. I used my hands to try to lift Drake's head up, but he moved my hands away.

"Don't," I whispered. Tears were starting to well up in my eyes. My entire body began shaking. I couldn't stop the thoughts of Matt from flooding my brain at that moment. Drake wouldn't stop. He moved his face and buried it between my legs. I felt like I would hyperventilate. It was too much. I was too emotional.

"Please don't," I said, this time with more force in my voice. Drake still didn't listen. My protests seemed to spur him on even further. I could feel his tongue probing my labia now. Suddenly Matt's face flashed on the inside of my eyelids. I shook my head left to right in an attempt to make it go away.

"Stop!" I yelled at Drake. I used my foot to kick him away. I was fully sobbing now.

"Ouch!" he growled. He stood up. His expression was crumpled in confusion as he held his face.

"What the hell, Lauriel?" he said, wiping my juices off of his lips with his hands.

I sat up and buried my face in my hands. I continued sobbing like I had just found out that a close relative had died. That's how I felt, too. It was like being away from Matt had opened up a huge chasm in my heart and my life.

"Shhh. What's the matter? What happened?" Drake asked, concern lacing his words. He bent down in front of me and tried to pull my hands from my face. "Look at me," he whispered, tugging on my hands. "C'mon, Lauriel. Tell me what I did wrong. Tell me what's bothering you so much," Drake pressed.

"I can't," I sobbed. "I'm sorry I did this to you. I just can't," I cried.

"You didn't do anything to me. But, I want you to talk to me. Look at me," Drake said softly. After a few minutes, I moved my hands from my face. With sad, pitiful eyes I looked into his gorgeous face.

"I can't tell you everything, Drake. There's just so much. Please don't take it personal," I said, my voice rising and falling with each word. "I just can't share everything right now. Some things take time and are just too painful to re-live."

"Okay. Okay. You don't have to tell me right now. We don't even have to talk. Let's just sit together in silence. As long as I can be near you I'm fine with that," he said with a sincerity I had never felt from anyone in my life, including Matt. Drake put his arms around me and just held me for hours. I felt like I had found the man of my dreams. At that moment, nothing could have convinced me of anything different.

"Where have you been all of my life?" I finally broke the silence.

"I've been around. We just had to find each other," Drake replied as he stroked my hair. "Sometimes finding who you're looking for is easier than we might think," he explained. The words flowed from his mouth so easy. I could tell that they weren't rehearsed. And that's what was so authentic about them. One part of me wanted to trust Drake, but the street side of me warned me not to. So the best course of action was for me to wait it out. The real him would reveal his true identity when the time was right.

MATT

I knocked on the door of the small Baltimore row house like I had a right to be knocking. At first there was no answer. I kept knocking, each time I banged a little bit harder. I remembered Lauren saying that Ryan never came outside and barely liked to answer his door.

Finally, I heard locks clicking on the door. The door creaked open a crack and I could see a sliver of Ryan's pale face.

"Hello?" he said in a soft voice.

"Ryan . . . it's Matt, Lauren's man. I need to speak to you," I told him.

"About what?" he asked. Then I could see him starting to close the door. I lifted my Timberland boot and drove it into the door. The chain that Ryan had left on the door didn't budge.

"Open the fucking door or I'll shoot your ass

right through this door," I warned, flashing my gun. Ryan unchained the door. I pushed my way inside.

WHAM! I slammed my gun into his head for disrespecting me at the door. I wasn't in the mood for none of the bullshit. I was there for a reason and I wasn't leaving until I was satisfied.

"Aghgh! Please don't shoot me!" Ryan cried. He held his hand up to his head and when he saw the blood from the long gash that had opened up on his head, he screamed again like a little bitch. Looking at his little frail, skinny ass didn't put me in the mindset of a skilled computer hacker.

"Please," Ryan begged. His white face turned beet red and his long, blond hair hung wildly over his eyes. "I don't even know what's going on. Why are you doing this?"

"I think you do know what's going on and why the fuck I'm here. Where the fuck did Lauren go?!" I gritted, leveling the barrel of my Glock at Ryan's head. I'm sure Ryan saw the fire flashing in my eyes. He was trembling like a leaf in a wild storm. "Don't fucking lie either because I have no problem spilling your brains all over this dirty-ass house of yours," I warned.

"I . . . I . . . really don't know," he replied shakily.

Ryan must've been one of those reclusive, pack rat, hoarder, genius computer geeks. His house was a fucking mess. I had never seen anything like this in person. I don't know how this nigga was living up in his nasty-ass place in those conditions. It stank like garbage that had sat out in the sun for ten days, human shit, dirty socks, and cat piss all mixed together.

I had to kick my way through the piles of takeout containers and fast food wrappers that littered the floors. Flies buzzed throughout the house. Roaches scurried around. I noticed rat droppings in the corners too. The dark brown, suede couch was barely visible amongst the garbage strewn over it. The only thing that looked organized was what I assumed to be Ryan's work space. There were four long tables set up with about eight computers on them—some laptops and some PCs. Each computer seemed to be in a different stage of work. Next to the computer table there were towers with routers, network drives, and what appeared to be an entire server set up along one wall. Ryan had about ten different cell phones and two landline phones. There were wires everywhere all plugged into socket strip after socket strip. This dude looked like he ate, drank, slept, and shit computers.

The more he denied knowing anything about Lauren's disappearance, the more I started feeling like he was trying to insult my intelligence. My jaw rocked feverishly and my free hand curled into a fist on its own.

"Yo, I'm only going to ask you one more time . . . where the fuck did Lauren go?" I gritted. I pressed the tip of the gun barrel down into his forehead until I saw his skin pucker. My heart was pounding and I could feel my muscles cording against my skin. I could actually see myself blowing this nigga's head off if he didn't help me. I was seeing red, which wasn't a good sign for him.

"I . . . I . . . swear. I don't know where she is," Ryan whimpered. "She came and paid me for helping her crack a bank account. I . . . I . . . had some IDs already made for her in the name of Lauriel Kelton because she said she would need them after the bank stuff was over. That was it. That was all she told me. When I hacked the accounts she had told me she needed the driver's license, passport, and Social Security card because she would be leaving town. She never said where she was going. All I remember her saying is she was moving up to the big time and that she always loved big cities. All along I assumed that you guys were going away together," Ryan told me.

Hearing his words hurt me more than Lauren's actual abandonment. I had assumed Lauren and I would be leaving town together too. Listening to Ryan now let me know that Lauren had plotted and planned her grimy shit out long before we even entered that bank to get that money.

Always loved big cities. I repeated silently in my head. That could mean anywhere. Lauren loved New York, but she had also talked about visiting Chicago and Boston, which were both big cities. My mind was racing with a million possibilities now. The more I thought about it, the more tense and on edge I became.

"Did you give her any phones or anything?" I asked Ryan. I hadn't removed my gun from Ryan's head, but I did ease it back a little bit so that it wasn't pressing into his skin any longer.

"Um . . . yeah. I programmed and sold her two TracFones," he told me. "I . . . I have the receipts and the paperwork with the phone numbers somewhere . . . if . . . if I can go find it," Ryan said with fear underlying his words.

"Yeah. Get the fuck up and do that. Don't try no bullshit like calling the cops or rigging shit or else you die," I snarled, moving the gun from his head, but keeping it trained on him leveled with his heart.

Ryan got up slowly, keeping his eyes on me the whole time. He didn't trust me and I didn't trust his ass either.

Ryan moved carefully so that I wouldn't think he was doing anything suspicious, I guess. Smart man. He kept his hands up until he made it to a small, rickety, metal desk that was situated at the side of the computer tables. He looked at me and nodded at the desk.

"Go 'head, man. Just hurry the fuck up," I gave him permission. He eased himself down slowly into a small metal folding chair. He slowly opened the big bottom drawer of the desk. I rushed over and peered inside the drawer to make sure he wasn't trying to get a gun or knife. I couldn't see shit but a bunch of papers and a bunch of roaches running out of the drawer.

"Nasty-ass nigga, damn," I grumbled under my breath. This dude's living conditions were fucking deplorable to say the least. I was planning on burning my clothes and my shoes when I left his crib. I ain't never seen no shit like this in my life. As I stood there stomping roaches

and dodging other little nasty rodents, Ryan ri-
fled through stacks and stacks of papers that
were just thrown haphazardly in the drawer. Just
like the inside of his house, the inside of the
desk drawer looked like a complete mess to me.
Ryan seemed to know exactly where everything
was located though. After a few minutes of shuf-
fling he sat up with a stack of papers in his
hands.

"Here! I found it!" he shouted like he was excited and relieved at the same time. I snatched
the papers from him. I examined every single
line. I knew that TracFones couldn't be traced
and there were no GPS features in the dispos-
able phones either, which is why hustlers and
scammers always swore by them. But since Ryan
programmed the phones for her, he had the
phone numbers for them so now I could call
that bitch Lauren and hear her voice. I'm sure
she wouldn't be expecting to hear from me. I
could just picture all of the color draining out
of her face when she picked up the line and
heard that it was me . . . the nigga she thought
she had stiffed and would never hear from in
her life again.

I was going to call her every minute of every
day until she got rid of both phones. I planned
on letting her know that I was going to find her
ass even if it was the last thing I did on earth. I
already felt like I was going to be closing in on
her real soon.

"Did she say what she was doing with the
money? She couldn't put that shit in the bank
so what was she going to do with all of it?" I

asked with the gun pointed back at Ryan's head. He swiped his long hair out of his face so that I was able to see his icy blue eyes. I would imagine him as a California surfer, not a computer hacker hiding out in the hood of Baltimore.

"Um . . . um . . . wait, I think I remember her saying something about her old foster mother being in a private nursing suite. Said the lady was the closest thing she ever had to a real mother, but that the lady was old and in need of round the clock care now. She asked me about safes and lockboxes. Maybe she was planning on hiding some of the money there with the old woman . . . you know, locking it up where no one could get into it except her," Ryan snitched. It didn't take much to get his ass to talk. I squinted my eyes into dashes. Partly because I was contemplating what he was telling me, but mainly because I was immediately disgusted by this snitching-ass nigga. If Ryan was singing like Billie Holiday to me, I could only imagine what he would do if the police came knocking.

"A'ight. Anything else you can think of that I should know?" I asked him.

He shook his head vigorously left to right. Of course he was going to say no. He wanted me out of his house. Little did he know.

"Where's the money she paid you?" I asked calmly. I was waiting for this dude to lie. "I know she was giving you three hundred thousand . . . where is it?"

"I . . . I . . . I don't keep money here. Um . . . I have a place up in the country that I keep my personal things," Ryan said, stumbling over his words. This nigga thought I was dumb or some shit.

I lifted my gun and cracked it down on the bridge of his nose.

"Ahhhhh!" Ryan hollered. He fell onto the floor writhing in pain.

"Now. Don't fucking play with me! I don't believe you. You gotta have a fucking safe around here! Take me to it or else the next thing you feel won't be the fucking handle of this gun," I gritted. I stepped closer to where he lay rocking on his side.

"I . . . I . . . don't have the money here! I swear! I've told you everything!" he mumbled like it hurt really bad to speak. I felt a rush of heat engulf my body.

"Yo, you must want to die today. Get the fuck up and show me where your safe is. I'm not fucking asking you, I'm telling you. Lauren told me you have a safe in this bitch," I growled. Sweat dripped down the sides of my face now. I could feel the large vein at my temple pulsing fiercely against my head. I felt like a monster at that moment. The thin strand of sanity I was holding on to was snapping with each minute that ticked by.

"Okay, nigga . . . we about to get on the same page," I snarled.

BANG!

"AGGGGGGHHHH!" Ryan let out a blood-curdling scream as the bullet from my 9mm Glock seared through the skin and muscle of his left thigh.

"Now, nigga, stop thinking I'm playing with you and tell me where the cash is," I said through clenched teeth. "Next time I'm aiming for your dome."

"Okay. Okay!" Ryan cried. "I'll tell you," he gasped. I grabbed the collar of his shirt and hoisted him up from the floor. I was only using one hand because I held my gun in my other hand so Ryan slipped from my grasp and fell back down.

"Get the fuck up," I spat. I pulled him up again. I held on to a fistful of his T-shirt and helped him walk. He limped toward his kitchen. I kept the gun on him just in case.

"Aww, gotdamn!" I gagged as soon as we crossed into the kitchen. I quickly put my forearm over my mouth and nose. The stench coming from the kitchen was unbearable. I swear it smelled like a decomposing corpse. I gagged a few more times. My stomach swirled with nausea. I had to fight against the urge to hurl. The rest of the house was disgusting but it was nothing compared to that fucking kitchen. I couldn't even see his stove because it was covered in black dirt, grease, and grime. There were dishes with decaying and moldy food on them piled up in the sink almost to the cabinets. There were flies buzzing all over. I had to swipe them away and duck a few times to keep those nasty shit from landing on me.

"Yo, nigga, you got dead bodies up in this bitch?" I wheezed.

"No," he whined.

"Stop whining like a bitch and hurry the fuck up and open the safe!" I didn't even want to breathe in the stale air lingering in that kitchen.

Ryan dragged his injured leg over to the refrigerator. I was looking at him like he was crazy.

"What the fuck you . . ." I started. My words went tumbling back down my throat when Ryan pulled back the refrigerator door and revealed that the inside was hollowed out and contained a huge safe door. That was the most creative shit I had seen in all my years of hustling and scamming. A refrigerator safe.

"What the fuck?" I gasped. These white people were something else with their clever inventions. It wasn't one of these electronic safes that niggas could just blow a hole in the keypad and get to your shit. Nah, this was one of those old, back-in-the-days joints made out of real reinforced steel and had the old combination dial to keep thieves out.

I rushed over and stuck my gun up against Ryan's spine just in case he was thinking about trying something funny. "Open it," I whispered harshly. "And don't try no funny shit because I will blow a hole in your fucking back so fast you won't know what hit you."

With his hands shaking fiercely, Ryan twisted the knob on the old-fashioned safe in several directions, some left, some right. It didn't work the first time.

"Don't play with me," I said gruffly with the heat of my breath on the back of his neck. He tried it again. A few turns to the left. A few turns to the right. CLICK. Finally the sound that made my day. My heartbeat sped up.

"Open it," I urged, sticking my gun harder into Ryan's back. When he pulled back the safe door I couldn't believe it. My eyes stretched wide and my jaw went slack. This motherfucka Ryan had stacks and stacks of cash in his safe. There had to be more than the three hundred thousand Lauren had paid him in that shit. I can't tell you what I was feeling standing there. I guess it was a mixture of excitement, fear, anger, and satisfaction all rolled into one. I couldn't even smell the odors in that kitchen anymore. Nothing else mattered except what was in front of me at that moment.

"Please . . . just take it but don't—" Ryan started to say.

BANG! BANG! Two shots to the dome from my Glock silenced his ass. He folded to his nasty, dirt-covered kitchen floor. Blood splattered on my face and onto the front of my clothes. The metallic scent of the blood was so strong I could taste it in the back of my throat. I was feeling invincible right then. My body was both hot and cold. Finally, my brain sent a message to my body: *Get the money and get the fuck out of there!*

I whirled around trying to find something to carry all of that cash in. There was nothing in that disgusting-ass kitchen that I could even try to use. All of the plastic bags that were strewn about had rat shit, roaches, or what looked like human shit in them or on them. I wasn't touching any of those.

I stepped over Ryan's body and raced back into his living room. I frantically spun around in circles trying to find a bag of any kind. That damn house was so junky and cluttered I couldn't find anything. Finally, I saw a laptop bag behind one of the computers. I raced over and picked it up.

"Ah." I quickly dropped it. About six roaches had scurried out of the bag and over my hand when I first picked it up. The bag was covered in rat droppings and cobwebs but it was my only choice. I picked it back up with the tips of my fingers. I raced back to the safe. I started stuffing the stacks of cash from the safe into the laptop bag. When every compartment on the bag was full, I stuffed more cash down my pants, down my shirt, and into my shoes. I had to take as much as I could carry. When everything was full, I looked back into the safe and it still had stacks inside. *This crazy dude was fucking rich and living like a fucking bum.* I just had to shake my head.

"I'ma have to let some of my niggas know this shit is here before five'o get wind of this stiff up in here," I huffed out loud to myself. I knew once the police found Ryan they would be stealing all of that cash themselves. Might as well had let niggas in the hood know before the crooked-ass cops got to it.

I raced toward the front door of Ryan's house. The bright lights of a couple of his computers caught my eye. I was suddenly struck by the idea that those computers could've been recording or booby-trapped, so I paused for a few seconds. Then I lifted the gun and let off one shot into each of Ryan's computers and into his server. If the cops came knocking, hopefully the computers would be fried and there would be no evidence left of our crime. I couldn't let the cops find me or Lauren before I found her first. Now that I was stacking things had just become much more promising for my mission to destroy Lauren.

LAUREN

I jumped out of my sleep to my cell phone buzzing on my nightstand. Instinctively my eyes shot over to the cable box. It was 7:45 in the morning. Who the hell was calling me? Barely anyone had the number to my TracFone so I just dismissed it as maybe a wrong number. A few minutes later, the phone was ringing again. It was apparent that somebody was trying to reach me.

I gently lifted Drake's arm off of my waist and carefully untangled my legs from his. He let out a grunting snore and turned over on his side with his back facing me. He was still asleep. I was jealous.

I cracked a little smile but that quickly changed to a frown when my phone began ringing again. This was out of hand now. *Maybe it's Daysha,* was my first thought. She was the only person aside from a few important contacts and Drake who had my number. With my eyebrows furrowed, I reached over and picked it up.

"Hello," I whispered, my voice still gruff with sleep. I slowly sat up on the side of the bed.

"Ms. Kelly?" a nasally female voice filtered through the phone. A flash of heat washed over me. I hadn't been called by my real name for almost three months now.

"Who is this?" I whispered, peering over my shoulder to make sure Drake was still asleep. With my face crumpled in confusion, I slowly stood up, but once I was on my feet I realized how shaky my legs were. I almost fell backward. I gripped the phone so hard it felt like the bones of my knuckles would burst through the skin on my hands. I walked slowly toward the bathroom, careful not to make any noise that might rouse Drake from his sleep.

"This is Mrs. Karrington from the Sunrise Assisted Living and Eldercare Center. I'm calling regarding your mother," the woman said. Her sharp, nasally voice was annoying, but it had a very familiar twang to it. A cold shiver went down my spine and caused me to shiver. I swallowed hard and closed my eyes. The call itself was very alarming. *Please let her be okay. Please let her be okay,* I started chanting silently in my head.

"Yes. What is it?" I asked in a barely audible tone. I could hardly find my voice because I was so afraid of what this woman had to say.

"Um . . . your mother, Clara Shepherd, has been admitted to Sentara Hospital. She's had a severe stroke. You should get to the hospital as soon as you can. They are not sure if she will be released because the situation seems very grave. I hate to sound crass, but our policy is that once a resident is admitted to the hospital and might be there long-term or is not expected to return, we need to have their room cleaned out."

"Um . . . I'll be there to get all of her things. Don't remove anything until I get there and see what is what," I snapped nervously, cutting the woman's words off. "It's going to take me a little while to get there. I am in another state . . . don't remove anything. I pay a lot of money every month to have my mother there so I would think a courtesy should be extended to me," I said in a low but gruff tone. I could feel my nerves tingling all over my body. A line of sweat beads cropped up at my hairline, too. This was the moment I was dreading, I just didn't expect it this soon.

"Okay . . . okay. We can give you twenty-four hours to get here, but I can't promise that my administrator will allow you more time than that. Please try your best. We will see you when you arrive," Mrs. Karrington said.

"Thank you," I huffed.

I hung up the phone and clutched it against my chest. I stared at myself in the mirror that hung over the sink. I didn't know who I was staring at anymore. I had different hair—it was now short and so light it was almost blond. I had different eyes, I popped in my gray contact lenses as soon as I awoke every morning. The fake lashes, the veneers on my teeth, the tattooed mole right above my lip—all of this was supposed to change me from Lauren Kelly to Lauriel Kelton but sadly as I stared at myself, I realized I was the same ol' girl. I was that baby who was born from what everybody told me was a trick my mother had turned. I was that little girl who'd been removed from her abusive and neglectful crackhead mother only to be placed in a dozen different foster homes where I was being treated badly. I came to realize that most of my foster parents only took kids in to get a freaking check. That's it. There were no safeguards in place to make sure you were treated well. If the foster parents liked you, then maybe you'd get three hot meals a day. If not, then you were either abused mentally or physically. I remember witnessing my sister getting touched by older male foster siblings and foster fathers who were supposed to take care of us. She was still a preteen when she'd gotten pregnant through rape in a group home and was forced to get a botched abortion. From there we were separated. I swear if I could turn back the hands of time, I'd do it. My sister meant the world to me. She was all I had. But my mother's drug addiction caused us to lose each other. I will blame her for that for the rest of my life.

Tears streamed down my face like a waterfall as I thought back on my past. I was frozen and couldn't move. I became so cold my teeth began chattering. Just the thought of returning to my hometown made a wave of cramps roll through my stomach. It had been so refreshing starting over in New York. I couldn't remember ever feeling this happy back in Virginia Beach.

I bit down into my lip until I tasted the acrid metallic sting of my own blood on my tongue. My mind was stalled on how I was going to maneuver this one. Going back to Virginia Beach so soon wasn't in my plan. I guess this was the one time I hadn't planned things out thoroughly. When I stashed the money at Sunrise, I figured I'd have at least a year before I had to go get the rest of the money from the safe I'd placed in the secure storage area at the facility. When I left it there, my foster mother, Mrs. Shepherd, was doing fine. She couldn't get around as well as she used to because she had had one of her legs amputated due to diabetes, but she wasn't deathly ill when I had last seen her. This stroke the lady from the home reported to me just seemed to come out of nowhere. What if she didn't make it out of this? I cringed at the invasive thoughts running through my mind. I didn't even want to think about something happening to her. I knew I would take it very hard if it did.

Mrs. Shepherd was one of the sweetest ladies I had ever known. She was a short, round, cherubic-faced lady who always wore housecoats even when she went outside. She laughed a lot and gave out lots of hugs and kisses too. I had always remained loyal to Mrs. Shepherd, even after I was forced to leave her house, because of all of the foster homes I had ever been shuffled around to, she was the only foster parent who had actually acted like she loved and cared about me. I closed my eyes and thought back. . . .

February 1996

I sat on the bathroom floor crying and rocking back and forth. I looked down at the blood. It was all over my legs, clothes, and hands now. I belched out more sobs. I jumped at the loud knock on the bathroom door. My eyes went round as dinner plates. I looked around for a place to hide the mess. I was twelve years old and I was about to die. That was all I kept thinking about.

"Lauren? Lauren, baby, what's going on in there? You all right?" Mrs. Shepherd called to me softly from the other side of the door. I was frantically trying to clean up the blood. It had smeared all over the white tile floor of the bathroom. It was starting to stain the grout in between the tiles, too. My body was covered in sweat. Cramps stabbed through my abdomen, too. On top of it all, my heart was hammering against the wall of my chest, which was causing blood to rush to my head. I really felt like I would faint at any moment.

"Umm . . . um. Nothing. I . . . I . . . um. I'm coming out now," I stammered. Really I didn't know what I was going to do. There wasn't even a window in Mrs. Shepherd's bathroom for me to throw the bloodied clothes out of. I spun around a few times trying to decide where to hide the soiled items. My eyebrows went into arches on my face when I spotted the back of the toilet.

Thinking quickly, I opened the back of the toilet tank and stuffed the clothes into it. I closed it down as quietly as I could but the heavy porcelain top clanged against the tank.

"Hey, baby . . . what is going on in there?" Mrs.

Shepherd said from outside the door. She jiggled the doorknob this time.

"Oh my God," I huffed.

"Um . . . nothing," I yelled back. Even I could hear the fear and panic in my own voice. I frantically rolled off wads and wads of toilet paper and balled it up. I wet it and began dragging it over the floor trying in vain to clean up the blood. I realized the wet tissue was making it worse, so I rolled off more tissue, this time I wiped it with dry tissue. All the while Mrs. Shepherd was gently trying to coax me to open the door. I'm sure any other foster home I had been in the parents would've busted the door down and kicked my ass for having it locked in the first place.

When I was satisfied that I had somewhat covered my tracks, I grabbed a towel from the back of the door, wrapped it around my waist, and opened the door.

"You okay, baby?" Mrs. Shepherd asked in a sweet tone. She was eyeing me suspiciously. I knew she was wondering why I had that towel wrapped around my waist, but as usual, she had a smile on her face. I didn't think I had ever seen her with a mean expression or evil look on her face since I had been there.

"Um . . . ye . . . yes," I stammered. I rushed toward the bedroom that Mrs. Shepherd had set up for me. I could hear her going into the bathroom. I was so scared that my entire body was burning up. I had come to the conclusion that whatever was happening to me was going to cause me to die. I just knew at any minute I would bleed to death. I put on a fresh pair of panties, a pair of pajamas, and climbed into the bed. I could feel another warm gush of blood rush from between my legs. I squeezed my eyes shut and clutched the pillow waiting for all of the blood to drain from my

body. Tears drained out of my eyes. I didn't want to die but I had only ever seen blood when someone was shot, stabbed, or dying.

I was sobbing. Not only because I was bleeding to death, but because I had been separated from my mother and my sister and now I was going to die and never see them again. After about ten minutes, Mrs. Shepherd opened my bedroom door and came inside the room. I kept my eyes closed . . . waiting for her to react angrily or worse.

"Lauren, baby. Sit up," she said softly. "Let me talk to you for a minute, honey."

Mrs. Shepherd flopped her ample body down on the side of the bed. I could smell her lilac perfume mixed with the Werther's caramel candy she always had in her mouth.

"C'mon, baby, sit up now," Mrs. Shepherd coaxed.

I shook my head no. I was crying. I was ashamed. But, most of all I was deathly afraid.

Mrs. Shepherd touched the side of my face gently. She wiped the tears off of my cheek.

"Shhhh. Ain't no need to cry. I know you're scared but let me tell you what's going on and maybe that will make it better," she said sweetly. I opened my eyes and saw that she had the wet, bloody clothes that I had stuffed into the toilet tank in her left hand.

"I see the blood on your clothes. I know it's nothing that you did on purpose. There was no reason for you to hide it. You can always come to me about anything that is going on with you," Mrs. Shepherd said with a sincerity I had never heard in any adult's voice. I sniffled back the snot and tears.

"It's called womanhood, baby. It's nothing to be afraid of or scared of. It happens to all girls when God *says it's time for them to become women,"* she said softly. *"Sit up. Come over here to me."*

Reluctantly, I did as Mrs. Shepherd asked. She reached over and pulled me into her ample bosom. She hugged me tight and rocked a little bit. I felt the tension easing from my body. I inhaled her scent. A warm comfort came over me like someone had covered me with a soft, cuddly blanket. I had never had a hug from an adult in my life. That's right, I know it sounds exaggerated or crazy, but up to that point I had never had a hug from a human adult in my entire twelve years of living. My mother had never hugged me. I had no idea who my father was so of course he never hugged me. My grandmother did nothing but beat me and her abuse was the reason my sister and I were in foster care in the first place. All of the other foster parents I had were grimy, abusive, neglectful pedophiles or just plain mean. I never trusted adults because of all of my negative experiences with them. I let my guard down when it came to Mrs. Shepherd, though. She was the first adult to ever show me real affection that wasn't followed by some sick attempt to have me perform some sordid sexual act on them or for them to perform one on me. I closed my eyes and melted against Mrs. Shepherd's warm body. I sobbed and sobbed. Not because I was scared about the blood anymore but because I was afraid that if she let me go I would never feel love like this ever again in my life.

"This happens to all women and it will happen to you every month from now until you're old like me," Mrs. Shepherd said sweetly as she held me close. "This means that one day you will be able to have babies so that means staying away from picky-headed boys and *their nasty willies," she continued. I asked her a few questions and she had all of the answers. It was the only talk I would ever have about sex. Everything proper I learned about being a woman I learned that day from Mrs. Shepherd. Everything else I learned at the hands of pedophiles or by trial and error when I started dating. I loved Mrs. Shepherd from that very moment and every day after that.*

I snapped out of my reverie and realized I was crying. My legs were trembling so hard I finally collapsed onto the closed toilet seat. I put my head in my hands and started thinking about my next move. There was no way I could allow Mrs. Shepherd to die without seeing her one last time. There was also no way I could allow that assisted living place to move my safe. Hell no!

But, now that I was practically living with Drake, he wasn't going to just let me up and go back to my hometown alone. He was very possessive over me.

I would have to tell Drake that I needed to go back to Virginia Beach, but I know he would insist on going with me. Which would mean the possibility of Drake finding out my real name and identity. I couldn't let that happen. All of this pretending would have been in vain. No other man had treated me like Drake had treated me in the few short months we had been spending time together.

I let out a long windstorm of breath. The more I sat and thought the more things I came up with that were just all wrong about returning to Virginia Beach. I mean, I couldn't forget that I hadn't left under the best of circumstances. I had to be very careful going back because I was sure that even after three months, Matt and Yancy were probably still searching for me. Not to mention, last week I had just gotten in contact with my best friend, Daysha, to let her know I was okay. Although the broken relationships I'd left behind were swirling in my brain, at the top of the list was the fact that I wouldn't be able to live with myself if I let Mrs. Shepherd die without seeing her one last time. And, my safe . . . there was still the fact that I needed my safe.

After about twenty minutes of being holed up in the bathroom, I finally returned to my bedroom. Drake was awake lying on his back staring up at the ceiling. When he heard me enter the room, he turned toward me and parted that sexy, lady-killer smile of his. He was too damn fine for human eyes, I swear. I had told him several times he should be a model.

"What's up, sweetheart?" he asked. My heart started pounding all over again. I had told so many lies that I couldn't just stop and go back to telling the truth. I hated to keep lying to him.

"Nothing, you sexy thing," I faked as I slid into the bed next to him. I snuggled my body against his, hoping that his touch would ease some of the angst I was feeling.

"You sure? You kind of look like you've been crying," Drake asked and told me all in one breath.

Damn, he noticed everything. I had never had a man who paid attention to every detail and was always so interested in my every move like this. It was flattering, but sometimes it was annoying and unnerving. Like now. I immediately grew annoyed with Drake's constant probing. I let out an exasperated breath.

"Nah. My eyes were tearing up because I had an eyelash stuck in my eye," I lied, thinking quickly on my feet. "Why would I be crying when you make me so happy," I said all phony-like.

"Good, because I can't have my lady crying and not knowing what I can do to make it all better. My job is to make you happy at all times. Remember that," he said. Then he pulled me on top of him.

"Now stop all of the talking and kiss me," he demanded. I cracked a halfhearted smile and let out a real phony giggle. I wasn't in the mood for sex, but it was the only way to really change the subject and make Drake feel that everything was normal. I lowered my mouth on top of his and kissed him passionately. His hands ran down my back and over my ass and back up again. Although I wasn't in the mood, my body began preparing for Drake. I felt myself getting wet and my nipples were hard and erect.

Within seconds I was on my back, legs bent, feet planted on the bed and Drake was entering my deep, moist center.

"Ahhh," I crooned as Drake moved inside of me rhythmically. I closed my eyes and tried to get lost in the ecstasy of his touch. It didn't work. The gears of my brain were still grinding on ideas of slipping away from Drake, going to

Virginia Beach to see Mrs. Shepherd one last time, grabbing the remainder of my cash, and getting away from everyone and everything forever. It all sounded much easier than it really was. I was really going to have to be smart about it this time or else everything I had planned might come crashing down around me.

MATT

I was pacing like a motherfucka during the phone call. My stomach was in knots. My fists were curled at my side and my jaw rocked feverishly. The adrenaline coursing through my veins had me feeling like I could rip someone's head off with my bare hands. I was listening intently to every word. This had to work. It was the only way I was going to get Lauren's ass back for what she had done to me. I could almost feel the satisfaction of getting revenge on her. The anticipation of it had me feeling invincible.

Finally the call ended. I rushed over. I'm sure the curiosity was written all over my face. I couldn't contain it.

"What did she say? Did she sound like she believed you? Did she say where she was at? Did she say she was coming back to VA? When she coming back? How long did she say it's going to take her to get here?" I shot off questions rapid-fire. I wanted answers to every single question and I wanted them now.

Daysha shot me an evil glare and sucked her teeth. She was such a mean little bitch I could've just snatched her by that fucked-up weave she had in her hair. I played it cool though.

"Yeah, she believed me. What? You think I can't sound like a professional over the phone?" Daysha shot back. I bit down into my jaw to keep from telling this dirty rat what I really thought of her ass.

"I'm not saying that but you know Lauren, she is real smart. Shit, for all you know she might've recognized your voice even through the disguise. I'm just fucking asking. You don't have to get all stupid about it," I retorted. This bitch was bugging, but she was so greedy she would've done anything for a little paper. Including betraying her best friend.

"Yeah whatever. She sounded like she believed every word that I said," Daysha snapped. "She's coming as soon as she can. Trust me, it worked. I don't do no half-ass work."

Daysha stomped over to me with her face folded into a frown. She extended the open palm of her right hand out in front of her and used her left pointer finger to point to her palm. Then she made the throat-clearing AHEM sound. I pursed my lips at that bitch and shook my head in disgust. I had seen opportunistic, money-hungry bitches before, but Daysha was the worst kind. She's the type of bitch that I would've had burned alive in my old life.

"Damn, I'ma pay you. Why you acting all pressed?" I grumbled in disgust. I hated thirsty-ass hood rat bitches. I never liked this trouble-making bitch Daysha anyway. It seemed like every time Lauren and I got into problems over other chicks, Daysha was right there in the middle of it. More than once she was the one who had carried the information back to Lauren. There were many times I argued with Lauren telling her not to trust Daysha's snake ass. But, no, Lauren was all about her so-called best friend.

"Look, this is about money. Or am I wrong about what all of this about? I mean, you think I would've been setting up my best friend for the downfall and for the likes of a grimy nigga like you? Too bad for her that she didn't look out for me with a few stacks before she snuck out of town because now it's fair game. What Lauren did to you and to me was grimy. And the way she played us lets me know that me and her must have never been *real* friends in her eyes. I mean you telling me she came off with almost three million dollars, the hood gossip is that she raked in more than that, and she ain't even try to hit me off with ten stacks? Shit, one stack would've done the trick. I'm not no hater chick, but I'm just going to keep it one hunn'ed with you right now. Lauren always did think she was better than everybody, but that was after she got with you. Before that she was on those struggle meals and struggle outfits just like the rest of you. She got with you and you upgraded her a little something. She never even tried to throw us nothing.

I mean, I got with my own version of a so-called hustler so I did a'ight for myself. I wasn't pressed. When your ass fell off I thought for sure Lauren would get humble . . . but nah . . . the bitch kept shopping, kept flossing, kept acting like me and her sister and all of us up in the hood were just rats compared to her. I didn't even know she had no credit-card-scam shit going on. She kept frontin' like you was still getting long paper in the streets. Well for me, this whole thing that's about to go down serves Lauren right. So yeah, I'm fucking setting that bitch up and I'm about to get paid to do it. Call me grimy but where I'm from only the grimy survive," Daysha preached, still holding out her hand in front of her.

I let out a long sigh. Irrational chicks like Daysha that had their own sense of right and wrong made my fucking head hurt, I swear. It really didn't take much convincing for her to turn on Lauren like a straight Judas. Money was all it took.

The day I approached her with the idea of helping me, I handed Daysha a thousand dollars as a deposit and promised her five thousand more. So, six thousand dollars to set up someone you called your best friend. I had to shake my head at this bitch.

"Here's another two stacks. When I'm sure this shit works and we get to the finish line, I will give you the rest," I told her.

"So what do we do now? Wait for Lauren to come to the assisted living place and snatch her ass off the street?" Daysha asked. "Because I'm not so sure she will even get in contact with me

when she gets to town. I can't predict for sure
that she will even let me know when she gets
here. I expect her to call me but what if she
don't?"

"Didn't you say she had called you like twice
to ask you to go see about the old lady?" I asked
her.

"I mean . . . yeah . . . she had me going down to
check on Mrs. Shepherd every now and then . . .
even though I never actually went. So, she might
call me and ask me to go down there. So if she
does, then what?" Daysha replied. She was so
damn dumb she had to be told everything.

"Well when she contacts you just act like the
old lady is real sick. Urge Lauren to come back
to Virginia Beach to see the lady. I mean the
point of all this is that we want the bitch to show
up. Maybe you can tell her to meet up with you
first and that you'll go with her to see the lady or
something like that. I need you to lure her to
me. It don't matter how it's done, I just need to
be face-to-face with her. Once I get my hands on
her, you can dip and I'll pay you after," I sug-
gested. Daysha let out a sarcastic giggle.

"Nah, nigga, you can pay me first and then
I'll lure her to you. Remember, I'm not new to
this stunt you're trying to pull off. Y'all hustler
types think y'all can swindle chicks like me. Well
not this chick. I ain't no dumb-ass," Daysha
snapped, rolling her neck like hood rats do.

"Ain't nobody tryna play you, Daysha. I'm
tryna think of what will be easiest for you and
what will get you out of it faster. I just need to
grab Lauren. Period. I'll pay you," I replied.

"But wait . . . if you grab her then how do you expect to get your dough? I mean, once you snatch Lauren up you really think she's going to hand the money to you and let you go about your way?" Daysha pointed out.

"Once I grab her ass I will put my gun on that bitch and go with her to get the money. Once she gets inside she will know that Ms. Shepherd ain't really sick, but I don't give a fuck. She's going to find out you set her up regardless. But, you won't care because you'll have six stacks in ya pocket," I replied.

Daysha fell silent for a few minutes, seemingly contemplating what I had just said. I could see that change-of-heart look coming over her face. Either way she was already knee-deep in this.

"It's either loyalty to your grimy-ass friend or loyalty to the almighty dollar. You can't worship two gods. You feel me? All I'm saying is your so-called best friend chose the almighty dollar over you already so think on that long and strong before you give me your final answer," I told Daysha. I waved a few dollars in front of her. She followed the money with her eyes like a horse being led by a carrot on a string.

"Yeah. I'm looking out for myself. Let's do what we gotta do," Daysha acquiesced.

I handed her two stacks. She snatched the money like she needed it to stay alive. Just like that I had bought her betrayal.

LAUREN

I was covered in sweat and my stomach was doing flips as I rushed around the apartment trying to pack a tiny overnight bag for my trip. It was so hard to think about what I might need because my mind was muddled with all kinds of thoughts. I was thinking about going back, thinking about Mrs. Shepherd dying. And at the top of my mental list were thoughts of dipping out on Drake. I hated lying to him but it had just become a way of life for me at this point. I couldn't even imagine going to him to tell him my real identity and explaining all of the baggage I was carrying from my past life.

I looked nervously over at the clock on the cable box. The time was ticking by faster than usual or so it seemed that way.

"Shit. I gotta get out of here in thirty minutes

or Drake will be back," I huffed. I didn't need much, but it was just a matter of getting my mind right in order to go back to my hometown. I was running off of no sleep. I hadn't slept one hour since the phone call. Fuck tossing and turning, I hadn't even been able to relax my mind much less my body since the call from the assisted living place.

"C'mon, Lauren. Get it together. In and out of that place. Drake will have to understand when you get back. He'll get over it," I peptalked myself. There was also the matter of what I would do with the money once I retrieved it. Just another thing to worry about. But, first things first.

I needed to slip away before Drake returned from his morning workout. I shook my head thinking about him coming back with that sexy sheen of sweat on his gorgeous face, flashing that bright white smile and holding my morning cup of coffee. I shivered just thinking about him. He was such a good man. I was really starting to feel like I was falling in love with him.

"Finally," I exhaled the word. I had enough stuff in my bag and I was ready to go. I grabbed my keys, Chanel purse, and cell phone. My cab was already outside. I took one last look at the note I had left for Drake.

Hey baby,
I had to make a quick day trip back to my hometown. I knew you would insist on going, which I would have loved, but I needed to do it

*alone this time. I'll explain everything to you
when I get back. Please understand. Please
don't be mad. I'll be back before you know it.*
  Smooches,
  Lauriel

It kind of broke my heart to have to leave
Drake something as impersonal as a note but I
had no choice. Sending him a text would've just
made him race back to the apartment and calling him would've just had him peppering me
with questions. I raced outside and hopped in
my awaiting taxi.

"JFK, please," I instructed.

As soon as the cab pulled away from the curb
and began moving down the street, I closed my
eyes and rested my head back on the seat. I was
trying to let all of my worries fall away for once.
I had been living so happily over the past three
months that I had become a different, more
carefree person. I had truly become my alias,
Lauriel Kelton. She was classy. She was happy.
She was carefree. She didn't steal. She was a totally different person.

I knew returning to Virginia Beach was going
to require that I transform back into street-
smart, hood-thinking, thieving, lying, conniving, watch-your-back–ass Lauren Kelly. It was so
exhausting having to be that person. All of my
life, I had to be a thief, a sneak, a grimy chick to
survive. I was very young when I was forced to
be a thief and scammer for survival. No one
wants to be a thief and a liar, but in my circum-

stance I didn't have much of a choice. It was either become ruthless or die. Tears cropped up in my eyes because a painful, intrusive memory slammed into my mind and I couldn't shake it away.

November 1992

"Lulu? You awake?" my sister Mariah called out to me in the darkness of our cold, empty apartment. It was Thanksgiving evening. We had no lights, no gas, no food, and most importantly no mother at home.

"Yeah," I whispered back. "You?"

I was so hungry it hurt to even speak. As soon as I opened my mouth a loud rumble of hunger pangs tore through my gut.

"Yeah, I'm up. But I'm hungry," Mariah whined. "I need food or I feel like I'm going to die."

"I'm hungry, too, Mimi, but what am I supposed to do? Mommy said if we leave the house the DFAS people will take us away and send us to a hole in the ground where rats will eat us alive," I told her. I heard her stomach rumble this time.

"Owwww!" my sister howled. Then she started crying hysterically. "Agggh! I'm hungry! I'm hungry!" Mariah screamed at the top of her lungs.

"Shhhh. Stop screaming," I said to her. Before I could say anything else Mariah scrambled up off the floor and raced for the apartment door. I jumped up and went after her. I knew I couldn't let her leave. I was responsible for her. I was the oldest.

"Mariah! No! We can't leave!" I screamed at her. I grabbed on to her shirt and tried to yank her away from the door.

"*I'm hungry! Get off of me!*" *She swung around and hit me in the face with the force of a man. It shocked me. I stumbled backward, slightly dazed but more surprised that my six-year-old sister had that much power behind her punch.*

"*I'm hungry! I need food!*" *she cried out. Before I could gather myself enough to stop her, she had unlocked our apartment door and bolted out of it.*

"*Mariah,*" *I yelled after her.* "*Please come back!*" *I knew I couldn't let her go out into the streets alone. I was so hungry that my body felt too weak to chase behind her. Every regular step, let alone having to run to speed behind my sister, felt like every muscle in my body would disintegrate. Thank goodness I was older and my legs were slightly longer than hers.*

By the time I caught up to Mariah I was so weak and winded I could barely speak. I clutched on to her shirt like my life depended on it.

"*Mimi . . . wait . . . I . . . will . . . get . . . us . . . some . . . food,*" *I puffed out each word through dry, cracked lips.* "*You have to let me do this. Just trust me.*"

My sister turned to me with tears making tracks down her ashy face.

"*Please don't let me die, Lulu,*" *Mariah begged pitifully.* "*I'm so hungry I'm going to die.*"

Her words broke my heart. At that moment I didn't feel like a little kid anymore. I felt like a mother who was responsible for her child. I grabbed on to Mariah and we stood in the bitter cold hugging for a few long minutes.

"*Okay. I'm going to find us something. I promise,*" *I assured her. I took her hand and we started walking toward the small general store that was up the road from where we lived. We were both frozen from having no coats and completely out of energy by the time we arrived at the store.*

"Mimi, you stay out here. If you go inside with me they will know something because you too little. I look kind of like a big girl so they won't think nothing if I go by myself," I told her. "Don't let nobody see you out here and be very quiet." I made her hide at the side of the store so nobody would snatch her. It was the small store because due to the holiday the supermarket wasn't open. I opened the store door and a wind chime that was hanging over the door tinged to announce my presence. I jumped and whipped my head around. The sound sent a flash of heat through my chest. The old white man behind the counter raised one eyebrow at me like he knew I was there to do no good. I quickly averted my eyes from him. Even at that young age I knew I couldn't let him put me on a guilt trip or I would lose the heart to do what I needed to do.

The store was practically empty inside but for a drunk man staggering to the counter to buy two more six-packs of beer and an old lady who looked like she had just purchased sixty scratch-off cards. I bit down into my jaw and mustered up as much energy and courage as I could. I rushed to the back of the store and looked around to make sure I was alone. It didn't seem like anyone was watching. I scanned the shelves with my eyes to see what I could get for us to eat that didn't need a can opener or a stove. I quickly stuffed a small box of Ritz crackers down my pants. The bulge was hard to hide since my pants were already two sizes too small. I grabbed two small bags of chips and stuffed both up my shirt. Then I grabbed some Oreos *and did the same thing. I knew I would never be able to just walk out of the store because now I resembled a pregnant eight-year-old. I was going to have to make a run for it.*

I swallowed hard, crossed my arms over my chest, inhaled, and bolted for the door.

"Hey! Hey!" I heard the store owner screaming behind me. I was already outside before the old man could even make it from behind his counter.

"C'mon, Mimi! Run!" I screamed to my sister. She had been sitting on the ground so it took her a few minutes to get up. She didn't move for a few seconds.

"Mimi! Run! Don't let them get you!" I hollered over my shoulder. My sister was too slow. It was too late. I was probably a half block up when I realized my sister wasn't coming. I stood in the middle of the road frozen by fear, anguish, and loss. I knew that the store owner had gotten her. I also knew that what my mother said was true . . . they would call the child welfare people to get her. I could barely think straight as I imagined my sister being put into a hole in the ground and rats feasting on her. I couldn't keep going without my sister. The thought of being without her was too much.

With tears running a race down my face, I turned around and started moving slowly back toward the convenience store. I had all of the things I had stolen in my hands, unopened, because I was no longer starving for food. All I wanted was to be reunited with my sister.

Halfway to the store a police car slowed down and pulled alongside me on the street. Without looking over at the cop car, I stopped walking. My legs gave

*out and I crumpled to the ground like a deflated balloon.
I sobbed uncontrollably. "I want my sister!" I wailed. I
wasn't looking for their sympathy. I was truly feeling like
our lives were over. For a quick second I thought about
my mother. The pain I felt from her neglect felt like
someone had stabbed me in the chest with a butcher
knife.*

*"Come with me, young lady," a fat, baldheaded
white police officer snarled as he grabbed my frail,
bony arm roughly.*

*"I hear you have sticky fingers. We don't tolerate
that around here. Not on my watch," the officer pon-
tificated with not even an ounce of sympathy in his
tone. It was clear that the cops in our city didn't care
about poor little kids like me and Mariah.*

*"Where's my sister?" I asked weakly. The officer
kept talking shit, but he didn't answer my question.*

*"Where's my sister?" I asked again, this time with a
little more feeling. Still, he didn't answer me.*

*Suddenly, every fiber in my body came alive. I ac-
tually felt like I had been jolted with electricity.*

*"Where the fuck is my sister?! I want my sister now!
Bring me to my sister!" I screamed, flailing my arms
and kicking my feet. The officer was caught off guard
so he lost his grip on me. I was able to land a perfect
kick. "I want my sister! I want my sister!"*

*"Oof," the cop coughed after catching a kick to the
nuts from my foot.*

*Before I knew it, I was surrounded by at least four
police squad cars. A bunch of officers circled me like I
was a mass murderer. They handcuffed me like I was
a criminal and took me down to the social services
building. I was completely out of energy by the time I*

got there. I was longing for my sister, some food, and a warm bed, all of which seemed impossible at that moment. I was led into a small room. Inside, there were two older ladies.

"C'mon, child. This is the search room. We gon' take you out of those old dirty clothes and give you a nice new sweatsuit," one of the women said to me. My mother was right! That place was like kiddy jail. I was stripped, washed down, and given a plain sweatsuit and some plain white skips. The other lady in the room blow-dried my hair and put it in three big braids.

"Okay, all done. Look how cute you look when you're clean," the first lady said proudly. "Now you gon' get some food and a warm bed. You look like you ain't been eating or sleeping, child."

I was led through the maze of hallways in the building. Finally, I arrived at the room.

"Lulu!" Mariah screamed when I walked into the big room they used to herd all of the abused and neglected children as we all waited for a home assignment.

"Mimi! Oh my God!" I cried, rushing into her with outstretched arms. We hugged so tight that we were stabbing each other with our bones.

"I thought I would never see you again," I huffed into her ear. We released the tight grasp we had on each other. I looked Mariah over. I could tell by the sparkle in her eye that she had finally had a decent meal.

"Mommy was lying," Mariah said, twisting her lips. "Ain't no holes in the ground and no rats here. This place is nice, Lulu. They have food here and TV. They have soap, toothpaste, and toilet paper, too,"

Mariah said excitedly. I knew better than to be tricked by all of that stuff. I knew at that moment that our lives would never be the same again. I was definitely right about that.

I couldn't stop the tears from falling during my cab ride to the airport.

"Miss. Miss. What airline?" the cabdriver called out to me, breaking up my nightmarish memory. I blinked a few times to shake it off.

"Oh, um, American," I said, finally opening my eyes to see that we had already made it to the airport.

I took a deep breath and hoped for the best. I contemplated backing out of the trip back to Virginia Beach but each time I told myself not to go, something tugging at my conscience would propel me forward. I was at the airport now. It was final. I was going back. It was up to God now.

I had spoken to Daysha and she had confirmed for me that Mrs. Shepherd was in bad condition. Daysha had laid it on thick with the guilt trip about me coming to see Mrs. Shepherd. By the time I had finished speaking to Daysha, I was an emotional wreck. I thought she would've still been mad at me from the gift card situation, but I guess she put it on the back burner because of what was going on with my foster mother. I was glad for that.

I will say that she didn't know the entire reason behind why I had left town. I had only told her that I was leaving Matt for cheating on me again. She knew how Matt could get, so the story and the fact that I needed to leave town just fit together perfectly. I told her I needed to hide out for a while and that when I got settled I'd let her know where I was so she could visit. That was the truth, though. I couldn't wait until I felt it was safe to let Daysha know where I was. I missed hanging with crazy-ass Daysha. She always knew how to make me laugh even when I was feeling depressed. I was definitely going to make sure I took care of Daysha after the dust cleared. She was my girl. I wanted so badly to give her some of the money when I first got my hands on it, but that would've meant telling her the entire story, which I couldn't. I loved Daysha to death but I knew Daysha's mouth ran like water, especially when it came to talking about money. If I had told her my plans about the lick and how I was going to steal all of the proceeds from Matt and Yancy, before long the entire hood would've known. Even with the credit card and check operation, I would've loved to add Daysha to the mix instead of that traitor Yancy, but I knew how much Daysha talked and bragged. She was never any good at keeping secrets. She was also a loose cannon when it came to spending money and showboating. Daysha liked to act like she had more than she actually did. I was guilty of that, too, so I couldn't judge her too much.

I did plan on hitting Daysha off when I got to the safe, though. After all, she was the only person I could trust. I would just have to tell her I hit the number or something. I chuckled just thinking about how she'd react when I told her I won the lottery.

Daysha had agreed to pick me up at the Norfolk International Airport. At least she sounded happy to get a chance to see me. I begged her not to tell anyone I was coming. I hoped she had kept her promise. I didn't even want my sister, Mariah, to know I was in town. It would open up a whole situation I wasn't prepared to deal with.

I was mentally fried by the time my plane landed in Norfolk. I hurried out of the airport wearing dark shades and a head scarf. I'd dressed up simply because I didn't want Daysha to think anything about me had changed. When I lived in Virginia Beach I always kept myself well put together so I had to keep it up.

I spotted Daysha waving at me. Instantly a smile spread over my lips. I happily rushed toward Daysha's little Hyundai. It felt so good to see her.

"My boo is back," Daysha cheered as I opened the back door and dumped my bag onto the backseat.

"Girl, damn. This was so unexpected. I'm so happy to see you, boo," I huffed as I flopped into the front passenger seat. "And damn you're looking good. Love the new hair," I said, smiling.

"Humph. You too. Looking mighty rich," Daysha said snidely.

"Oh please. Far from it," I replied with a little chuckle. "And what? You don't miss a bitch enough to give me a damn hug?" I joked.

"Girl, you know my mind be all over the place," Daysha said. We both reached over from our seats and gave each other a quick hug.

"Are you hungry?" Daysha asked as we pulled out of the airport.

I looked at my watch. I was on a time restraint. I needed to get to the hospital and then to the assisted living place so I could get the hell out of town before anybody got wind of me being in town.

"No, girl, I ate in the airport," I answered quickly. I looked at my watch again. I didn't want to make Daysha feel like I was just using her for a ride.

"Well I'm hungry and we are not going anywhere until we stop at our spot and grab some food. We have a whole lot of catching up to do. Shit, you've been gone three damn months. I'm not letting you get away that easily for three more long damn months," Daysha said. She was leaving me no choice. I let out a long breath.

My heart sped up. I balled my toes up in my shoes.

"Um . . . I . . . I . . . really can't stop, boo," I said nervously. "This was not a pleasure trip. I have to check on Mrs. S., take care of a little business, and bounce before anyone gets wind that I'm here. Which I hope is still a secret," I said. I hated to disappoint her like that. Guilt immediately trampled on my mood.

"Uh-huh. First of all it is still a secret because who was I going to tell? But you are not going to just come into town and run back out without at least having lunch with me. Hell no, Lauren. I will be putting your ass in the used-to-be-friends category if we can't even sit down for a few minutes and chat," Daysha snapped. I knew she was serious, too. I didn't want to lose her as a friend.

"Okay. Okay. But look, we have to eat, catch up a little bit . . . and then I really have to run, Daysha. I'm not even spending the night in town," I told her. "Deal?"

Daysha let out a long, exasperated breath and twisted her lips.

"You know you get on my damn nerves being so damn bossy all the time. Okay, deal. You spoiled damn brat," Daysha relented jokingly. I laughed at her.

"You're the one that just threw a tantrum because I said I couldn't do lunch and you're calling me spoiled? Your ass is still as crazy as ever," I replied with a laugh. Damn, I loved Daysha. A true ride-or-die chick who never let me down.

"So to make the most of our time, start catching me up now," I said as we drove toward downtown. "I know your Ms. Benita ass got all of the scoop for me." We both laughed.

Daysha smacked her lips, and sang in the ghetto bird way she always did, "Shit, girl, it's so much stuff going on in the damn hood I don't even know where to start . . . Okay. Wait. Let me start with the craziest shit to happen. Your man—" She stopped and rethought her words when she saw the hostile side eye I gave her. "I mean Matt. That condo he was living in burned to the ground and it was real suspicious. Suspicious as in Randy's lil brother says he saw two hulking dudes walking away from your place just as smoke began shooting out." Daysha paused and smacked her lips again, so I knew the next bit was going to be even more juicy . . . . or tragic, judging by what she'd just told me.

"And then he saw Matt crawling from the place looking like he'd just lost a fight with The Rock. I mean, he was beat up like hamburger. Crazy, right? And would you believe his boys on the block, I mean his ex-soldiers, just stood by and let them dudes get away with . . ."

I just stared at her. Blank. No expression. But inside my mind was whirling, like what the hell was going on!? Leaving Matt high and dry was my revenge; I really hadn't had any fantasies of Matt getting a beatdown. I'm not saying he didn't deserve it for all the dirty he'd done to me, but I didn't want that kind of karma. No, I didn't want to lay a hand on him, I just wanted him to be broke, desperate, and miserable because he'd fucked up a good thing. But back to what Daysha was saying.

". . . and word on the other side of the block is that Yancy is pregnant with Matt's baby," Daysha said in a gossipy old lady voice. "Mmmm hmmm. Yup. They saying she is big-time pregnant, like seven months along. Like Matt is going to be a father any day now type of shit," Daysha reported. "If he ever tried to deny it, there's your proof there. That baby proves that they were fucking on the side. That bastard!" Daysha finished up her news with a wave of her hand, like she was Vanna White revealing the final letter.

My entire body got hot. I shifted uncomfortably in my seat. I was immediately feeling crushed, but I put on my brave face. I was not going to let this throw me off from what I'd come back to accomplish.

"Oh really? Well I guess he's her problem now. Good fucking luck with that. Matt is selfish so he won't even be able to give of himself enough for a child," I replied as if the news didn't even bother me. In actuality, I felt like someone had driven a knife right into the center of my chest and kept turning it and turning it. Daysha could've kept that little tidbit of information to herself.

"Mmm-hmm. That's what I said when I heard about it. I know everything you been through with that nigga. But I ain't gon' lie. If I was you I would feel some kind of way. Especially because you couldn't hold one in for the nigga after all of those tries," Daysha said. The end of her statement landed in my brain like a hard kick to my skull. A sharp pain literally exploded at my temple when she said it.

I whipped my head to the side and shot her a dirty look. I didn't even realize that my chest was heaving, but I could feel the wave of emotion swelling in my throat in the form of a hard lump that had formed there.

"Why the fuck would you say such a cruel thing!" I shot back. I could not believe she had brought up the three miscarriages I'd suffered over the years. "My struggles have nothing to do with Matt and his nasty bitch. That was nothing to bring up," I said, my voice rising and falling with emotion.

Daysha of all people knew how painful those experiences had been for me. Even now, I felt like screaming and crying just thinking about it. Especially the one I carried and didn't know that I was pregnant. It had taken me months to recover from that. Matt reacted like an asshole too. He had spent days out drinking with his friends. I guess he didn't know how to deal with his grief either.

My head was swirling with the pain of thinking about my failed pregnancies on top of hearing that Yancy was pregnant by my man. I really felt like crying when I thought about it. Yancy was going to give Matt the most precious gift a woman could give a man and I had been unable to do that. I was crushed inside. Once again those feelings of inferiority I had experienced when I first found out about Matt and Yancy were back. It was the first of many things that made me regret coming back.

"That was so fucked up, Daysha. I'm really thrown off by that coming from you," I said, breaking the awkward, tension-filled silence that had enveloped the inside of the car.

"Oh oops. My bad, boo. I didn't realize that still bothered you. I mean you left the nigga like a thief in the night . . . or so I heard. I didn't think you'd care what he was doing now," Daysha said matter-of-factly. I had to do a double take and make sure this was my best friend, my road dog, my ride-or-die who I was riding with and not an imposter. Not even ten minutes earlier she was all saying how she missed me and wanted to catch up. Now, she had turned into a bitch.

"Damn. Whose side are you on, Daysha? You sound real crazy right now," I said, my eyebrows furrowed in confusion. "Just real unexpected coming from you. Especially because we haven't seen each other in forever. I thought this little quick visit was going to be all about laughs and catching up."

"Ohhh, boo. Don't take it the wrong way. I'm always on your side. Always. But, sometimes we all need a little reality check about life. I am just stating the facts and giving you the scoop . . . nothing more . . . nothing less. This is not about sides. I don't have to pick sides when I'm telling the truth," she said flatly. Then she let out a raucous laugh. Something wasn't right about my best friend, but I didn't have time to piece it together.

I just fell silent. I was still going to have a quick lunch with her, but after it was over I would just go about my business. I had decided I didn't need her to chauffeur me around. I'd take a taxi to the place. Something about her was different in a way that I couldn't place a finger on. Maybe she was mad that I left town and didn't give her much detail? Maybe she was mad that I looked so good? It wouldn't be the first time Daysha had gotten jealous of me. I didn't know what her problem was and in my assessment, I didn't have time right now to figure it all out.

In and out of Virginia Beach. That was my plan. Little did I know a bunch of other people, including my so-called best friend, had different plans for me.

MATT

I pulled my fitted cap down farther on my head and slid down a little bit in the driver's seat of the rental car I had Daysha rent for me. When I spotted Lauren for the first time since she had betrayed me, something inside of me started ticking like what I would imagine the inside of a bomb to feel like right before it exploded. The feeling I was experiencing was surreal to say the least.

So much shit had happened to me since the last time I saw Lauren. I felt like someone's eyes were constantly on me. I noticed it after the condo burned down, and even though I tried to ignore it, there was no mistaking that I was being hunted. I coulda sworn I was about to get jacked as I left Ryan's house, but the SUV tailing me did nothing. Spooky as shit to not know why I was being followed and why those thugs left me for dead in my burning condo. All I knew was this situation had something to do with Lauren. She either set me up or . . .

I squinted my eyes into slits and blew air out of my flaring nostrils like a bull on attack. Up until that moment, I didn't know how I would feel or react if I had ever laid eyes on Lauren again, but now I knew. I was having an out-of-body experience because I could actually see myself rushing from the rental car, running up to Lauren, pulling out my gun, and murdering her in front of thousands of witnesses while she stood outside at the cab stand of the airport. I blinked a few times and realized that I was still sitting in the car. I touched my waist where I had my burner locked and loaded. My hands were shaking fiercely trying to keep myself from pulling that shit out.

"You so lucky, bitch," I whispered harshly. I bit my bottom lip so hard I could taste the sting of my own blood on my tongue.

I swear on everything I love it was taking everything inside of me not to run up on Lauren with my burner and blow her fucking head right off her shoulders. Besides there being too many witnesses, I knew it would be wise to wait. I knew she didn't have the money on her but I also knew that it had to be very close. Sometimes it felt like I knew Lauren better than she knew herself. I took her in when she was just a teenage girl looking to be taken care of. I watched her become the woman she is today, so it baffled me why she thought she could ever get away from me after she stole my fucking money.

I watched her every move until Daysha showed up and picked her up. My body felt hot all over watching that Lauren's smug ass saunter toward her car like she was a fucking celebrity. She walked like one of those rich chicks that didn't have a care in the world. She probably felt like it too. I'm sure Lauren most likely thought I would never have a reason to be near the airport and that she could dip in and out of town without me ever finding out. The fucking joke was on her. Little did Lauren know she was about to be sitting in the car with Daysha—the worst traitor since Sammy "The Bull" Gravano.

I snorted and shook my head left to right in disgust. Lauren looked real good in all of her designer threads, with her head and eyes covered like some high society, black version of Jackie O. She was always good at fronting like she had it all together. Most people admired her but I knew the real Lauren Kelly. The Lauren Kelly who was thrown around from one foster home to the next. The Lauren Kelly whose mother was the neighborhood ho and back-alley-sucking-dick crackhead. Lauren was one of those chicks that I considered the lowest of the low in the hood. I had only chosen her because she was gorgeous and most of the niggas in the hood wanted her but couldn't have her. At first it was a competition thing for me, but I can't front, I fell in love with her after a while. I had bitches back then that were real high class, not fakes like Lauren became. I had chicks who went to college, had degrees and were professionals. They might've been attracted to me for the money I had at the time, but so was dirty-ass Lauren. I was so furious now that I didn't realize I was gripping the steering wheel so hard the veins in my wrists were cording against my skin. There was no anger worse than a broken fucking heart. I see now why niggas ended up doing life behind a chick. Some say it was ego but I say that it was truly being heartbroken that men couldn't handle. I was feeling that shit right then.

"If you run up on the bitch right now you'll never get the money. All you will end up with is a life sentence. Stick to the fucking plan. Go home, smoke a blunt, and chill until you get the call from Daysha," I grumbled out loud to myself. It was taking a lot of convincing because my trigger finger was itching.

I watched Lauren throw her bag in Daysha's backseat and get into the car. There was a bit of a pause before Daysha's car pulled away from the airport's pickup curb. My hands were itching against the steering wheel and my foot was tapping on the gas pedal. "Don't do it. Don't do it."

I sucked in my bottom lip. I had to exercise great restraint to keep myself from pulling out behind that fucking car. The way I was feeling, there was no telling exactly what I would've done to Lauren. I was liable to bust shots into Daysha's back windshield, which would've only landed my ass back in the clink. I sat there staring and thinking until I could no longer see any traces of the car.

When Daysha's car was fully disappeared

from the airport, I sent Daysha a quick text message:

Yo, I'm heading to my condo. Make sure you hit me when she gives you a hint about where the money is. Don't slip up.

I pulled out of the airport and turned up some Rick Ross in the rental. I needed something to keep me calm, but also keep my head in the game. All of this shit was almost over. I would have the money soon and Lauren's ass would be in the morgue.

Back at the condo I couldn't rest. I tried all types of shit to make my mind relax. Even a full blunt of the best bud in Virginia ain't do that trick. My nerves were on a wire's edge and my whole body still hurt from the beatdown I got from those strange dudes. I could not sit still to save my life.

First, I paced Buddha's condo at least ten times going over the plans in my head incessantly. I rearranged shit in my closet and made a pile of the shit Lauren had left behind so I could burn it later. I counted the money I had took from Ryan. I rolled a couple more blunts for my reserve stash. None of those things could stop my imagination from running wild about what was going on with Lauren and Daysha. I must have checked my cell phone every minute since I had gotten home. All of this hard-pressed, stressing behavior wasn't me. All of these years I had prided myself in always being cool under pressure. I was a boss so why the hell was I acting like a straight-up bitch?

"Yo, nigga, you straight trippin'. You a boss, nigga. Shit is going to work out," I told myself. Even I couldn't convince myself that everything was going to be all right. By the time I finished moving around the condo like a crazy person I was sweaty as hell.

I went and took a shower to calm myself down. As I got out of the shower I heard my cell phone ringing.

"Oh shit!" I huffed, breaking into a run to get the phone from my nightstand.

"Hello?" I wolfed into the phone. "Hello?" I said again. There was no voice on the line but I could hear background noise and breathing. My whole body went cold. The last time I answered the phone and got no response, I got jacked and almost torched. This couldn't be happening a second time—this had to be a coincidence. I racked my brain for someone who could be playing this silly phone game.

"Yo, stop fucking playing, whoever this is. I can fucking hear you breathing, you stupid-ass cunt," I barked. My damn nerves were too touchy for games at that moment. I hung up the call and looked at the screen. Unknown. I had been getting mad unknown calls and the person just always breathed into the phone but didn't say shit. Honestly, I thought for sure it was Yancy this time. It was like I just couldn't get rid of that crazy bitch.

"Fuck!" I cursed. I slumped down on the

couch and flicked on the TV. I needed to find something funny to watch so I could shake the edgy nerves and the bad mood I was in. As soon as the TV screen came on, the news was the first thing popped up. Just as I was about to change the channel I heard some shit that caught my attention. . . .

"In a story we have been following for three months now, police say they may finally have a break in the case of three million dollars that was stolen from the bank account of local businessman and community activist Nikolai Kudrin. Police believe the masterminds behind the missing money are a drug dealer out on parole and a high-tech hacker. Police report that their break came after a cooperating witness, who claims to know the man pictured here, came forward this week. A suspect has been identified as forty-one-year-old Matthew Connors. The cooperating witness identified him, but does not know his exact whereabouts. Based on information they received, the police also report that in a bizarre twist in the case, twenty-five-year-old expert computer hacker Ryan Stiltsky was found dead in his Baltimore home. Police believe his death may be directly linked to the stolen millions. During the homicide investigation into Stiltsky's death, detectives also uncovered electronic evidence—some type of electronic diary Stiltsky kept—that linked Stiltsky to the crime. The evidence also points directly to Connors. Police report that with the help of the cooperating witness they hope to close in on Connors, but they are still looking for tips on locating him. If you have any information regarding the whereabouts of the suspect, please contact the Norfolk Police Department's crime tip line at 1-800-LOCK-U-UP."

Yo, it was like a bomb had just exploded in the room. The reporter's words resounded like firecrackers in my ears.

"Ain't this about a bitch!" I sprang up on my legs like a jack-in-the-box. I literally had to pinch myself to make sure that I wasn't trapped in some crazy-ass nightmare. I couldn't believe that my fucking name and picture were floating around on the news. But, worst of all, I couldn't believe that police were calling me out as the sole suspect. I don't know how they figured it out, but since they did, how could they not know Lauren was involved? How did that bitch manage to get away free and clear?

This score was supposed to put me on top, but at every turn it looked like I was digging my own grave. I looked around the living room, suddenly paranoid. The cops were on to me, so I had to be careful. They could come crashing in the door any minute to drag me back to the pen. Crashing at the condo Buddha had set me up in was now more than temporary housing— it was my hideout. It would take the cops a while to go down my list of known associates and question everyone about my whereabouts. By the time they dug in and tracked me to Buddha's condo, I planned to be long gone.

"Argh!" This could not be happening to me right now. Not when I am so close to catching this bitch Lauren and getting all of the money back. This shit could not be happening!

"Argh!" I growled again, sending the TV remote crashing into the wall across from me. "I can't fucking win!" I howled. "Argh!" I swiped everything off the coffee table onto the floor and then like the Incredible Hulk I hoisted the entire table up and threw it over onto its side. "Argh!" The bookshelf went crashing to the floor. I sent more things flying across the room and into the walls. I went on a rampage tearing the condo up until I was finally exhausted.

I stalked to the bedroom and plopped down on the side of the bed. I put my head in my hands and squeezed my scalp. I had to think now. The more I thought, the more I could see my world going up in flames. I was a wanted man and my name plus my face was all over the news. The news report played over and over in my head. The news reporter had said the police have a cooperating witness, which in the hood means a fucking snitch. In my assessment, that could only be one person . . . fucking Yancy. She was the only person alive, aside from Lauren and me, that knew about the lick.

"That bitch. I will kill her, too," I huffed.

I knew I should have at least tried to make shit right with Yancy two weeks ago when she came by the condo to tell me she was pregnant. I couldn't process that information at the time. I was looking dead at her swollen stomach but I couldn't even grasp the fact that the baby was mine. I guess it was a knee-jerk reaction when I had told her that it wasn't no fucking baby of mine and that she better go find the trick she had gotten pregnant by. I knew it was wrong when I was saying it, but I couldn't help it. I was wrong for dissing Yancy like that, but after Lauren lost our babies I had completely given up on being a father. When Yancy brought that shit to me, I was just thrown off. Losing those babies with Lauren had really hurt 'cause I had always wanted a seed of my own. Now, chances were I was going to be a father for the first time and I would be on the run and never see my seed at all. All of this stress had me contemplating putting my own gun in my mouth and pulling the trigger.

As I sat there regretting ever getting involved with Yancy, my cell buzzed with a text from Daysha:

> I'm downtown at lunch with her now. She's talking about going to the place alone and then bouncing. She hasn't mentioned the money. I think you might have to show up at the place or else you chance missing her. I can only stall her for so long. Get here now.

"Fuck!" I growled. I text Daysha back.

> Yo, 5-O is looking for me right now so I've got to lay low until dark so I can make my getaway. It's all over the news. You might want to ditch that bitch in case the suits are looking for her ass. Yancy snitched. I'll catch up with you later.

There was no way I could get caught right now after what I'd heard on the news. I was positive the cops would be swarming around that assisted living place, thinking I might come through there with Lauren. The entire plan to get Lauren's ass back and to get the money back was a bust. Now, I was going to have to wait for it to get dark, take what I had left from my raid of Ryan's safe, and bounce. Leaving Virginia Beach was my only option right now, but that was going to be real hard with the good and the bad guys searching for me.

"You really put me in a fucked up position, Lauren. After all I did for you, this is how I end up . . . on the fucking run for my life and for my freedom. Even after all of this a nigga stayed having mad love for you, but not now. Consider yourself lucky that I couldn't confront you today. I swear they would be tagging your toe had I gotten to see you up close and personal," I spoke through my teeth aloud as if Lauren was standing right in front of me. All I could do was hope that I could make it out untouched.

LAUREN

I downed my third mojito with the hopes that it would lighten my mood or at least help to change the tense atmosphere I was in. It didn't work. Trust me, I could have used about ten more drinks with the way I was feeling at that moment. It was hard enough being back in town without all of the added little stress from Daysha.

Lunch with Daysha was painful to say the least. We were barely conversing. I really had nothing to say to her after her little remarks in the car about my miscarriages, so there were long bouts of silence between us. When there was conversation it seemed forced and strained. I thought I would be excited to share news about my new relationship with Drake, but I had completely shut down on her.

Daysha, who usually runs her mouth non-stop, spent most of the time texting on her phone and whipping her head around like that shit was on a swivel. If I didn't know any better, I would've said Daysha was acting like she was expecting someone to come join us. If I didn't trust her so much, her suspicious behavior would have had me thinking she had called Matt down there or some shit. Nah, I knew Daysha hated Matt so I wasn't worried about that.

When Daysha wasn't looking around all crazy suspicious, she was undressing me like one of the hater chicks we always talked about back in the days. Even without asking I was sure Daysha probably knew which designer had made every piece of clothing, the shoes, and the bag that I wore that day. It was disgusting how she was acting.

As soon as we sat down earlier, Daysha had made a comment about my Chanel purse. "Damn, bitch, that's the big-boy Chanel. That's about ten Gs, right? Must be fucking sweet, whatever you're doing for loot," she had said. I had ignored her. Thank goodness our waitress had come over to break up the tension. Then, Daysha kept it up. She was like, "Mmm. Mmm. Ms. Lauren Kelly the superstar. Life must be treating you good, you out here wearing a Balmain skirt and them new Loubs that ain't even hit the stores down here yet."

Okay, I couldn't ignore her snide comments anymore. I crumpled my face in disgust and shot her an icy glare.

"Girl, please. You know *we* like nice shit so why you acting like that? You ain't looking too shabby. New Gucci bag. New Michael Kors sneakers. True Religion jeans. Romeo and Juliet top. I mean we always been about the fashion so what's the problem today?" I had shot back at her. Daysha tried to laugh it off like she had only been joking. I didn't return the fake laughs with her. I was trying to make it through lunch so I could ditch her ass anyway.

Now, I shoveled a forkful of my teriyaki salmon into my mouth and looked across the table at Daysha. Of course she was in the middle of texting or receiving and reading a text, I should say. I watched Daysha's eyes go wide. She looked over at me and cracked a phony, nervous smile. Then, once again she was looking over her shoulder like she was afraid someone was after her. I sucked my teeth. She was getting on my nerves. As a matter of fact, she was making my damn nerves bad. I had had enough. I looked at my watch and decided it was time for me to go. But, first, I needed to ask Daysha what the fuck was up with her. I would hate to leave things with my best friend with tension if she needed to say something to me. I loved Daysha like a sister.

I dropped my fork and finally asked, "You a'ight, Daysha?" I just couldn't take the phoniness and tension for another minute. "It just seems like things are different between us. I'm not sure if I did something to you or what," I said, looking Daysha dead in her eyes. Daysha averted her eyes from mine and lowered her head. She picked up her fourth Hennessy and Coke and threw it back. It was like she was trying to use the drink as liquid courage or something. Daysha opened her mouth like she was about to say something, but just then our waitress interrupted to ask if we were okay.

"Yes, we are fine," I said, cracking a fake smile. I turned my attention back to Daysha. She was looking over my shoulder like she was distracted by something behind me.

"Okay . . . so back to my question. I need to clear this up before I'm gone again," I said to her.

"I have to use the bathroom. I'll be back, Lauren," Daysha said, abruptly cutting me off. I opened my mouth to say something but Daysha quickly got up and rushed from the table, leaving me there alone. I folded my face into a frown. Suddenly, it was like a lightbulb went off in my head. Daysha was definitely expecting somebody.

I was a lot of things, but stupid wasn't one of them. I slowly turned around in my seat and I spotted the first dude staring at me. He stood out in the restaurant like a sore thumb. He was tall with low-cut hair and was wearing a dark suit. Definitely not the type of dude you'd see in a local chain restaurant. I turned back to the table and noticed another dude, dressed similarly, staring at me too. *What the fuck? Nah, not more than one* Men in Black *nigga in the same place. Something is up,* I told myself. It was time for me to bounce. Clearly, I was going to have to dip out on Daysha.

I slowly dug into my purse and pulled out two one-hundred-dollar bills. I threw them down on the table. My heart was racing. My hands were shaking. I wanted to wait for Daysha but she was taking too long. I slowly stood up, picked up my purse, and slid it on my shoulder. I was trying to play it cool but my legs were trembling with fear. My steps were kind of unsteady. My waitress rushed over. I guess she wanted to make sure I wasn't bouncing out without paying my bill.

"Oh, was everything to your liking?" she asked in that cheery I-want-a-tip-bitch way. Her little eyes were scanning over the table to make sure she saw some cash for the bill.

"Yes, everything was perfect. Keep the change. I have to get going," I replied with a shaky, phony smile myself. I quickly scanned the room and those dudes in suits were still there. I could feel the heat of their gazes bearing down on me. *They are definitely here for me! Shit!* I said to myself.

Play it cool, Lauren. Play it cool, Lauren. Just get out of the door. Just get out of the door, I chanted to myself.

I swallowed hard and started heading to the door on unsteady legs. As soon as I moved, I saw the men moving in my direction. I dug down deep and got a burst of energy. Suddenly I was much more steady on my legs. My fear had turned into determination. I knew they were following me now, but I wasn't going that easily. I got to the door, pushed it, kicked off my heels, and bolted from the restaurant. Just like I suspected the men in suits bolted after me.

MATT

"Calm the fuck down! I can't understand shit you're saying, Daysha," I yelled into the phone. Daysha was yelling and screaming into the phone. I could only understand every other word. I was on my feet pacing nervously.

"Yo! Calm the fuck down and tell me what you're saying!" I boomed. I couldn't take it anymore. My nerves were already on crazy edge. I stopped moving for a few seconds so I could listen intently to what she was saying.

"Okay," Daysha said, sucking in her breath so she could speak properly.

"I . . . I . . . shouldn't have . . . I . . . I . . . didn't mean to . . . they probably got her. Oh my . . . my . . . gawd," Daysha stammered and cried at the same time.

"What? What happened? Something happened to Lauren?" I asked frantically.

"Three men came into the restaurant. Um . . . they came to get her. When I came out of the bathroom she was running out of the restaurant and they were chasing after her," Daysha relayed through sobs. "This is crazy. We're the only ones who know she's in town, so who were those dudes? I can't believe I betrayed her and made her come back here!"

"Daysha! Are you sure they weren't five'o? Who were they? What did they look like?!" I barked into the phone. I was up on my feet and pacing again now. I had to know because whoever was after her, they were probably coming after me next. Again.

"I don't know," Daysha cried. "They just . . . just . . . you shoulda seen the way they went after her. My best friend is probably dead by now."

"Think, Daysha! Fuck, man! Tell me exactly what they looked like! How did they act?!" I screamed, my voice going high like a bitch.

"They were wearing dark suits and dark shades. They were big . . . like tall and big. I . . . I . . . don't know. They could have been cops. I just didn't see them long enough. But they started chasing her." I could barely understand what Daysha was saying. She was breathing so hard into the phone I would swear it was inside her mouth. "Oh my gawd! It was all because of me. I was the reason she came back here! Me being greedy, I set up my best friend. All for some funky-ass money! Now somebody might kill her," Daysha screamed. This bitch was straight wigging out, which meant she might go running her damn mouth. I felt like I was caught up in *The Matrix*. The way shit was falling apart seemed unreal, like some shit out of a movie.

I was gripping the phone so tight my hand began to cramp. Sweat dripped down the sides of my face and all of the muscles in my body were tense.

"Yo, Daysha, you talking crazy. This is because of snitching-ass Yancy, not you. Look, I gotta go. I can't give you the rest of your paper because as soon as it gets dark I'm bouncing. You ain't never speak to me or see me. I got niggas that will come after you if you try anything funny, too," I told her. I hung up the phone.

"Fuck!!!" I screamed. This time I smashed my cell phone into a million little pieces. I stalked through my condo and loaded up all of the weapons I could find. Cops or those thugs that were tailing me . . . this time I wasn't going to be a sitting duck for whoever decided to come after me.

"A nigga is not going out without a fight. I ain't no punk bitch," I grumbled. I got up and peeped out of the mini blinds hanging from my bedroom window. I needed nightfall to come so I could get the fuck out of Dodge. But waiting . . . the suspense . . . and counting on it taking a while for the cops to track me down . . . I was tense as shit. I needed to calm down before my nerves sent me bolting out of the front door. If folks saw a crazy-looking nigga running down the street, they'd have the cops giving chase in ten seconds flat. I couldn't let that happen. No way.

I paced over to my bed and lay down. I lit up a blunt to calm my nerves while I figured out an escape plan. As the weed worked its way into my system, I leaned back on my bed and stared up at the ceiling. I hadn't had this ill feeling of fear in the pit of my stomach since the day I woke up and found my moms murdered in our apartment. When shit got tough for me like it was now, that memory always came crashing back down on me like a brick falling from the sky. Today was no different. . . .

August 1984

My mother had put me to bed with her usual kiss on the head and a quick tickling session. I was laughing raucously and rolling all over my bed. When she stopped for a few seconds I looked at her lovingly.

"Ma . . . I'm gettin' too old for you to be ticklin' me. My friends said that's gay," I had said to her. I was ten years old, but I was still my mother's baby.

"Whaaat, boy?" my mother sang in her sweet soft voice. "What you and your friends know about calling something gay? You my baby and I will tickle you if I want to. When you're a grown man I will move your wife aside and tickle you right in front of her. Now, I'm gonna keep tickling you," she said jokingly. Then she bent down and tickled me again. I laughed. The bond I had with my mother was unbreakable. She was there every morning when I awoke and she made

sure to tuck me in every night. It was just she and I against the world. I had never known any father.

"Okay. Okay. Enough now. You go to bed so you can be sharp in school tomorrow. That education is the only way out of this place and it's the one thing nobody can ever take from you," my mother said with feeling. She bent down and planted another kiss on my face . . . this time on my cheek.

"I love you, little boy," she said.

"I love you more," I replied.

"I love you morer and morer," she said with a chuckle. That was another one of our nighttime rituals.

"Uh uh . . . I love you morer, morer, morer, and morer," I said back, opening my arms as wide as they would go. My mother threw her pretty head back and laughed heartily.

"Okay. It's really time for bed now. Stop trying to stall to stay up later," she said. Then she gave me another kiss. A warm comfort filled my chest and spread all over my body like the coziest blanket I had ever felt.

"G'night," I said to her. She smiled. She clicked off my light. I lay awake for a little while. I heard when she went and opened up the door. I heard her giggles and the man's voice. I also could tell it was a different man than the night before. Every night I would lie awake listening to my mother and her male "company" as she called the different men that frequented our house at night. I would listen until I could no longer keep my eyes open. Usually by the time I awoke the company would be gone.

That next morning I jumped out of my sleep. Usually, my mother would wake me up for school and I would purposely give her a hard time. This morning, she hadn't come into my room. I knew it was later than usual and my mother hadn't come to wake me up for school like she always did which was really strange. I sat up in my bed and rubbed my eyes. The sun was shining brightly through my bedroom window and I could already hear the hustle and bustle of school buses outside. A pang of panic shot through my chest. As young as I was I knew that I was supposed to be outside before the school buses came.

"I'm late," I mumbled. I guess I was experiencing a mixture of apprehension and elation because the only time my mother didn't wake me up was when she'd decide to let me stay home for the day to do something special with me. I opened my bedroom door and dragged my feet down toward my mother's bedroom. Her door was still closed. That was strange too. My mother was always up early. She used to always say, "Money never sleeps, baby, and closed legs don't get fed." I never knew what she meant by that.

"Mommy," I called out as I knocked lightly on her door. As soon as I hit the door it came open slightly. I peeked through the crack between the wall and the door. I could see my mother's bare legs hanging off the side of her bed. My eyebrows dipped on my face. Everything seemed off to my little young mind.

"Mommy? We late," I called out to her. I still didn't enter her room without permission, though. My mother had always forbidden me from coming into her room unless she told me to come in after I knocked. And, if her door was locked at night during the time she had "company" I was not to knock at all. Whatever problem I had she would solve it when she was done. But at that moment she was clearly in her room alone.

"Mommy! Can I come in? We are late for school!" I yelled, this time a bit more frantically. Still my mother didn't answer. I noticed that her legs didn't even move at the sound of my voice. Up until that moment my mother had never ignored me for any reason. "Mommy?!" I called out to her again. I could feel panic rising from my feet and climbing into my consciousness.

Looking through the crack in the door I followed my mother's legs and trailed my eyes down to the floor. There was something wrong. I sucked in a lungful of breath when I saw a dark red pool of blood on the floor right under her legs. A cold feeling came over me and I couldn't stop my teeth from chattering.

"Mommy!!" I shrieked in a panic. I pushed the door with all of the strength inside of me. I almost died of a heart attack when I saw the rest of my mother's body sprawled on the side of the bed with a blanket of blood surrounding her. Her head was turned in an awkward position that looked like it hurt. Her eyes were open and so was her mouth. She looked like she was in extreme pain.

"Mommy!!" I let out a bloodcurdling scream. "Mommy! Mommy! Mommy!" I continued shrieking until the back of my throat itched and burned. I didn't care about the blood. I ran over and began shaking her lifeless body frantically. I couldn't tell at that moment where her injuries were, but I did see the long metal object sticking out from between her legs. I felt

*myself fading. Suddenly my world went black. Later I
was told that I went into shock and collapsed right on
top of my mother's bloodied body. I can't remember how
my mother and I were found. But, a week after I'd
found her, during her funeral service, I heard people
talking and whispering about how one of my mother's
johns had slit her throat and drove a metal pipe up
into her vagina so deep it had busted up her organs.*

I jumped up soaked with sweat and with my
chest heaving. I guess I had fallen asleep and
that memory about the morning I had found
my mother murdered had turned into a nightmare. I sat up and swiped my hands over my
face. I looked at the cable box, it was almost
midnight.

"Damn. I gotta get out of here," I grumbled. I
got up from the bed and walked into the closet.
I hoisted the duffel bag I had packed contain-
ing the money I stole from Ryan, two guns, and
a few pieces of necessary clothing items. I kept
my Glock out and shoved it down the back of
my pants. I took a deep breath.

"Now or never, nigga. Time to blow this joint
for good," I said out loud. I stepped out of the
closet and walked through the bedroom.

BAM! CRASH!

"Oh shit!" I huffed. I heard the thunder of
what sounded like a million pairs of feet stam-
peding in my direction. I dropped my bag and
went for my gun. I pulled it out but it was too
late.

"Drop that shit!" a voice barked. I was definitely outgunned. I hung my head and let my
Glock drop to the floor. Before I could do or say
another thing, what seemed like a million dudes
put hands on me. I folded to the floor as a storm
of punches and kicks rained down on me. They
left no part of my body untouched. I quickly realized that this couldn't be the police. I was about
to die and there was no escaping it.

LAUREN

My feet moved at the speed of lightning. I could feel the wind beating on my skin so hard it made snot wet the inside of my nostrils. My entire body was covered with a thick sheen of sweat and I could feel it burning my armpits. My breath escaped my mouth in jagged, raggedy puffs and my chest burned. My heart felt like it would burst through the front of it. Even feeling as terrible as I did, I would not and could not stop moving.

"Move!"

"Get out of my fucking way!"

"Watch out!"

"Move!"

I screamed command after command at the nosy-ass people who were staring and gawking and being in my damn way. My legs were moving like those of a swift and agile cheetah as I swerved and swayed through the throngs of people on the downtown Virginia Beach street. I was met by more than one mouthful of gasps and groans and I could faintly see more than one wide-eyed, mouth-agape stare as people gawked at me like I was a crazy woman. I guess I did look crazy running through the high-end shopping area with no shoes on (I had run straight out my Louboutins), my expensive embellished Balmain skirt was hitched up around my hips, my vixen weave blowing in the wind, and my Chanel caviar bag strapped around my arm like a slave chain. I could feel that my makeup was a cakey, smudged mess all over my face and eyes. But I didn't give a damn. I wasn't going to stop running. No matter what. Looking crazy was the least of my worries.

I had run track in high school and it was still paying off now, but clearly I wasn't in the same athletic shape. Still, I wasn't about to go out like this. I wasn't going to get captured on the street and probably murdered for something that wasn't totally my fault. I had been pushed and provoked to do everything that I did. All of the mistakes. All of the grimy shit I had done over the years. All of it was because I was born at a disadvantage from day fucking one.

I didn't want to die. I had always seen myself growing old with a few kids and grandkids surrounding me when I was ready to be settled. I would've given anything to be old and settled at this moment. But, of course, life threw me a curveball.

I could hear the thunderous footfalls of the

three men chasing me. If they weren't so damn gorilla big and slower than me they would have caught me by now.

"Hey! Are you okay?" I heard a man on the street yell at me as I flew past him nearly knocking him over. Why the hell was he asking me such a dumb question when you could clearly see that I was being chased by three hulking goons dressed in all black with their guns probably showing on their waists or maybe even in their hands? Thank goodness I am always so alert or they would've walked right up on me while I unsuspectingly ate my lunch at the posh restaurant and grabbed me. It was the fact that I had only been back in town for a few hours, the disappearance of my lunch companion, and the suspicious looks that had alerted me in the first place. How could I have been so trusting? So naïve and stupid, too.

I could feel the look of terror contorting my face, so I knew damn well passersby could see the fear etched on every inch of it.

Finally, I dipped through a side alley and the first door I tried allowed me inside. Thank God! With my chest heaving up and down I rested my back against another cold metal door inside and slid down to the floor. My legs were still trembling and my muscles were on fire in places on my body I didn't even know existed. I tried to slow my rapid breathing so I could hear whether the men had noticed me dipping into the alley but the more I tried to calm myself the more reality set in about the grave danger I was in. I was probably about to be murdered or worse, tortured and then murdered right in a dank alleyway in the place I thought I would never return to. If I hadn't gotten that call, it would have been years before I crept back here. I thought about Matt and wondered if he was the one who had sent these men after me. But how would he have known I was back? I knew Matt had a lot of selfish ways about him and although shit had gone south with us, I never thought he would try to do something like this to me. I expected that if he wanted to confront me, he would come himself. Even if it was Yancy who had sent the goons, I would think Matt would have tried to spare me.

CLANG!

A loud noise outside interrupted my thoughts and caused me to jump. I clasped both of my hands over my mouth and forced the scream that had crept up my throat back down. Sweat trickled down my face and burned my eyes. My heart jackhammered against my chest bone so hard it actually hurt. My stomach knotted up so tightly the cramps were almost unbearable. I dropped my head. Suddenly I felt like vomiting.

"I don't see her! She's not down here!" I heard one of the goons outside of the door scream to the others. I swallowed hard and started praying under my breath.

Dear God, I am sorry for all of the things I've done. I don't know how things got so far gone. I never meant anything by any of it. I just wanted to live a better life than I had as a child. I guess with the mother You gave me and the hand You dealt me, I should've just handled it. I should've worked harder

*and not try to take the easy way out all of the time. I
know stealing is wrong. Since the first time I stole a
credit card from my foster mother's purse, I knew it
was wrong. But I got addicted to the feeling that I'd
gotten over on someone. I felt powerful. I remember the
times I'd hear her talking to my foster father about
some of the fraud scams she witnessed by working as a
bank manager. It was interesting to hear how bank
and credit card frauds were being committed on a
daily basis. It all seemed too easy, too intoxicating. I
had to test the waters. . . .*

*So here I am today. I'm literally running for my
life. Maybe this is Your way of teaching me a lesson.
Trust me, I hear You loud and clear. If You let me get
out of this, I swear I will change my life. I don't even
know how things got this far. . . .*

Those last few words of my prayer resonated
with me the longest. I truly didn't know how I
had gotten to this point. I immediately started
to think back on everything that had happened.
I had definitely done my share of dirt but did I
really deserve to die like this?

My mind raced with a million thoughts but at
the forefront was the fact that I believed that
Daysha had set me up. Tears streamed down my
cheeks as I crouched down and hid. My own
friend had turned on me in the worst way. A hic-
cup of sobs escaped my mouth before I could
even control it. I quickly clasped my hands over
my mouth.

"In here! Here!" I heard one of the men
bark. My shoulders slumped and I just closed
my eyes.

"Get her!" I heard another one yell. I felt

them pushing the door against my back. I gave up. I gave up on trying to run. I gave up on trying to find happiness. I gave up on trying to find love. I gave up on trying to have money and survive. I just finally gave it all up.

I was still sobbing, but I was going to face these dudes like a woman. I stood up and turned toward the door. When the first goon pushed it in he jumped because he didn't expect to find me standing there ready to go with them without a fight.

"I got her!" he called out to the rest. I shot him an icy glare as my entire body trembled. For all I knew he was going to pull out a gun and shoot me down right there. He didn't. The second goon rushed through the doorway and clamped down on my arm roughly.

"The boss wants her brought to him alive," he told the others. "He wants to do the honors himself."

They dragged me out of the building and into a black SUV. They didn't bother to tie me up, handcuff me, or anything.

"Where are y'all taking me?" I croaked out, my throat sore and my mouth dry.

"To hell if you don't pray," one of them answered with an eerie finality that sent chills down my spine.

When the SUV they had forced me to ride in pulled into the desolate area, my heart thumped against my chest bone. I stretched my eyes and saw that there were nothing but warehouses and factories surrounding the entire area. This couldn't be a good sign, I was thinking. I looked around and right away I knew this was the type of place thugs like these took people to kill them. We were near the port, that much I could tell. In the distance I could see the water and the ships behind the buildings. It was a place that was familiar to me since I was from the Tidewater area.

You might as well consider yourself as good as dead, Lauren. My imagination ran wild and was telling me that there were probably many bodies in the murky green water behind the warehouses. I surmised that I would be joining them soon enough.

When the SUV rolled through the tall, silver chain-link fence each pop and crunch of the gravel under the tires unnerved me. The tension inside of the car was palpable, to say the least. My teeth began chattering uncontrollably. My body trembled as well. I wrung my hands in my lap and swung my legs open and closed nervously. None of the goons said anything once we arrived, but I could feel a different type of vibe envelop the car. It was ominous and dark all of a sudden. They knew the fate that awaited me.

I was praying in my head but the words weren't really clear to me. I had already started to wig the fuck out mentally. Everything was muddled and blurry. Even my hearing was blocked by a ringing noise that suddenly exploded inside of them. I guess this was what happened when a person felt like they were looking death directly in the eyes. The best I could describe it was a dizzying fear that threatened the very fiber of my sanity. I could actually feel the fine strings of my mental stability coming loose.

When the vehicle finally stopped moving something inside of me seemed to click on as if someone flipped a light switch inside of me. Or maybe it was more like something snapped in half like a twig being broken in the middle. Whatever happened, it caused my body to come alive like I had been pumped with a billion watts of electricity. I guess my fight-or-flight instinct kicked in because I started fighting like I was in the center of a boxing ring with my toughest opponent. I swung my arms and caught the goon to my left right across his face. He clearly didn't see it coming nor did he expect it.

"Oh shit! This little . . ." he balked, quickly throwing his hands up to his face. The goon sitting on my right side tried to grab me but he wasn't able to get a good grip on me before I was first able to claw a chunk of skin from his cheek.

"Ahhh! Get this bitch!" he howled. I kicked wildly and swung my arms just as wildly. They weren't ready for me. I may have been a woman and short in stature, but my will to live made me as big and tall as every motherfucka in that vehicle. I was moving so wildly that I couldn't see nor did I really know who or what I was hitting with each crazy swing.

"Calm that bitch down! Y'all letting a bitch fuck y'all up!" the goon that was driving yelled from the front.

"This bitch is crazy," the goon on my left

huffed. "I'm about to put two in her fucking head!" he growled.

That's right. I wanted them to know I was crazy . . . crazy about my life. It didn't matter who was trying to capture and kill me, I wasn't going down without a fierce fight. I had been through a lot in my lifetime and through it all I knew one thing for sure . . . I was a fucking fighter. I didn't lie down easily for nobody. I swung at the goon on my left again but I missed. He grabbed hold of my wrists and squeezed them so hard it made me buckle over at the waist. I just knew he would shatter all of the bones in my wrists.

"Ahhh," I said, wincing, but I didn't stop fighting. I couldn't move my arms but I sure kicked and bucked my body like a wild animal being carried to slaughter. The goon on my right scrambled out of the door.

"Grab this bitch! I'm sick of her," the one holding my wrists demanded. His partner leaned back into the car from outside of the door and stuck his hands under both of my shoulders and began pulling me out of the SUV.

"Get off of me! Agh! Get the fuck off of me!" I screamed at the top of my lungs. My prayer was that someone, somewhere nearby would hear my cries. The other goon finally released my wrists. He shouldn't have. I jutted my foot out forcefully and caught him with a perfect kick in his side. He made a noise but he kept on coming. My kick didn't faze him but it sure did infuriate him.

"That's it! She's a dead bitch! I'm sick of this

bitch!" the goon boomed, pulling his gun from his waist.

"No! Don't fucking shoot her right here!" the driver barked. The other goon sucked in his bottom lip and slowly put his gun away. I kicked at him again but I couldn't get to him. I turned my head to the side and tried in vain to bite the goon who was holding me under the shoulders.

"This little spitfire is trying to fucking bite me now," he grumped.

"Get her the fuck inside so we can do what we gotta do. She's lucky the boss wants her brought to him alive or else I would've put this bitch on ice," the driver growled. Before anything else was said I was dragged from the vehicle. As soon as my feet hit the dirt I started bucking, kicking, biting, and spitting again. I was exhausted and my body ached, but I would not stop fighting.

"Let go of me! Get off of me!" I kicked, screamed, and flailed as all the three men tried in vain to drag me toward the door to the ware-house-looking building.

"Get off of me!" I wasn't going in there that fucking easily. I felt like I was on death row being led to the chamber. No wonder it took so many guards for the death row inmates. It was a different kind of fight when you felt like your life was on the line.

"Ouch! Little bitch!" One of the goons growled. I had kicked him in the stomach as he tried to lift me onto his shoulder.

"This little bitch is a fighter," one of the others commented. The tallest of the three gorilla goons finally hoisted me, kicking and screaming, onto his shoulder. I began pounding my fists into his back. My small hits didn't faze him at all. He began walking swiftly to the door. I couldn't let them take me inside. I turned my head and was able to latch onto his ear with my teeth. I bit down with the force of a mighty lioness. I moved my top and bottom teeth side to side while my sharp teeth were clamped down on the goon's cartilage.

"Arrrrggghhh!" the goon screamed out. "Agggghhh! Get her off of me! Get this bitch off of me! She's fucking biting me!" he hollered, his voice going high-pitched like a woman's. I was taking great satisfaction in inflicting this type of pain on him. He was trying to dump me over but I wouldn't let go of the jaw lock I had on his ear. I could taste his blood on my tongue now. The scent and taste made me feel animalistic. The adrenaline made me feel powerful. Even with all of that going on the goons still managed to take me inside the building. The scent of sawdust, burnt flesh, and blood shot up my nose as soon as we entered. Blood covered my lips and made a red smear that extended from my mouth across my cheek. I was breathing like a wild beast.

WHAM! The force and pain from something hard slamming into the side of my face forced my mouth open. I finally let go of the clamp I had on the goon's ear. The man quickly threw me down onto the concrete floor with a thud.

"Agh!" I cried out as a foot slammed into my rib cage as soon as I was on the floor. I also hit the back of my head and was seeing stars for a few seconds. Dazed and confused, I was still very aware that my life was about to end.

"This fucking little bitch took a chunk of skin off my ear," the goon I had bitten whined as he carefully put his hand on his injury. When he brought his hand back to the front of his face and saw all of the blood covering his fingers . . .

"Aghhhh! Look at this shit! I should kill this bitch," he shrieked like a woman. He drove his huge foot into my stomach.

"Awwg," I gagged. My legs instinctively shot up toward my chest, forming a cover for my stomach. He went to kick me again but one of the other goons stopped him before he could.

"Nah. We had instructions to bring her here alive. We can't do shit until the boss says so," another of the goons answered.

"This bitch is so lucky. I would rip her fucking head off and shit down her neck, I swear," the goon with the missing ear chunk snarled. I started laughing like a crazy woman. I was losing grip with my reality and I think shock or delirium was setting in on me. Was this how it was all going to end for me? After all of the shit I had survived growing up . . . I was about to die in some warehouse behind some stolen money?

"Go get the boss," the other goon said to the one holding his ear. "Let him decide what to do with her." The injured goon scrambled out of the door. I began praying in earnest.

God, if You spare my life I will change. Only You know my heart. Only You know this was all about survival and not hurting anyone. Matt got what he deserved for years of his abuse. God, if You spare my life I will change.

My prayer was interrupted after a few seconds. I opened my eyes when I heard the click of more than one pair of shoes ringing out against the concrete floor like gunshots. From the sound of it there was more than two people entering the room.

"Oww," I howled as I was snatched up from the floor by my hair and forced into a hard metal chair.

"Fuck off of me!" I growled as both of my arms were forcefully pulled behind my back so far that my shoulders bulged. I moved my body up and down but to no avail. My ankles were roughly tied to the legs of the chair. It was no more use in fighting. I finally went still. I kept my head down and my eyes closed. I didn't want to see whatever they were going to do to me coming.

Just do it. Get it over with. Take me out of my misery, I said in my head as if those killers could somehow read my mind.

"Look at him!" one of the goons growled, clutching onto a fistful of my hair and forcing my downturned head upward. "He wants to look into the eyes of the bitch that took his money! Show him some respect!" My eyes fluttered open and I squinted against the bright light that was hanging from the ceiling. At first all I could see was the silhouettes of two men. I could tell they were dressed in suits. I knew from the sound when they entered that they also wore hard-bottomed dress shoes. All of these assessments told me that whoever had captured me wasn't Matt and his rough-around-the-edges-ass friends.

The first man stepped closer to me. His chin was square and his face was hard, his expression twisted in a cruel sneer that was nothing like the playboy businessman I'd seen in the magazines and on TV. The man we'd stolen three million dollars from. Nikolai Kudrin.

I was shocked. I never imagined that one of my marks would actually come after me. My hustles were supposed to be safe. My victims probably got all their money back from their banks after I hit them up. Plus, they'd never be able to track me. How did Kudrin find me?

"So this is her? The genius behind the whole operation," the man said. "Look at her now? All pitiful," he continued. He summoned the other man over. When the second man stepped closer, I felt warm urine escape down my legs. I shook my head no. My body was wracked with the shakes. Suddenly I could no longer breathe. I felt like I would hyperventilate. *Can't be? This can't be!* I screamed in my head. I told myself that I had to be hallucinating.

I sucked in my breath when I looked up and my vision finally came into full focus. Tears sprang to my eyes immediately and I could literally feel my heart crumbling to a million little pieces in my chest. My head started pounding like somebody was using it for a drum. My stomach swirled with nausea. Before I knew it, I leaned over in the chair they had propped me up in and threw up. I gagged and gagged over and over again until I had nothing left to give. I couldn't stop the dry heaves from coming. I literally felt like my entire world had crashed in on me. *This can't be! No! No!* My mind raced at the speed of light.

"Dr . . . Dr . . . Drake," I rasped, my throat burning as if I had just swallowed a firelit sword. *No! This can't be true! No! It can't be him!* I screamed inside of my head. No words would come out of my mouth. The shock was tearing me apart inside. I literally felt like someone had set all of my organs on fire.

I blinked a few more times just to be certain that my eyes were not deceiving me. I couldn't believe that Drake was standing there, dressed in a suit. I had just slept with him the night before. He had just told me he loved me the week before. I had just made love to this man every night for the past two months. He was a part of my new life, not the Virginia Beach hood I'd been born into. Our whole relationship flashed through my mind and I still couldn't figure out how my old life and new life collided. My mouth hung open in shock.

"You thought that you could just get away that easily?" the other man snarled at me. I had come to the quick conclusion that he was the boss. Maybe Drake was his right-hand man? I didn't care what the boss was talking about, I simply could not take my eyes off of Drake. He refused to look me in the eye.

"You bastard! Fucking bastard!" I shrieked. It just came out of nowhere. It had bubbled up from the pit of my soul. The scream zapped all of my energy. The pain I felt from Drake's betrayal was enough to kill me. When the pain subsided and I was able to look up again, Drake was looking at me like he didn't know me. I was in too much shock to even call his name out. Drake probably wasn't his name anyway. I was in love with the enemy. He had been so perfect. I had never had a man treat me like he had. Just like everything and everyone else in my life, it was all temporary, all a lie. I guess I wasn't good enough to find someone who would really love me. If I wasn't good enough to be loved by my parents, why should anything else be different?

"Oh she's a tough one, huh?" the boss gritted. "But what she didn't know is that you don't fuck with Nikolai Kudrin. Get her the fuck up. I want to show her what she can expect."

My eyes went wide. I knew it was time for me to be killed. I wondered how Drake was going to feel watching me suffer. I wondered if any of his feelings for me were real.

The same three goons untied me and roughly pulled me up from the chair. It didn't matter what they did to me at that point, I still could not and would not take my eyes off of Drake. I locked eyes with him and we both exchanged a long, telling glance. There was a serenity in his eyes that changed something inside of me. It was like all of the hurt and pain faded away in that instant. Although he had betrayed me in the worst way, for some reason I wasn't afraid to die anymore. I had accepted my fate. I guess everything had come full circle for me. There was no more need to fight. I was finally ready to accept the karmic consequences of my actions for all of these years. Stealing from people. Lying to people. Tricking Matt and Yancy out of every dime of the money although they had worked for it too. All of the shit I had done was coming back to me.

When Kudrin's minions took me out of the chair, I didn't even fight. I had accepted my fate, therefore I had no more fight in me. I was forcefully led into another room. The lights were dimmer in this other room and the air in the room was freezing. Even with the bitter-cold air stinging the inside of my nose, I could still smell the acrid, tinny odor of old blood. It was like raw meat gone bad.

"Take her over there. Show her what she did. Show her what's about to happen to her if she doesn't start talking about where the fuck they put my money," Kudrin demanded. I was dragged to the other side of the room. I was shivering so fiercely my muscles started to seize up. It was painful being that cold. It was like they had me inside of a meat freezer.

"Look! Look at what you caused! This is all you," one of the goons growled, while he held my neck in the direction of what he wanted me to see.

I sucked in my breath. My eyes went round and my mouth fell open when I saw him. My knees began knocking against each other. More urine trickled down my legs and my stomach knotted up. I had to squeeze my sphincter muscle to keep from literally shitting myself.

"Matt!" I screamed. I felt the blood rush to

my face, which caused my head to swirl. "Matt!" My knees finally buckled and I almost fell to the floor. The goons held on to me tighter and kept me from hitting the floor.

"Look! Look at him and don't turn your fucking face away!" one of the goons snarled, holding my face roughly and forcing me to look down at Matt. I felt like throwing up again. I couldn't stand to look at him. It was too much. Guilt kicked me in the head. I was responsible for this. I tried to look around the room to see if they had gotten Yancy, too. There was just me and Matt. In the end, we had started out together and now it looked like we were going to end things together.

"Oh Matt," I cried, and shook my head.

Matt was beaten so badly I could barely recognize him. His nose was completely flattened, his lips were like two pillows, and he could barely open his eyes because his battered eyelids were so swollen. As dark as Matt was I could still see blue, green, and purple bruises cropping up all over the sides of his forehead. Blood covered his face, which made it even harder for me to make out his features. I could see huge knots on his head that had begun to swell to the size of golf balls. It seemed like blood was leaking from everywhere—gashes in his head, his mouth, the inside of his bloodshot eyes, and from the inside of his ears. The way Matt lay curled into a fetal position, I knew he was probably dying. I had seen that before. Once when I was a kid I witnessed a boy get hit by a truck and when his body flew up in the air and hit the ground it immediately curled in on itself. Mrs. Shepherd later told me that it was the body's natural defense against danger, but it was also how the body began to react when a person was about to slip away. I had never forgotten. And now it looked like that was going to be my fate, too.

MATT

"Ooof," I gagged as another fist slammed into my stomach, causing all of the wind in my body to involuntarily escape through my mouth. Acidy vomit leapt up into my throat and spewed out of my mouth right after.

"Hit 'em again!" a deep baritone voice commanded. With that, another sledgehammer-sized fist slammed into my left jaw. I felt the blood and spit shoot from between my lips. The salt from the blood stung the open cuts on my split bottom lip.

"Until he tells me where the fuck every dime of my money is I want his ass to suffer," the deep voice growled. "Break every bone in his body if you have to."

"Agh!" I belted out as a heavy-booted foot crashed down on my ribcage. I think hearing the crack and crunch of my own bones disturbed me more than the excruciating pain I felt.

I coughed and wheezed trying to will my lungs to fill back up with air. Each raggedy breath hurt like hell. I knew then that some of my ribs had been shattered. More fury came right after.

"Ugh!" I coughed as a front kick with a pointed, steel-toe boot slammed into my back. I swore I heard my spine crack. My insides felt like they were being shuffled around by the punches and kicks I'd been subjected to since these dudes had snatched me from my hideout in the thick of the night. I had tried to bounce before they could get me, but I was too slow. Lauren was lucky I hadn't snatched her ass outta that restaurant and brought her here to beat the money outta her. Although I wanted to kill her myself right now, I could only pray that she was someplace safe . . . maybe with the police or back on the run. But if these dudes were after me, I would think they would be after her and Yancy as well.

"Where is my fucking money!" the voice boomed again. This time, I forced my battered eyes open and looked at the sharply dressed man who was standing over me. In dim light I couldn't make out his face. But I could see from the flash of his sparkly diamond pinky ring, solid-gold cufflinks, and a clearly expensive tailor-made suit, this dude hadn't even broken a sweat. He obviously took great satisfaction in commanding his goons to torture me over and over. And like good little soldiers, they did just enough to hurt me, but not kill me.

"I'll ask you one more time, Matthew Connors . . . what the fuck did you and your bitch do with my fucking money?" the boss man growled. His money? Me and my bitch? What the . . . It finally hit me like a hammer to my head. My entire body went cold like my veins had been injected with ice water. The score that was supposed to put me back in the game and set me and my woman up for life had turned into my worst nightmare.

The man who'd been our mark let out a raucous, maniacal laugh. "You petty fuckin' thief," he spat as he moved closer to me. "Stealing instead of going out there and working for your own shit. I can respect a man who hustles for himself, but a man who steals from another hardworking man is a waste of fucking sperm. Your mother should've just swallowed."

The heat of anger that lit up my chest from his words was probably enough to make me kill him with my bare hands. I bucked my body out of anger but that just made shit worse.

I couldn't believe our big score, that pussy-ass playboy businessman Nikolai Kudrin, was delivering the worst beatdown I'd ever known. Even worse than the smackdown I got at my condo. It was all coming together now. How my whole life started to go down the toilet right after we stole dude's money. I can't believe Lauren's hustle had gotten into a situation crazier than anything I'd done out in the streets.

"Aggh!" I screamed. Kudrin crushed one of his hard-bottom Salvatore Ferragamo loafers down into my balls. The famous Ferragamo buckle glinted off the bright lights and taunted me. I guess this was payback for all of the times I had purchased expensive Ferragamo shit with other people's money and identities. Maybe Kudrin was right, a man who is a thief is the worst type of motherfucka alive.

"Now, you little bitch. I want to know how you got the balls to steal my money and where it is now. I'm not going to keep playing so nice because this . . . this little bit of ass-whooping and pain is nothing compared to what I do to niggas like you who I see as the scum of the earth," Kudrin growled. Then he stomped down on my balls with what felt like the force of a ten-ton boulder.

"Hmgh!" I screamed out and panted for breath at the same time. The pain was unbearable. I could barely catch my breath. Small squirms of light flitted through my eyes. I was literally seeing stars.

"That's what I thought. Now, if you want to make it out of this alive you better fucking start talking," Kudrin snarled. "You must've realized by now that you and your little female crew of thieves fucked with the wrong man," Kudrin hissed. "I just look like a square businessman. You have no idea who I really am. Not even now."

"Agggh!!" I shrieked as the square heel of Kudrin's shoe slammed into my nuts again. This time with so much force I felt like my ball sack had busted open. I opened my battered and swollen eyes and stared up at the blinding light dangling from the ceiling. I was praying and inviting death to just come take me away from this pain. I could feel the walls closing in on me but before the darkness and the shock engulfed me I thought about Lauren and Yancy and all the shit we had done to get to this point. Suddenly I was thrust back in time to how all of this shit started.

If I had my way a nigga would've bypassed that fucking lick and just stuck to the credit card shit until I could get on my feet and back in the game.

"We got a little surprise for you . . . maybe this will jog your memory about where my money is," Kudrin snarled.

"Uh! Ah!" I screamed as freezing cold water was dumped on my battered body. The icy water shocked me back into consciousness. I was shivering. I felt like my heart was going to explode. The pain that was wracking my body was unbearable. Every inch of me ached . . . even my hair follicles.

"Bring her in!" Kudrin demanded.

I think I smelled Lauren before I even saw her. It was her familiar scent that forced me to open my battered eyelids although it hurt like hell to do it.

"Matt!" Lauren screamed out. I could hear that she was sobbing.

I could barely see her. My vision was blurry and clouded.

"Lauren," I garbled through my swollen lips. Blood leaked from my mouth and burned the cuts on my lips. "T . . . T . . . tell him," I rasped. "Wh . . . where . . . the mo . . . money is." It hurt so bad to talk. My left jaw was definitely broken. I had to fight through the pain. I needed Lauren to understand that if she didn't cooperate I was going to die and she was also.

"Oh my God, Matt! I'm so sorry!" she cried out. "I'm so sorry for everything! I'm going to fix it! I'm going to make it right!"

"Get her up. Fucking torture her until she tells me where my fucking money is," Kudrin snarled. Lauren started screaming again. I saw Lauren's hand extending toward me like she was trying to touch me. She never made it. She was snatched away. That was it for Lauren. Her life was about to be over.

I closed my eyes because even after all Lauren had done to me, I couldn't stand to watch them torture her.

BANG! BANG!

I jumped from the loud roar of a gun. "Lauren," I called out painfully. I couldn't get enough air in my punctured lung to put any force behind my words. I couldn't hear her anymore. Just the idea of Kudrin killing Lauren sent enough adrenaline through my veins to make me go crazy.

"Lauren! No! Lauren!" I screamed. I rolled onto my side in an attempt to get up.

WHAM! Something slammed into my side. When I hit the floor again darkness finally took over. For good.

LAUREN

I wanted to kill everybody in the room and save Matt, even if it meant dying myself. It was partly because I was concerned about him, but mostly because I wanted to send a great big fuck-you to Drake. I wanted Drake to see my concern for Matt so it would make him jealous. I wanted to pretend that I had never fallen in love with Drake's traitorous ass. The ache in the center of my chest kept reminding me that I was indeed still in love with him.

"Get her up. This is bullshit. We didn't bring her here for a fucking lovefest reunion. Fucking torture her until she tells me where my fucking money is," Kudrin snarled.

"Aghgh!" I cried as I was dragged up from the floor. I caught a glimpse of Drake standing there watching this all unfold. Like a brick falling from the sky, it finally hit me. I could picture Drake's taxi pulling up right behind mine outside of the bar in New York. I could picture him racing to hold the door open for me. I could picture him watching me inside the bar. The moment he approached me also played like a movie in my mind now.

"You motherfucka!! You lying motherfucka!" I barked with my eyes trained on Drake's gorgeous face. I had figured it all out just like that. Drake had followed me that day I was shopping in New York. He knew all along who I was. He had also followed me back to Virginia Beach. He may have even listened to all of my conversations with Daysha. One thing he didn't know . . . that no one else knew . . . was where the rest of the money was stashed. I wasn't telling them either. If I couldn't have it no one could. I made up my mind about that.

"Strip her, tie her up, and hang her from the rafters. I got some shit for her that will be like truth serum," Kudrin growled. "I want my money."

"Agh! Help me! Don't do this!" I screamed when I felt a bunch of hands all over me. All the while I was staring dead at Drake. I am sure he could see the devastation and pain in my eyes.

I jumped and started shaking when the sound of the material of my shirt ripping resounded loudly off the hollowed walls of the warehouse. The freezing cold air in the room slapped at my naked skin. My nipples betrayed me and became erect as if I was turned on.

"Nice tits," one of the goons said, followed by a cruel chuckle. Another one came over and squeezed a handful of my breasts. The goons surrounded me like buzzards over a dead carcass. They were jeering at me and taking a free-for-all fondling my body. I stood stock still and let them have their way.

"Nice and suckable," the other goon said lecherously.

"Aye, boss, with a body this fine, you should let us all have a piece of her before we kill her," the third one with the chunk missing from his ear joked as he cut my skirt away from my waist. I was shivering even more now, more from fear than cold. I closed my eyes and began to pray.

"Matter of fact . . . I'm about to make her beg me to treat her like the whore she is." The same goon leered. He pushed me forward and started dropping to his knees from behind me.

BANG! BANG!

The goons were cut short by gunshots. His body lurched forward onto my back. I jumped up.

"Agh!!" I shrieked. The booming sound of gunshots had made me completely deaf. Instinctively, I threw my hands up to my head and covered my ears.

BANG! BANG! Two more shots rang out but they sounded muffled to me. I didn't even realize I was jumping up and down. Then I felt a strong hand latch on to my left arm with a death grip.

"Get off of me!" I wailed. I didn't know what was going on. I could hear the faint sound of a voice in my left ear, but I couldn't understand what it was saying. I looked up with fear dancing in my eyes. It was Drake. He was the one holding on to me. He was pulling me but I was too frightened to move.

"Come on! Let's go!" he was screaming but it looked to me like he was just mouthing the words. "Let's go!" He took his suit jacket and hung it around my quaking shoulders to cover me. I was shaking my head no and trying to pull away from him. I didn't trust him. Wasn't he with these goons? Hadn't he set me up? Didn't he work for Nikolai Kudrin? Then I realized that it was Drake who had shot the goons. Kudrin was lying on the ground too but I wasn't sure if he'd gotten shot.

"Lauren," I heard Matt call out to me one last time. I tried to turn around, but Drake tightened his grasp on my arm.

"C'mon," Drake urged, pulling me in the opposite direction from Matt. "You can't do shit for him now! Let's go!" Drake barked at me.

"Lauren! No! Lauren!" I heard Matt scream. I turned in his direction. I watched him roll onto his side in an attempt to get up. One of the goons who was on the ground nursing a gunshot wound extended his foot and kicked Matt in the ribs. I saw when Matt toppled back over.

"Oh my God! Matt! He's going to die!" I hollered as I watched him fall flat to the floor.

"You don't fucking listen," Drake roared. He grabbed me around my waist and hoisted me up onto his shoulder.

BANG!

"Agh!" I screamed as I felt a bullet whiz right past my face. They were shooting at us.

BANG! BANG!

With me on his shoulder Drake whirled around and returned two shots in the direction of the goons and Kudrin. It was like some shit out of a movie how perfect those shots hit their intended targets. One of the goons dropped to the floor again. This time I could see that he wouldn't be getting back up.

"Let me go! I can't leave him like this! It's all my fault!" I cried out. "I don't trust you! You are a fucking liar!" I yelled as I punched Drake in his back.

Drake ignored my cries and my little hits didn't faze him in the least. Carrying me like a rag doll, Drake raced through the warehouse doors to a black Bentley. He opened the door and dumped me into the passenger seat. Then he raced around and got into the driver's seat. He still had his gun in his hand.

"Let me go! Please! Let me go!" I cried out. I was rocking back and forth and hugging myself. I had just experienced something that was too surreal to believe. I think I was still in shock.

"I'm not letting you go," Drake said calmly. "Now just sit tight and be quiet. I will explain everything. We've just got to get away from here first."

"I hate you! You liar! You set me up! You're a fucking liar!" I cried. I was experiencing so many mixed-up emotions. Drake had betrayed me but he had also just saved my life. It was all too confusing.

"You think I betrayed you, but I saved your life, Lauren. My ex-boss Nikolai Kudrin was going to torture and kill you for stealing from him. It wasn't even about the money. He didn't need the money . . . for him it was the principle. It was the fact that someone like you had the balls to steal from him. It was his pride and ego that was injured more than his pockets. You had outsmarted him. He never likes to be outsmarted. What he had planned for you wasn't fit for a human . . . so you can thank me later," Drake explained.

"But you . . . you lied to me. You let me believe that we had something," I sobbed until my shoulders quaked. "You let me fall in love with you. You made me believe that you loved me, too. You're a fucking liar!"

"Shhh. You're right. I lied. In the beginning it was all about finding you and finding Kudrin's money. Yes, I was standing as his right-hand man so I was sent to follow you. To find out where you lived. To see where you had the money hidden. I was assigned to do all of that . . . but once I found you, followed you, spoke to you, kissed you, and made love to you . . . Lauren, knowing you made it impossible to follow through with my assignment. At some point it became more about protecting you from what I knew was coming rather than turning you over to Kudrin. I could've told him where you were the day I followed you, but I didn't. I knew when you left the letter at the apartment in New York that you were coming back to danger. I knew that Kudrin would find you as soon as you stepped foot back in Virginia Beach. . . ." Drake paused as he focused on swerving around the traffic ahead of us. I had no idea were he was going and I didn't care. Everything he was telling me was crazy. The worst I thought could happen was that the police would track and find me. Not that my score would end up being a crazy thug, as bad as any street hustler about his money.

I grabbed on to the door handle to steady myself as the car continued to swerve. Drake continued. "They had been following your friend Daysha practically since you'd left. They knew eventually she would be the one to lead them to you if I didn't. I had never told them that I had found you. I wanted to move you as far away from the danger as I could. They knew Matt didn't have the money or else he would have been dead a long time ago. When you left New York, I knew what was up so I came right away. I came to save you, not betray you," Drake said with feeling and a sincerity that no man had ever shown me. No one had cared that much for me since Mrs. Shepherd. I continued to cry uncontrollably—a mixture of fear, love, confusion, and surrender all rolled into my emotions. Inside I felt all warm and mushy from Drake's words.

"But who are you?" I croaked through my tears. "I feel like I am in love with someone I don't even know. Who the fuck are you?" I sobbed.

Drake pulled the car over on a desolate country road. He put it in park and turned toward me. His handsome face melted my insides and I looked away. I was scared of my feelings for him, especially with all the deception between us.

"Look at me," he demanded in a soft tone that was almost a whisper. I hung my head and shook it left to right. I squeezed my eyes shut and let the tears drain out of the sides. "I can't look at you. I don't know you."

"Please. Look at me, Lauren," Drake said again in a soft whispery voice. This time he extended his hand and put it behind my head to urge me to turn it toward him. "Just give me that . . . at least."

"I can't," I sobbed. "I just can't. It hurts too much."

"You can and you will. What I have to say I need to be looking into your eyes to say," Drake said. With sobs hiccupping through my chest, I finally relented. I slowly turned my head and gazed into Drake's eyes. A flash of heat lit up my face as I stared deep into his beautiful chestnut eyes. I swear his face was so damn fine that it made everything I was feeling even more intensified.

"My name is Derek Hague. I've been working as a cleaner for Kudrin for two years. I gained his trust and I became his right-hand man. When Kudrin sent me to find you, then follow you to the money and then to bring you to him, it was just another assignment for me."

I grabbed the handle of the car door, ready to open it and make my escape. His confession made me feel like I'd traded one bad situation for another. My pause gave him time to hit the automatic door locks, trapping me in the car with a man I loved but didn't really know. I squinted my eyes closed as he continued.

"But after I met you, I knew I couldn't . . . do what I knew he'd eventually ask me to do. And as we grew closer, and I began to fall for you, protecting you became my first priority. Not Nik. Not completing my assignment." Drake leaned over and tried to pull me into his arms. But I wasn't ready yet to forgive him.

"A man in my line of work has a lot of contacts and people who owe him favors. That's how I know that right now police officers are swarming that warehouse. They will save Matt's life so he can be prosecuted. There are also police officers swarming Yancy's place and bringing her in. I made sure that I worked behind the scenes to clear your name. I was the cooperating witness. I got you off, simply because I want to be with you. And if you want to be with me, we have to leave this place for good. Will you go with me?" Drake . . . I mean Derek explained everything to me. My head was spinning from everything he had just said. My heart was thumping wildly and I began sobbing like crazy.

"Nobody has ever cared about me enough to go through all of this. I . . . I . . . don't even know what to say," I said through tears.

"Then just say yes," Derek whispered.

Then he pulled my head toward him and leaned closer to me. "Wait, it hurts right there," I said, referring to the bruises I had alongside my face.

"I'm sorry," he said as he loosened the grip on my face. When his lips finally touched mine, the kiss was different from any other one we had exchanged. Our tongues danced together and our hearts, bodies, and minds connected on a level I could never explain with words. I was still scared, but I had also never been this happy in my life. Everything I had been through began to fall away in that moment. Derek stopped kissing me and leaned back.

"Will you go with me?" he asked again.

"I will go with you," I whispered.

He smiled and I saw his shoulders slump with relief. He started the car and we began to drive. I didn't know where we were going or what life was going to be like for us, but I knew that the feelings I had for this man were totally different than anything I had ever experienced. I thought about Mrs. Shepherd and how I wasn't going to be able to see her. I sent a prayer up for her, hoping that she wasn't in pain and that she'd be able to recover from her stroke. And I tried to keep my last vision of Matt out of my mind's eye. I felt awful about it and I hoped to God what Derek had said was true about the police swarming the warehouse and saving Matt's life.

After a few long minutes, Derek broke the silence inside of the car.

"I have the money from the safe that you had stashed at the assisted living home," he said like it was no big deal. My eyes went wide and I whipped my head in his direction. He smiled. "Oh, and Mrs. Shepherd has been moved to a safe place. She didn't have a stroke. She was never sick. I will arrange for you to see her soon."

I let a huge smile spread across my lips. "Who are you? Are you sure you're not an angel?" I asked. Derek laughed.

"I also have the money that you stashed in all of the different gym lockers. And from the safe-deposit box. All of your stash spots have been emptied for you," he continued.

My eyebrows shot up. This dude had really been trailing me. Thank God he'd fallen in love or I would've been fooled.

"But . . . but . . . how?" I stammered.

"I told you I was following you. I told you I knew everything. Including the fact that your best friend had tried to set you up," Derek said. His words were like a hard slap to my face but he'd only confirmed what I had already suspected.

"Yeah, she was working with Matt to get you back to the area. She was pretty grimy," Derek said.

"I knew it. I knew something wasn't right with her," I agreed. I felt a pang of hurt flit through my stomach about Daysha but for some reason I wasn't that surprised.

"That's all behind you now," Derek said, smiling. "It's just us and the money. Looks like you were the last one standing out of your crew," he said, and winked.

I turned my head and looked out of the windshield at the road ahead. All I could do was pray that what Derek had just said was true. I knew things always had a way of coming back to haunt you.

LAUREN

One Year Later

"Push! Push!" Derek urged as I clamped down like a vise on his hand. I bore down and pushed as hard as I could. My entire bottom felt like it was going to explode.

"Huh, huh, huh." I threw my head back on the pillow and panted for breath. "I'm so tired," I whined. "I can't do it."

"Come on, baby. You can do this. You got this," Derek said encouragingly.

"I'm exhausted," I huffed. I could feel the sweat wetting my scalp and draining down the sides of my face. My entire body was hot like I was sitting in a sauna.

"Agggh!" I hollered as another wave of body-shattering contractions crashed through my abdomen.

"Okay, Mrs. Hague, it's time to push again," the doctor said. He bent down between my legs. "Come on. I see the head. A few good pushes and it'll all be over."

"Mmmmm. Grrrrrr." I bore down, held my breath, and pushed again. I could feel the vein at my temple throbbing. This time I felt so much pressure in my anus and vagina I just knew it would explode. "Grrrr." I kept pushing. I could hear Derek cheering me on. It felt like a fiery bowling ball coming through my ass. I squeezed Derek's hand until I almost broke all of the bones in it but he never complained.

"Great job! It's a boy!" I heard the doctor scream. Next, I heard the sweet, musical sound that was the wail of my son's cries. The sound was the sweetest thing I had ever heard in my entire life. I felt an overwhelming rush of warmth fill me up inside. I flopped my head back on the pillow and closed my eyes. I started crying but these were definitely tears of pure joy. I had finally been blessed with a child. It was what I considered the greatest gift I had ever received in my entire life. I felt like I didn't really deserve such a great gift from God, but I guess God had seen things differently. I was a mother now. There was nothing more I could accomplish in my life.

"You want to hold him?" the nurse asked, smiling warmly.

"Yes. Right away. And I never want to let him go," I replied. I opened my eyes and accepted my baby boy into them. I belched out a mouthful of sobs, but this time, they were happy ones. He was beautiful. He already had Derek's perfect complexion and his almond-shaped eyes. He had my tiny ears and my heart-shaped lips.

"He's so perfect," I said, keeping my eyes on my brand-new baby boy. Derek walked over to the side of the bed and stroked my hair. He leaned down and kissed the top of my head.

"You did it, Lauren. After all of the treatments and hard times we had to get here, you did it. He is perfect and so are you," Derek cheered me on.

"No, we did it. You were so great through everything. You knew this is what I needed to make my life complete and you never complained. You are really a gift from God, Derek. I never want to be without you a day in my life," I told my new husband. The nurse came over and helped me put my son on my breast so that the first thing he got to nourish his little seven-pound body would come straight from me. It was an overwhelming tsunami of love that crashed through my entire body as my baby boy suckled my breast.

"I'm going to run home and take a shower, baby. I have been dying to for the two days we have been here. I won't be long. You know I can't stand to be away from you but for so long," Derek said, planting a kiss right on my forehead. Then he gently kissed our son.

"Hurry back," I told him. "I can't stand to be without you, either."

With that, Derek rushed out of the hospital-room door. I was alone with my baby. I stroked his hair and counted his tiny fingers. I hummed a song to him too.

"Now this is what love is. My life is finally complete. I will be the best mother I can be. I will be nothing like my mother," I said, speaking to myself out loud. I held on to my son tight and closed my eyes. I could feel myself drifting off to sleep. The exhaustion was finally taking hold of me. I heard the door to my hospital room creak open and I could sense someone walking in. I was so exhausted I didn't even want to open my eyes. With my eyes still closed, I cracked a smile.

"What did you forget this time, Derek Hague? I think your head is attached to you so it can't be that but if it wasn't you would've forgotten it," I joked. I didn't get a response from Derek. I heard a chair move to my left.

"Derek?" I called to him. He didn't answer, which wasn't like him. I figured then maybe it was a nurse coming in to check on us.

Finally, I opened my eyes and turned toward the presence. I jumped so fiercely I almost dropped my baby. I sucked in my breath and swallowed hard. Suddenly my exhaustion had faded into sheer panic when I saw Matt's face. But how? I thought he'd gone back to prison. I opened my mouth to say something . . . anything . . . or even to scream but no sound would come.

"Congratulations, Lauren," he said with a sinister grin on his face. I couldn't speak. I felt the air going in my open mouth, but no words would come.

"Finally, a baby for you. Damn, after all of this time," he said evilly. "I guess life is treating you well. I should've known you thought you would be the last one standing."

I just blinked rapidly. I was clutching the baby so tight to my chest I might've been smothering him.

"I just wanted you to know that you didn't actually get away with it," he told me. Then he parted an ill smile that sent a cold chill down my spine.

"No one ever does," he followed up, smirking.

"Wh . . . what . . . do y . . . you want?" I stuttered in a barely audible tone. He threw his head back and laughed maniacally.

"What I want you can't give me. It's too late to buy your freedom with the money. It's past that now," he said after abruptly stopping his laughter. His face was deadpan. The look in his eyes scared me to my core.

"Please, I will do whatever you want, just don't hurt Derek or my son," I said, my voice quivering.

He started laughing. "It's too late for that, Lauren. Everything you love has been tainted by the karma of everything you did." He stood up and held his cell phone out toward me. I was puzzled. What did he want me to do with it?

"Take it, someone wants to speak with you," he insisted.

I grabbed the phone from his hand and pressed it against my ear. "Hello," I said.

"Hello," I heard an elderly voice speak. Right

then and there I knew it was my foster mother Mrs. Shepherd.

"It's me, Lauren," I told her.

"Hi, baby, how are you?" she asked.

"I'm good. What about you?" I asked, looking at Matt, still puzzled why he wanted me to talk to Mrs. Shepherd.

"I'm fine, darling. I've got this nice young man over here standing next to me. He said you wanted to talk to me so he used his phone and called you," she explained.

"What's his name?" I asked her.

"I don't know. Let me ask him. What's your name, sir?" Mrs. Shepherd said.

"Buddha," I heard him say. Then he said, "Tell her good-bye."

"Well, I think he wants his phone back because he told me to tell you good-bye," she said, and before she could utter another word I heard a BOOM. The sound ricocheted through the phone. I screamed and dropped Matt's cell phone from my hand. "He killed her. You had him kill her! I fucking hate you!" I sobbed.

"That was only the beginning," he said, and tore my son from my arms. My baby began wailing.

"No, Matt!" I screamed. "No! Please give him back to me! Please! I beg you."

He held my screaming baby up against his face and inhaled deeply. "Was it worth it? Was it all worth it?" he asked me evilly.

"Please," I pleaded. I tried to get up but my body was too weak.

"Shhhh . . . don't worry. I'll give you a chance to get your son back," he said.

"What do you want?! I have money. I have things. . . ." I said pleadingly. He let out a cacophony of laughter.

"You damn right I want my money, bitch! Don't try to bring the cops into this and don't try to get any of the doctors or hospital security involved. If you do, I'm going to make the call to my other dude who just kidnapped your new husband outside the hospital," Matt warned.

"If I give you the money, you promise you'll let my husband and son go?" I asked him.

"Do the right thing and you'll find out," he said with finality.

Looking into Matt's eyes, I knew two things. This was not entirely about the money and my life would never be the same again . . .

Kiki Swinson's "tension-packed" *(Library Journal)* and "unrelenting" *(Publishers Weekly)*, bestselling novels deliver startling twists, unforgettable characters—and a stark, unforgettable portrait of life in the South. Now she detonates an explosive tale about a couple who can't get enough—and a risk that will exact a merciless price . . .

DEAD ON ARRIVAL

Enjoy the following excerpt . . .

PROLOGUE
DAWN

Where the fuck was he?

I looked at the clock and noticed that I'd been sleeping for a couple of hours. I'd dozed off waiting for Reese to come home so we could talk about where we were going when we left town. He told me he was leaving his grandmother's house and was gonna make a quick stop at NIT. Then he was coming straight here. So, where the fuck was he?

Before I could grab my cell phone and dial his number, my phone started ringing. I picked it up from the nightstand next to my bed and looked down at the caller ID. I let out a sigh of relief when I saw that it was Reese calling me.

"Hello," I said.

"Did I wake you up?" he asked. He sounded kind of weird.

"Reese, where are you?" I asked, ignoring his question.

"I'm about to pull up to the house, so put on something and meet me outside," he instructed.

"Meet you outside for what? *Do you know what time it is?*" I screeched. He was making me angrier by the second because he was displaying some very odd behavior.

"Please don't ask me any questions. Just do what I said," he replied calmly.

"Bye," I said, and then I disconnected our call.

I was furious at the thought that I had to get out of my bed and meet him outside. What kind of fucking game was he trying to play?

I grabbed a sweatshirt and a pair of sweatpants from my dresser drawer and a pair of sneakers from my closet and got dressed. After I grabbed a jacket from the hall closet by my bedroom, I headed toward the front door. My adrenaline was pumping. I was already thinking of what I was going to say to him if he was making me come outside for nothing. He was going to feel my wrath.

Blinded by the headlights of Reese's car parked in our driveway, I blinked my eyes a few times and held up my left arm to shield my eyes. I saw the silhouette of Reese's body sitting in the driver seat, so I closed the front door behind me and walked over to his car. I was heading toward the driver side, until he rolled his window down halfway and told me to get into the car from the passenger side.

I obeyed his instructions and got into the car with him. As soon as I closed the door, I turned around and looked at him. "What the fuck is so important that I had to come outside and get into the car?" I asked him.

Reese wouldn't open his mouth to respond.

"What's wrong with you?" I questioned him.

A voice from behind me said, "He's dead!"

I turned my face slightly to the left and saw an Asian man with a gun and a silencer pointed directly at me. My heart dropped in the pit of my stomach. Anxiety and fear crippled me as I slowly moved my eyes away from the Asian man, back to my husband's face. At that moment, that's when I noticed the blood seeping from the hole in his head. I instantly froze. I knew then that this man was about to take my life too.

1
REESE

I knew Dawn was going to jump down my throat when I walked through the front door of our home. Not only did I not come straight home from work, I didn't answer my cell phone when she called me over a dozen times, and I didn't have the $800 I promised her I would have. Shit hasn't been going right for us these last six months, so she'd been breathing down my neck because of it. To be more candid, we'd been having some financial problems for the last couple of years. Our car payments were past due, our credit cards were maxed out, our light bills had more than tripled, and our home was in fucking foreclosure. Taking a boatload of flat-screen smart televisions, laptop computers, and

fur coats here and there helped me pay a few of
our bills. It also helped me get into a few poker
games at my homeboy Edward Cuffy's spot,
which was exactly where I was when Dawn called
me earlier. Edward was one of the senior opera-
tors at the Norfolk International Terminal. So
far, he's got twenty-four years under his belt. In
other words, he had seniority, so nothing got by
him. If anything was stolen out of the shipping
containers and sold for a handsome profit, Ed
definitely got his cut. No ifs, ands, or buts about it.

Edward was like a big brother to me. He wasn't
a big guy, but he made up for it in height and
walked around like he owned the world. He was
like Samuel L. Jackson. Sixty-five percent of the
longshoremen on the pier liked Edward, but
the other thirty-five percent hated him. My wife,
Dawn, was one of them. "Did you just come
from Ed's house?" she didn't hesitate to ask as
she walked toward me. I knew she had just come
from the kitchen because I smelled the aroma
of tomato sauce, she wore a cooking apron, and
she held a plastic mixing spoon in her left hand.

"Why are you asking me that?" I instantly became defensive after I locked the front door.

"Because I called you over a dozen times and
you kept sending me to your voicemail," she
spat as she stood before me. Dawn and I got
married two years ago. We dated for a year before I popped the question. When I first met her,
she was gorgeous. She resembled Toni Braxton.
She was sexy too. Plus, she wasn't this fucking
nagging. I remember when she used to walk
around our house almost naked, on a daily basis.

Now I can't get her to take off her terry-cloth robe. She went from looking like a Playboy bunny to a Catholic nun. She assumed on several occasions that I was cheating on her because I complained about her appearance, but my guilty pleasure was gambling.

"I was at the pier. This new guy named Nate needed some help with a few containers, so I stuck around and helped him," I lied as I passed her and strolled into the kitchen. She knew I was lying, so she followed me.

"So, if I call down to the office and ask Porsha' to check your time sheet, it's gonna show that you were still at work?"

I gave her a head nod and then I turned my attention toward the pot of boiling water. When I looked closer and saw spaghetti noodles, I knew I was having spaghetti for dinner.

I changed the subject. "When will the food be done?" Dawn knew that I wasn't confrontational. I'd do anything to stay away from an argument, especially with her. She was famous for backing me into a corner, and I hated it.

"As soon as you hand over the eight hundred dollars you promised to bring home to me," she answered as she stood two feet away from me.

Hearing her ask me for the money hit me like a ton of bricks. Anxiety consumed me. I literally felt like a fucking little kid that just got caught stealing money from my mother's wallet. I tried to think of a good excuse as to why I didn't have the money, but my mind went totally blank.

"Reese, where is the money?"

"I don't have it yet." I dreaded my own words.

"What the fuck you mean you don't have it yet?" she roared. I could tell that she was at her wit's end.

"Listen, Dawn, I've been working on a few things, so as soon as it comes through, I'll get the money," I tried to explain.

"You're still stealing from those shipping containers, huh?"

"Why are you concerning yourself with that?"

"Because I don't want you going to jail," she said. "Do you know that the port police are doing a lot more patrolling than usual?"

"Stop being so paranoid. I know what I'm doing," I assured her.

"So, how much longer am I gonna have to wait for the money?"

"Give me until tomorrow. I'll definitely have it by then," I told her, even though I wasn't sure. I needed to say something to get her off my back, at least for now.

"Reese, I'm telling you right now that if you don't have the money tomorrow, I'm taking your fucking Rolex watch down to the pawn shop and pawn it," she threatened, and then she turned around and walked to the stove.

I didn't comment one way or another because if she knew that I had already pawned my Rolex, she'd really be breathing down my neck. It was important to her to get this money from me because for one, she lent the $800 to me a couple weeks ago and two, she needed it for a fertility treatment. Having a baby was the most important thing to her. I had children from a previous relationship, but I didn't have any children with Dawn.

I've told her time and time again that if she and I don't ever have kids that I won't love her any less. But she doesn't believe it. She thinks that having a child with me will bring us closer together. I don't believe that. I think things are good the way they are. We don't need another mouth to feed. Shit! I bring home around $85,000 a year and Dawn about $50,000. But we're still in fucking debt. She pays the little things like the light bills, gas bills, and her $750 BMW car note. I pay most of the bills, like our $2,500 mortgage payment, $700 a month in child support for my other kids, my $1,300 truck payment, and then I gamble up the rest. So, tell me how bringing home another mouth to feed is going to bring us closer together? It won't.

I headed to the bathroom and took a quick shower. After I was done, I slipped on a pair of shorts, a white T-shirt, and then I headed back to the kitchen. Dawn had my plate of spaghetti on the kitchen table waiting for my return. She was already sitting down and eating when I walked in. "Looks good," I mentioned as I took a seat in the chair across from her.

Instead of thanking me for the compliment, she rolled her eyes and continued to eat. We sat there in an awkward silence for at least five minutes. I started to get up a few times and take my plate in the living room so I could watch a little TV, but I knew that would send her up the wall, so I decided against it. Thankfully, the doorbell rang. I pushed my chair back to get up, but Dawn insisted that she answer the door while she got to her feet. So I scooted my chair back toward the table and continued to eat.

I heard Dawn as she walked across the hardwood floors to the front door. And when she yelled through the door and asked the person on the other side to announce themselves, I listened for their answer. "It's me, Alexia," I heard the lady say, and then I heard Dawn unlock the front door and open it. "What brings you by?" I heard Dawn ask Alexia.

"I was in the neighborhood," she replied.

Alexia was Dawn's older sister. She was five years older, to be exact. She closely resembled Gabrielle Union. She had this overly confident personality. When she walked in a room, she always commanded the attention of everyone there. I personally didn't like her because she always had something negative to say about Dawn's and my marriage. And to keep from cursing her ass out, I did my very best to avoid her.

"Wait, I smell food," she continued, and then I heard two sets of footsteps walking in my direction. I knew that at any moment I was going to come face-to-face with Alexia, so I needed to keep my composure. She knew how to ruffle my feathers, but I wasn't going to let her get to me today. I had too much other shit going on in my personal life, so I refused to let her add anything to it.

"Look at what we have here," she commented after turning the corner to enter the kitchen. She gave me this cunning look.

"What's up?" I said, and then I buried my face back into my plate.

"Nah, what's up with you? I see you got my sister slaving over the hot stove again," she replied sarcastically, as she sat down in an empty chair at the table.

"Isn't that what a wife is supposed to do when she has a family?" I told her.

"Speaking of family, Dad's been complaining about how he's been giving you guys money so you can make ends meet around here," Alexia said while she gave me the evil eye.

I got defensive immediately. "I don't know why you're looking at me. I don't owe your daddy shit!" I roared, firmly gripping my fork.

"Alexia, Reese didn't go to Dad to get the money, I did," Dawn chimed in.

"He might as well have gotten the money from Daddy, because if he was handling his business with the money he made from the terminal, then you wouldn't be in this situation."

"Bitch, why don't you just mind your fucking business!"

"You're the bitch! Got my sister around here running to my parents for money so y'all won't lose your house and cars. You aren't a real man. Real men take care of their family and make sure there's nothing lacking in the household. Not you. You rather throw your money away gambling while your wife does what she can with the money she makes and the money she gets from my parents."

"Alexia, you promised that you wouldn't say anything else!" Dawn yelled.

"He started it with me."

"Fuck her! She out of line, coming in my house talking all that fly shit out of her mouth."

"Nah, nigga, fuck you!"

"Reese, please stop. You too, Alexia. Y'all are about to give me an anxiety attack!" Dawn yelled once more.

"So, it's okay for her lonely ass to walk in here and start talking her shit to me?" I hissed.

"Stand up and be a man, and then I wouldn't talk shit to you," Alexia spat.

Dawn walked over toward Alexia and grabbed her by the arm. "Come with me, please." She led Alexia out of the kitchen. I realized that Dawn had taken Alexia outside after I heard the front door open and close. I heard bits and pieces of their conversation, with Alexia talking louder than Dawn, of course. Their spat only lasted a couple of minutes and then they came back in the house. This time when Alexia entered the kitchen, she focused on carrying on a conversation with Dawn, instead of me.

Alexia started talking about some bullshit-ass nigga she just started dating who wanted to have kids with her already. "We've only been dating for a month and a half and the nigga wants me to have a baby. I told him he was crazy."

"I thought you couldn't have any kids," I blurted out. I swear I couldn't let her slide by with that bullshit-ass statement, especially since she started running her mouth at me as soon as she walked into my kitchen. In my eyes, this was the perfect time to put her ass back in check.

"Don't worry about me. Worry about the fact that you haven't gotten my sister pregnant." Alexia hurled her words at me. I swear, I wanted to ignore her and not feed into her bullshit, but she started hitting nerves I didn't know I had.

Dawn jumped to my defense. "Come on now, Alexia, that's hitting below the belt. And besides, it's not his fault that I haven't gotten pregnant."

"Well, who's fault is it, my sister? He's a fucking loser." Alexia pressed the issue.

My blood was boiling. I wanted so badly to stand up and slap the shit out of her no-job, meddling ass. But I knew that putting my hands on her would be a huge mistake, so I got her where I knew it would hurt, and that was her personal life. All the niggas she fucked and continued to fuck.

"You got a fucking nerve coming in my house and disrespecting me. If you weren't Dawn's sister I would drag you by your hair and haul your ass out of here," I told her.

"Do it, nigga! Do it!" She stepped closer to me.

Dawn stepped between us. "You're a lucky-ass bitch!" I said.

"Nah, nigga. You're the lucky one because if I had it my way, I would file the divorce papers for my sister myself."

"Well, thank God you're not. Now mind your business before I call the cops and have your ass thrown out of here," I replied while clenching my teeth. I had so much other shit I wanted to tell her. For starters, she was a fucking unemployed high school dropout and a whore. Everyone down at Norfolk International Terminal had fucked her. Talking about Dawn not being able to get pregnant, she can't get pregnant either. So for her to come in my damn house and start stirring up drama between my wife and me is unacceptable. This bitch needs to know who's really in charge.

"I swear I can't believe that you married this nigga! You would've done so much better if you'd married that nigga Blake," Alexia continued.

"Well, she didn't, so deal with it," I snapped.

"I don't have to deal with that shit."

"Well, I'll tell you what, deal with the fact that you had to have over a dozen abortions because you were fucking two and three niggas at one time and you had no idea who the father was." I hissed like I had venom spewing from my mouth.

"Nigga, you don't know shit about me!" Alexia shouted.

"Reese, are you fucking kidding me right now?" Dawn said as she stood between us.

"I know you're a fucking ho! And I know every nigga you slept with. I mean, hell, every nigga at NIT know who you slept with," I continued. I was digging deep in my bag of information so I could humiliate the hell out of her. Judging from her facial expression, my tactic was working, but I could also tell that my words were hurting Dawn.

"Reese, stop it right now! I fucking mean it!" Dawn yelled at me.

I stood on my feet. "Tell *her* to stop it! She started this whole fucking thing!"

"Fuck him, Dawn! He's a fucking loser anyway!"

"Bitch, you're the fucking loser! That's why you can't keep a man! Nobody wants you," I roared.

"Oh, but you wanted me," Alexia said. She and I were standing at opposite sides of the kitchen table.

"Bitch, I never wanted you!" I protested, but she was right. About one month before I met Dawn, I met Alexia at the nightclub Upscale in Chesapeake. I was with one of my friends, who pointed out that he knew Alexia and that she was easy to get into bed. So, being the adventurous man that I was, I bought her a few drinks and then I tried to talk her into coming back to my apartment so I could fuck her. Now the only reason it didn't happen was because she was with two of her homegirls, and she drove. So she gave me her number that night. I can't tell you why I never called her, it just didn't happen.

"I want both of y'all to shut the fuck up right now!" Dawn roared as she stood between us.

"I'm not doing shit! This is my fucking house. Just send that bitch on her merry way."

"I ain't gotta go nowhere! This is my sister's house too," Alexia griped as she stood her ground.

"Dawn, get that ho out of my house right now! I'm not gonna say it anymore," I warned her.

Without saying another word, Dawn grabbed Alexia's hand and tried to pull her in the direction of the front door. "Come on, Alexia," she said.

But Alexia snatched her arm away from Dawn. "Are you scared of this nigga or something?" she blurted out.

"Nah, she ain't scared of me. She ain't got a reason to be," I told her as I took a step toward her.

"So, whatcha about to do?" Alexia asked me while Dawn grabbed her arm once again and started pulling her.

"I'm not about to do anything."

"So, why you walking toward me like you're about to do something?"

"Bitch, just get out of my fucking house! You're not wanted here," I concluded, and then I walked around her and Dawn. I started walking down the hallway toward my bedroom so I didn't have to hear Alexia's mouth anymore. I swear, if she were my woman, talking to me like that, I would've choked all the breath out of her body and gladly taken the thirty-year prison sentence to go with it.

I closed the door after I entered my bedroom. I heard Alexia utter a few more words to Dawn and then I didn't hear her voice anymore. I didn't hear Dawn's voice either. I figured she must've walked outside with Alexia, or even left for that matter. Either way, silence was something I needed to unwind. With the drama surrounding my relationship with Dawn, the bills we had and the gambling debt I couldn't get rid of, I needed this time to think. I needed to figure out how I was going to get things back on track. I needed a plan and I needed it right now. I just hoped that whatever I came up with eliminated my problems completely. If it didn't, then it would be a waste of my time.

Connect with Us

Visit us online at
KensingtonBooks.com
to read more from your favorite authors, see books
by series, view reading group guides, and more.

Join us on social media

for sneak peeks, chances to win books and prize packs,
and to share your thoughts with other readers.

facebook.com/kensingtonpublishing
twitter.com/kensingtonbooks

Tell us what you think!

To share your thoughts, submit a review,
or sign up for our eNewsletters, please visit:
KensingtonBooks.com/TellUs.